LEONIE OF THE JUNGLE

JOAN CONQUEST

1st WORLD
LIBRARY
Literary Society

Leonie of the Jungle

Joan Conquest

© 1st World Library, 2007
PO Box 2211
Fairfield, IA 52556
www.1stworldlibrary.com
First Edition

LCCN: 2007924144

Softcover ISBN: 978-1-4218-4283-7
Hardcover ISBN: 978-1-4218-4185-4
eBook ISBN: 978-1-4218-4381-0

Purchase *"Leonie of the Jungle"*
as a traditional bound book at:
www.1stWorldLibrary.com/purchase.asp?ISBN=978-1-4218-4283-7

1st World Library is a literary, educational organization
dedicated to:

- Creating a free internet library of downloadable ebooks

- Hosting writing competitions and offering book
publishing scholarships.

Interested in more 1st World Library books?
contact: literacy@1stworldlibrary.com
Check us out at: www.1stworldlibrary.com

1ˢᵗ World Library Literary Society

Giving Back to the World

"If you want to work on the core problem, it's early school literacy."

- James Barksdale, former CEO of Netscape

"No skill is more crucial to the future of a child, or to a democratic and prosperous society, than literacy."

- Los Angeles Times

Literacy... means far more than learning how to read and write... The aim is to transmit... knowledge and promote social participation."

- UNESCO

"Literacy is not a luxury, it is a right and a responsibility. If our world is to meet the challenges of the twenty-first century we must harness the energy and creativity of all our citizens."

- President Bill Clinton

"Parents should be encouraged to read to their children, and teachers should be equipped with all available techniques for teaching literacy, so the varying needs and capacities of individual kids can be taken into account."

- Hugh Mackay

TO

THE SPLENDID NATIVE OF INDIA,

THE LIVING

MADHU KRISHNAGHAR

CONTENTS

"And never the twain shall meet."

BOOK I

THE WEST

CHAPTER I

"To deliver thee from the strange woman!"
—The Bible.

"Who found the kitten?"

"Me," quavered the childish voice.

Lady Susan Hetth tchcked with her tongue against her rather prominent teeth at the lamentable lapse in grammar, and looked crossly at Leonie, who immediately lifted up the quavering voice and wept.

Sobs too big for such a little girl shook the slender body, whilst great tears dripped from the long lashes to the tip of the upturned nose, down the chin and on the knee of the famous specialist, against which she rested.

"Stand up, Leonie, and push your hair out of your eyes!"

The thin little body tautened like an overstrung violin string, and a shock of russet hair was pushed hastily back from a pair of indefinable eyes, in which shone the light of an intense grief strange in one so young.

"Leave her to me, Lady Hetth!"

The surgeon's voice was exceedingly suave but with the

substratum of steel which had served to bend other wills to his with an even greater facility than the thumb of the potter moulds clay to his fancy.

"Leonie is going to tell me everything, and then she is going to the shop to buy a big doll and *forget* all about it!"

"Please may I have a book instead of—"

"Leonie, that is very rude."

"Please, Lady Hetth. Go on, darling—what kind of book."

"'Bout tigers an' snakes, oh! an' elephants. Weal animals. Dolls, you know"—she smiled as she confided the great secret—"aren't weal *babies*, they're just full of sawdust."

He lifted the child on to his knee, frowning at the weight, and smoothed the tangled mass of curls away from the low forehead with a touch which caused her to make a sound 'twixt sob and sigh, and to lie back against the broad shoulder.

It was a long and disjointed story, told in the inconsequent fashion of a child of seven unused to converse with her elders; and continually interrupted by the aunt, who, fretful and dying for her tea, jingled her distracting bracelets and chains, fidgeted with the Anglo-Indian odds-and-ends of her raiment, and disconcerted the child by the futile verbal proddings; which are as bad for the infant mind as the criminal attempts to force a baby to use its legs are to the infant body.

"So! and you found the dear little kitten lying quite still in the nursery this morning?"

"Yes! Stwangled!"

"Do pronounce your *r*'s, Leonie."

The child shivered in the man's arms.

"Who told you it was strangled?"

"Auntie!"

The man's hand closed for a moment on a heavy paper-weight as he looked across the room at the woman who was waggling her foot and knitting her scanty brows at the sound of the rending sobs.

"Auntie was mistaken, darling. Kitty was asleep, tired out with playing or running away from the dog next door."

Leonie shook her head. "Kitty's dead," she wailed, "lying all black and quiet, like—like my dweams!"

There was a moment's pregnant silence, during which Leonie turned round and snuffled into the great man's collar, and he frowned above the russet head as he drew a block of paper and pencil towards him.

"What dreams, darling?"

"Don' know—dweams I dweam!"

The specialist sat still for a second and then laughed, the great kind laugh of a man with a big heart who adores children.

"Let's play a game, Leonie! You tell me about the dreams, and I'll tell you about my new motor-car, and the one who tells best will get a big sweet!"

With a child's sudden change of mood Leonie sat up, swinging her black silk legs to and fro, her eyes dancing, her lips parted over the even little teeth.

"I *love* sweets!" said she. "You begin!"

"My car's grey!" said Sir Jonathan Cuxson. "What colour are your dreams?"

"*Black*!" was the unexpectedly decisive reply. "Black with lots of wed—wet wed—and gween eyes—lots and lots of eyes—and—and soft things I can't see, and—noises like kit—kit—kitty makes when she purrs!"

"Yes?"

"Yes! and people with soft feet like the—the slippers Nannie wears at night so that I can't hear them. And—and that's all!"

She laughed like the child she ought to have been as she bit the end off a big pink fondant which had materialised out of one of a dozen little drawers in the desk, then holding up the other end to the man laughed again spontaneously and delightfully as he pushed the sweet into her mouth.

Then he put her on her feet, tilted the little white face back till the strong light shone into the opalescent, gold-flecked eyes, kissed the curly head and told her to run round the room, open the cabinet doors and look at the hidden treasures.

"May I touch them?"

"Of course, sweetheart!"

"I'm vewy sowwy *you* didn't win," she said in her old-fashioned way, "because you are vewy, vewy nice. And"—she continued, suddenly harking back as a child will to a previous remark—"and it is all vewy, vewy black, with a teeny, weeny light like the night-light Nannie lights, and—!"

She stopped dead and buried her head in the middle of Sir Jonathan's waistcoat, fumbling his coat sleeves with her nervous little hands.

"Yes, darling!" said the man, without a trace of expression in his voice as he held up a finger warningly to the woman who had rustled in her chair.

"And—and sometimes there's a black woman. And I'm—I'm fwightened of her 'cause she calls me, and—and—pulls me out of bed by my head."

"How do you mean, darling? Does she catch hold of your hair? It must hurt you dreadfully!"

Leonie suddenly stood up, nervously pulling at the man's top waistcoat button as she furtively glanced first over one shoulder and then over the other.

"No! she doesn't touch me," she faltered, "and I—I don't always see her. But—but"—she laid her open palm against her forehead in a curious little gesture suggestive of the East—"but she pulls me through my forehead, and when she pulls I've— I've *got* to go! May I *hold* that elephant?"

The brain specialist looked straight into the strange eyes which smiled confidingly back into his.

"Just a moment, sweetheart," said he. "What do your little friends, and Nannie, and Auntie say when you tell them about the dreams?"

Leonie leant listlessly against the arm of the chair, and sighed as she flashed a lightning glance at her aunt who was turning over a periodical on a table by her side.

"I don't tell Nannie because I think she wouldn't weally understand, and—and—"

Silence.

"Well, darling?"

"Auntie," she spoke in the merest whisper, "got awful cwoss the first time I did tell her. She was going out to a dance, and I was telling her whilst she was dwessing—it was a lovely dwess all sparkles and little wosebuds—and I upset a bottle of scent over her gloves. The scent too was like my dweams, just like—like—oh! I don't know, and I haven't any!"

Once more the man intuitively bridged the gulf.

"No little friends? How's that?"

"Bimba died," she announced casually. "She liked books, too. It's vewy silly thinking dolls are babies, isn't it; that's why I love weading, it—it seems weal!"

Lady Hetth broke in hurriedly.

"We simply can't keep her away from books when she's in town. Of course when we are in the country she simply lives out of doors. It is very difficult to keep her amused. She sulks when she goes to a party and always wants to go home!"

"I don't sulk weally, Auntie, I jus'—jus' don' seem to know how to play!"

She smiled a wan little smile at the woman who had no children of her own, and moved away slowly with a backward doggy look at the man.

"Good God!" he muttered. "Will you come here, Lady Hetth!"

CHAPTER II

"When your fear cometh as a desolation."
                              —*The Bible.*

Susan Hetth rose.

She had always intensely disliked her brother-in-law's old friend, failing utterly to perceive the heart of gold studded with rare gems that was hidden under a bushel of intentional brusqueness.

But as she was under an obligation to him she decided to make herself as pleasant as possible, and to obey his orders, however irksome.

Great brain specialist, great philanthropist, she had rung him up in a panic that morning after having vainly ransacked her memory for some other human being in whom she could with safety confide her fear, and from whom she could expect some meed of succour.

She knew, as everybody knew, that years ago he had given up the hours of consultation which had seen his Harley Street waiting-room filled to overflowing; that little by little, bit by bit, indeed, he had given himself up entirely to research work, travelling in every quarter of the globe in his quest for the knowledge necessary to the alleviation of the mental troubles of his fellow-beings. And that when he found it or some part of it he had hurried home, and having brought it to as near a state of perfection as possible, had flung it broad-cast to the suffering; just as he flung the immense sums of money he made among the destitute for whom he loved to work without thought of the morrow.

A genuine case of trouble he had never been known to dismiss, and Susan Hetth had heaved a sigh of relief into the receiver when he fixed an immediate appointment.

The spook of fear is not the cheeriest companion of the early cup of tea, and Nannie's words, allied to Nannie's face when she entered without knocking, had caused the silly, invertebrate woman to take immediate action for once in her life.

Not for anything would she confess it, but she wished now she had listened to Nannie when, just a year ago, she had so fervently urged a visit to the doctor the first time she had discovered the baby girl walking downstairs one step at a time in her sleep.

She remembered the way the ever-changing house-parlourmaids had furtively looked at the child when she came in to dessert; how one after the other they had given notice, declaring that although they really loved the child their nerves would not stand the ever-recurring shock of finding her sitting in some corner in the dark; or the pattering of her little feet on the stairs when she occasionally evaded the nurse and walked about the house in her sleep; and she remembered how other nurses who brought baby visitors to tea had watched the child, surreptitiously touching their foreheads and wagging their heads at each other.

But, as is the way of the supine, she had put it off and put it off until her negligence had culminated in the frightful scene of this same very early morning, when Leonie, waking in the day nursery to find her kitten dead, had screamed and shrieked hour after hour until the house-parlourmaid had rushed in and given instant notice, with the unsolicited information that the

Joan Conquest

servants thought, and the neighbours said, the child was mad and ought to be sent to a home.

Then, indeed, had terror suddenly tweaked Susan Hetth's heart, the social one, the maternal one having long since atrophied through want of use; for the shadow of lunacy is about the blackest of all the shadows that can fall across a butterfly's sunny, heedless path.

Ten years ago she had lost her husband, in the year following most of her capital had gone in a mad-cat speculation, and three years later her gallant brother-in-law died, leaving her a yearly income sufficient for expenses and education if she would undertake to mother his little daughter. Since then she had led the usual abortive life of the woman who lives on the past glamour of her husband's success and a limited income, upon which she tries ineffectually to dovetail herself into a society to which she does not rightly belong. Having noticed an increasing plenitude of silver among the ash-gold of her hair, a deepening of the lines of discord between her brows, and the threads of discontent which were daily being hems-titched into her face by the sharp needles of make-believe, covetousness, and a precarious banking account, she had recently decided to try and annex, or rather try and graft herself on to a certain unsuspecting male being *en secondes noces*.

And that simply cannot be done if there is the slightest shadow upon one's appendages.

So she sat down in the chair with as good a grace as she could muster, and arranged her big picture hat so that the spring sun should not draw Sir Jonathan's attention to the methods she employed to combat the rapidity with which what remained of her prettiness, prematurely faded by the Indian sun, was vanishing.

For a long and trying moment he sat silently staring at her, wondering as he had always wondered what had induced his old friend to place his little girl in such inadequate, feeble hands.

To break the tension Lady Hetth clanked a silver Indian bracelet bought at Liberty's against an Egyptian chain sold by Swan & Edgar's, and the man frowned as he drew a series of cats on his blotting-paper.

CHAPTER III

"Against stupidity the very gods Themselves contend in vain!"
—*Schiller*.

"Let me see," he said slowly. "You have been in India I believe. I wonder if you know anything about it!"

"I lived *ten* years in the Punjab." This information was given with the intense self-satisfaction peculiar to the feminine Anglo-Indian. "With my husband," was added after a rather damping silence, "who was knighted for certain—er—work he did in the Indian Civil Service."

"That doesn't mean that you know anything about the country, Mam. Leonie has been with you almost seven years, please correct me if I make any mistake. She is seven this month you say. She was four months old when she came over from India. Did her ayah come with her, by the way? No! Had she been good to the baby—yes! yes! I know, they always are, but these dreams indicate that the child has been badly frightened some time or another!"

"But she *couldn't* be frightened at four months," vacantly interrupted Susan Hetth, who could not see the trend of the conversation, or the need of the detailed interrogation. "She would be *far* too young!"

"Too *young*!" snapped Sir Jonathan. "Rubbish! Do you know

why you are afraid to-day of falling from a height?"

"No," replied Susan Hetth, cordially loathing the man, his methods, and his manners.

"Because," he answered roughly, "you were frightened of falling from your mother's or your nurse's arms when you were a few months old, and the impression of height and fear made upon your baby mind is still with you, *that's* why!"

"The brute!" she thought, as she smiled the propitiatory smile of one who is afraid and murmured, "How very interesting!"

"Is there anything else you can tell me about your little niece? no matter how trivial a detail! Has she ever screamed for hours as she screamed this morning? Does she get angry? I mean mad angry!"

"No!" replied the aunt. "From what her nurse and daily governess tell me she seems to be *remarkably* sweet-tempered. You see I don't—I haven't—I don't see much of her. I'm—I've—you see I have *so* many friends over here!"

The man snorted.

"I must say," she continued, "I have *never* met a child so averse from being kissed or being made a fuss of—she *hates* anyone to touch her, even—even *me*, her *mother*, as you might say; but they say she is tractable, and has never been known to lose her temper, or slap, or scratch, as some children do—no! there is *really* nothing to tell about her—of course she walks a bit in her sleep, at least so her Nannie says!"

The specialist's hand crashed on the table. "Good God, woman!" he flung at her, "what in heaven's name *are* you modern women made of? How long has she been walking in her sleep? Tell me all you know *at once*—and remember it's your niece's *brain* and her future you are talking about, so try and describe this sleep-walking with as much interest and regard to detail as you would if you were talking about a new dress. Why in heaven's name didn't you send her with the nurse—the *servant*—instead of coming yourself—I might have learnt something about the child *then*!"

It seemed that Leonie while still quite a baby had walked about the night nursery in her sleep; that she had been found in the day nursery and on the lower landing, but had always gone back to bed without waking; that she muttered a lot of rubbish which the nurse could not understand, and was always very tired next day. That now that she was older she slept in a room by herself as she became unaccountably restless and wide awake if anyone slept in the room with her. No! the nurse had never noticed the hour or the date, or anything, and that was really all, and "couldn't you give the child a dose of bromide."

Which sentence served to finish the history and to bring Sir Jonathan with a bound from his chair.

"Bromide," he snarled, "*bromide*! Now, Lady Hetth, listen to me. There is something more than nerves and a highly strung temperament in this. Next week I want Nannie, not *you*, to bring the child here on a visit. I know India and her religions as far as any Englishman dare say he knows anything about that unfathomable country—yes! Mam! religions—Hinduism—Brahminism—Buddhism—why, I've passed the best part of my life trying to unravel certain physical and psychical threads knotted up in India; but the years are slipping by, and time is getting shorter and shorter, and but a tithe done out of all there is to do; but thanks be, my boy has inherited my love for this work, and will carry on here when I have crossed the threshold and found the solutions to my problems on the other side. Though I'm sure I don't know why I'm telling *you* all this," he finished brusquely, "we will return to India."

"Yes! India is very, very interesting!" piped Lady Hetth, rising and standing on one foot so as to rest the other suffering from an oversmall shoe.

"Very, *very* interesting!" she continued unctuously and with the enthusiasm she reserved as a rule for the S.P.C.K.I, which letters stand for an attempt to graft a new creed on to the tree of religion in India which was bearing *fruit* at a period when we were hobnobbing in caves, with a boulder or good stout club as reasons for existence.

"I'll write and tell you when to send the child and her nurse, and between us we'll manage to keep her amused. And in the meantime stop all lessons and let her do exactly as she likes, and feed her up, Mam, feed her up, her bones are simply coming through her skin."

Again he laughed a great rumbling laugh, as lifting the child from the ground he felt the little hands in his mane of white hair.

"You're nice," she decided, "vewy nice."

"Like to come and stay with me?"

"Oh, yes! if you won't—won't make me—!"

She stopped short.

"Well! what—won't make you what?"

"Nothing—Auntie pulled my dwess!"

The door closed softly.

CHAPTER IV

"The kindest man,
The best conditioned and unwearied spirit
In doing courtesies."

　　　　　　　　　　　—Shakespeare.

They met on the threshold.

Swinging back the door to let Leonie and her aunt out, Ellen, the middle-aged maid, almost an heirloom in the family of Cuxson, bristling in starched cap and apron, let in the erstwhile plague of her life, but now as ever the light of her eyes, Jonathan Cuxson, Junior.

He took Lady Hetth's hand in a mighty and painful grip when after a moment's hesitation she introduced herself.

"Why, of course! You must be Jan! Except for being bigger you haven't changed a bit since I saw you years ago one Speech Day at Harrow!" She looked with open admiration at the very personable young man before her who loomed large in the hall with his height of six feet two and a tremendous width of shoulder. His eyes were grey, and as honest as a genuine fine day; the jaw was just saved from a shadow of brutality in its strength by a remarkably fine mouth; the ears were splendid from an intellectual point of view, and the set of the head on the neck, and the neck on the shoulders, perfect. The nose was a good nose, rather broad at the top, with those delicate sensitive nostrils which usually spell trouble for the owner.

"I don't believe you remember me!"

Happily the reply which must have been untrue or given in the negative was averted by the hilarious arrival of a puppy.

Having heard the deep voice associated in its canine mind with bits of cake and joyous roughs-and-tumbles, it had forsaken the happy though forbidden hunting ground of the upper storeys and negotiated the stairs in a series of bumps and misses.

Arrived in the hall it hurled itself blindly against Leonie's ankles, and ricocheted on to its master's boots, where it essayed a *pas seul* on its hind legs in its efforts to reach the strong brown hand.

"Oh!" said Leonie, as she fell on her knees with her arms outstretched to the rampaging ball of white fluff and high spirits, the which thinking it some new game squatted back on its hind legs with the front ones wide apart, gave an infantile squeak, and whizzed round three times apparently for luck, as tears welled up in the child's large eyes and trickled down the white face.

"Hello, kiddie! You're crying!" said Jan Cuxson, who like his father had a positive mania for protecting and helping those in trouble, which mania got him into an infinite and varied amount of trouble himself, and led him into unexpected boles and corners of the earth. "I'm—I'm not crying weally!" choked Leonie, "it's—it's my kitten!"

"Oh! do stop, Leonie!" said her aunt, leaning down to catch the child's hand and pull her to her feet. "She's coming to stay with you," she added, as Leonie stood quite still with that piteous jerk of the chin which comes from suppressed and overwhelming grief, as she watched the puppy play a one-sided game of bumblefoot in a corner.

"That's jolly," said the young man.

"Oh! she's coming as a case. She walks a good deal in her sleep, and as my brother-in-law, Colonel Hetth, if you remember, was such a—"

But Jan Cuxson was not listening.

He too had put his hand on the curly head and tilted it back gently so that the light shone into the sorrow-laden eyes encircled by shadows.

Then he smiled suddenly down at the mite, and she, perceiving that a ray of light had suddenly pierced the all-pervading gloom, smiled back, and catching his left hand in both of hers pressed it to her forehead.

"Good Lord!" he muttered, as a thrill ran through him at the unexpected and oriental action.

And Fate, plucking in senile fashion at the loose ends which lay nearest her old hand, knotted two tightly together with a bit of rare golden strand she kept tucked away in her bodice.

"And what shall we do when you come? Can you ride? I know of a lovely pony a little boy rides!"

Leonie shook her head mournfully, feeling unconsciously but acutely the penalty of her sex for the first time in her life.

"I can't wide astwide," she sighed, "I haven't any bweeches. Jill and Maudie Wetherbourne always wide in skirts. But I can swim," she added quickly, "an' jump in out of my depff. I learnt in the baff at the seaside!"

"Oh! come along, child, *do!*" broke in her aunt to her own undoing.

"Auntie jumps in too, though she says she doesn't," proceeded

Leonie in a gallant effort to shore up her family's sporting reputation.

"I do *not*, Leonie! I can't imagine how you ever got such an idea into your head!"

But Leonie, nothing daunted, shook back her russet mop of hair and gave direct answer, to the confusion of the domestic who happily stood out of Lady Hetth's eye-range.

"But, Auntie! I've *often* heard Wilkins tell Nannie that you've been in off the deep end before bweakfast! Oh! do let me hold him just for ever such a little while!"

To save the expression of his face Jan Cuxson had bent and lifted the pup by the scruff of its neck, and upon the piteous appeal put it squirming and wriggling in the outstretched arms.

Great tears dripped all over the animal though Leonie stood on one foot, bit her underlip, and squeezed the puppy to suffocation in a valiant effort to restrain this appalling sign of weakness.

"Tell me what makes you cry like that?"

"My—my kitten was—was stwangled by—by someone this morning, an'—an' she was all soft an'—an' fluffy like—"

The words ended in a paroxysm of sobs muffled in the puppy's coat whereupon it ecstatically licked every visible part of the child's neck, whilst Ellen, throwing decorum to the winds, knelt down and drew the shaking little figure into her arms.

"Anybody in there!" suddenly and very gruffly asked Jan Cuxson, jerking his head in the direction of the room where the few and favoured awaited the pleasure of the specialist.

"No, Sir," replied Ellen, as she disentangled one of the puppy's claws from the lace on Leonie's sleeve. "I'm going to call my father! I don't think you understand your little girl very well!"

He spoke quite gently but his face was white with anger, that almost terrifying rage which surges over and through the mentally and physically strong at the sight, or thought, of cruelty to the small and weak.

He whistled two exceedingly sharp notes and plunged his hands into his pockets, where he scrunched up his keys and some loose change.

CHAPTER V

"The liberal soul shall be made fat."
— *The Bible.*

"Well! well! well!"

Sir Jonathan walked over to the child and knelt down beside her as the maid rose and straightened her crumpled apron.

"Let me have the doggie, darling!"

"No!—no!—*no*! I—I love him. He's all soft and cuddley. I want to hold him for jus' a little, little longer!"

The child's voice was shrill with excitement as she pulled back from the encircling arms, her lips quivering, her eyes staring distractedly first at the younger man then at the dog.

"Would you like to have Jingles, kiddie?"

The change in the child's face was electrifying, and Sir Jonathan, rising with his eyes fixed upon her, touched his son's arm to draw his attention to it.

Tears like dewdrops on brown pansy petals hung heavily from the lashes, but the corners of the mouth turned up in an adorable smile, and waves of gratitude and delight swept up from chin to brow obliterating the agony of the past hours.

Joan Conquest

"For *me*—to *keep*?" she whispered, as she stood on her toes in an instinctive effort to make the body reach and unite with the mind at the highest point of this most perfect moment, whilst her little breast heaved with the repressed sobs of her fully laden heart.

"Yes! for keeps, little one!"

The three elders stood silently, the specialist watching intently the light which kindled in the child's eyes as she looked from one to the other before she bent her head over the dog she had completely surrounded with her arms.

Jan Cuxson made a movement to end a situation which was bordering on cruelty when Lady Hetth anticipated him with her customary dire tactlessness.

"There now, Leonie! *Now* perhaps you'll be satisfied. Give Mr. Cuxson a kiss and say thank you nicely!"

Leonie would have cheerfully put her hand in the fire to serve this wonderful being who royally distributed gifts, and *live* ones at that, and only hesitated for the barest fraction of a second before, her face suffused with crimson, she walked up to him.

"Of course if—if you want me to—I'll—I'll kiss you," she said heroically, unconsciously squeezing the puppy under the stress of the awful moment until it yelped, "but I'd—I'd wather—" She stopped and looked up hurriedly into the understanding face of the elder man.

He nodded as he caught her eye so that she finished all in a hopeful burst.

"But I'd wather not if you don't mind!"

Lady Hetth frowned and put out her hand, murmuring something about really having to go.

"I'll send for her and Nannie, Lady Hetth. And keep her out of doors as much as possible. Why don't you take her to the Zoo this afternoon?"

"I couldn't *possibly*!" came the prompt and irritable reply.

"What about me!" interrupted Jan Cuxson. "Eh! kiddie? You and I riding big, fat elephants at the Zoo!"

"*You*—and *Jingles*—and *me*!" said Leonie, disengaging her hand from her aunt's. "And you," she said sweetly, laying it on the elder man's coat sleeve.

Heaven had opened wide its gates and she was for pulling everybody in with her, and her eyes danced, and so did her patent shod feet on the rug.

"It's *too* kind of you, Jan!" broke in her aunt. "I really don't like to let you waste your time with a child!"

"Not at all, Lady Hetth! I love kids—and the Zoo. Where shall I bring her to afterwards?"

"Oh! Yes! bring her to the Ladies' Union Club where I am staying. No! you'd better take her to her Nannie as they don't allow children in the Club, thank goodness. They are staying in York Street, Baker Street, quite convenient for you."

She trailed through the door as she spoke, pouring out a cascade of vapid thanks and announcing also that she had shopping to do at Debenham and Freebody's.

She hadn't, she was going to catch an omnibus in Cavendish Square, being of those who, blindly extravagant in most things, think they economise when spoiling their clothes and temper in a penny ha'penny bus, instead of keeping both unruffled in a taxi, at two shillings.

Ellen, returning later triumphantly with a taxi, held wide the

Joan Conquest

door, a wide and loving smile across her plain face.

"You come too, Sir," said Jan Cuxson. "Do you heaps of good to ride an elephant!"

"I only wish I could, boy," said the man as he laid one hand on the shoulder of the son he loved, and the other on Leonie's head. "But I've much to do in that opium case, and I'm dining out, and shall read a bit when I get back—"

"And I'm dining out too, more's the nuisance, otherwise I could help. Sure to be awfully late as it's a farewell dinner to a fellow at the hospital—"

"Well! See you in the morning! Good-bye, sweetheart, I won't forget the book, and just you make that lazy fellow show you everything!"

He bent and kissed Leonie as she lifted her face, which was an unheard-of thing for her to do, and watched her as, hugging the struggling dog, she ran down the steps and was lifted into the taxi by her companion.

With his foot on the step Jan hesitated, then turned and walked back to his father.

"I don't know why. Sir, but I do wish you'd come too," he said slowly, looking at the man he loved with a love past the comprehension of the younger generation of the present day.

He put out his hand as he spoke and gripped the elder man's hard, then ran down the steps, jumped in beside Leonie, and turned to wave hilariously with her as they sped away to the Zoo.

The brain specialist went back thoughtfully to his room, and when he had closed the door stood for a long time looking out at the little garden with its one big tree.

"I wonder, I *wonder*," he mused. "I'd give a good deal to get at that ayah—well! why not?—I could start for—" He looked round suddenly, then laughed as he passed his hand over his eyes. "Funny! I thought someone opened the door."

He moved to his desk and turned over his diary, showing blank page after blank page.

"Strange," he muttered. "There is nothing written down after to-day, not a single engagement. I must have entered them in some other book; very careless of me."

CHAPTER VI

"And the wild beasts of the islands shall cry
in their desolate homes."
                                        —*The Bible.*

"Gawd!"

Mrs. Henry Higgins called upon the Almighty in the
vernacular of Seven Dials, sought gropingly for the members of
her progeny who clutched her skirt, and fortunately kept her
head.

"'Enery James—no! Gertrude Ellen—you've gotter better
headpiece, jest yer slip along to the keeper an' tell *'im* to look
slippy and come along quick *h'and* quiet!"

Gertrude Ellen, puffed up with pride at the pull she had had
over her brother, slipped off, as her mother continued in a
raucous whisper, "Now if that young miss don't deserve a
thorough good 'iding! I'd take the skin off yer if any of yer did
such a fing, strite I would. Drat yer, keep stilt cawn't yer—
you'll rouse the brute!"

She shook her skirts so that the half-dozen clinging children
rattled like a bunch of keys, pushed her jet bonnet back from
the shiny wrinkled forehead, and waited, her motherly heart
aquake in spite of her drastic language.

Jan Cuxson was standing in front of the lions' cage at one end of the lion-house, talking to his old friend the keeper, under the impression that Leonie was close beside him; but she, having taken advantage of their conversation and a practically empty house, had slipped quietly away, climbed the barrier near the far window, and was *also* holding conversation—with a tiger from Bengal.

The animal lay outstretched with his wonderful head close to the bars, and his unblinking opalescent gold-flecked eyes staring straight into the opalescent gold-flecked eyes of the child as she stood on tip-toe so that her face was almost on a level with that of the animal.

"*Poor* tiger!" she was saying. "I'm vewwy sowwy for you—I'm sure you're not so vewy, vewy wicked, an' if you will bend your head I will stwoke you behind the ear same as I did Kitty."

Mrs. Henry Higgins gasped.

Holding on to one bar tightly just near the tiger's mouth so as to steady herself, Leonie stretched, and thrusting her hand inside began to rub the tiger's head quite forcibly behind the ear.

"Nice?" she inquired as the animal closed its eyes under the unexpected and unexperienced caress, then opening them lifted the beautiful head and yawned to the full capacity of the huge mouth, affording Leonie a front row view of the splendid ivories and pale pink tongue.

"Oh—h—h!" said she admiringly, standing flat and patting the nearest paw. "I *do* like you though you *do* fwighten me when you walk so softly in my dweams—oh—h—h!"

She shivered with ecstasy as the tiger rolled on its back, displaying its soft white belly as it bit its hind foot with the abandon of a baby, then turned on its side, and leaping side-ways to its feet, slunk off to the far corner of the miserable den, which is all a civilised country gives a wild animal in exchange for its jungle home.

Meanwhile the Higgins brood, like hungry sparrows on a rail, were sitting open-mouthed on the lower steps provided for the benefit of those spectators who wish to revel with safety in the degrading sight of the royal beasts fed with lumps of bleeding meat pushed through the lower bar on the end of a prong.

Rendered somewhat incoherent by fear, and haste, allied to the ghastly English she had acquired in the streets and been allowed to retain in the Council School, Gertrude Ellen had found it somewhat difficult to arouse the keeper to a realisation of the impending disaster.

But when he *did* look over his shoulder in the direction her dirty little hand was pointing he swore a mighty oath and acted promptly.

"Keep still, Sir, for the love of heaven!" he whispered, catching hold of Jan Cuxson's arm as the latter made a step forward. "Don't let that there animal see yer, he's the blamedest, cussedest brute I've ever had to do with. Never had a civil growl from him since he came here over three years ago."

Whilst speaking the man had hurriedly discarded his boots and climbed inside the barrier, whilst Cuxson held the child quiet by her thin little shoulders.

"Damn that woman," went on the keeper, "why can't she keep still. Sure as blazes if that there tiger sees her, which don't mean if he's *looking* at her, he'll go nasty and have that missy's 'and off."

Mrs. Higgins, having clumped her brood into silence, was making frantic and what she imagined to be surreptitious signals of distress with her left arm, keeping her eyes glued on Leonie, who was clinging to the bars with both hands whilst calling upon the tiger to come back.

He came back, half crouched, noiselessly, stealthily, the hair of the belly almost touching the ground, for all the world like a cat about to spring upon an unsuspecting sparrow.

He came to a standstill within an inch of the bars and threw his pointed ears straight forward so that they stood out at right angles to the beautifully marked face; spasmodically twitched back the mouth without a sound issuing therefrom, and then lay down and pressed his head against the bars.

The tiny hand was stroking the silky ears, patting the head, and prodding contentedly into the thick fur of the neck when suddenly with a mighty heart-quaking roar the tiger leapt up and back, and then hurled himself at the bars.

The keeper had crept, bent double, along the inside of the barrier, and had most suddenly and surprisingly seized Leonie by the waist and wrenched her free from the bars to which she had tried to cling, holding her like a vice in his arms where she vainly kicked and struggled for freedom.

CHAPTER VII

". . . that man could not be altogether cleared
from injustice in dealing with beasts as he now
does."

—Plutarch.

The whole house was in an uproar.

The lions were trotting round and round, stopping to listen and snuff in the sawdust near the bars; the stumpy jaguar, black as ink, with a body like a steel case, was rushing up and down, rubbing its forehead fiercely as it turned; a lion and his mate were rearing themselves one after the other against the walls, half turning from the middle to fall almost backward in that peculiar movement which reminds one forcibly of great succeeding waves stopped and thrown back upon themselves by some bleak rock.

People were pushing and straining to look in at the windows, and rattling the doors which had been hurriedly locked by the keepers who had rushed to ascertain the cause of the tumult, whilst the tiger made the place resound with its terrific roars as it hurled its huge weight again and again at the bars of its cage.

"Come *on*, Mother," shouted the keeper above the din, "bring all those children and let's get out. They'll quieten down when we've gone. Can't you *read*!"

He shook Leonie slightly under the stress of his agitation as he hauled her in front of the notice which commands you to refrain from climbing the barrier.

"Of course I can wead," she replied with dignity; "I'm weading the little—"

"Well! read *that*!"

"But—but"—stammered Leonie, having read with difficulty—"but I knew the tiger, Mr. Keeper!"

"*Oh*! yes! of course! You were tiger 'unting and brought him from the Sunderbunds about four years ago; it wasn't the gentleman, of course not!"

"But weally," pleaded Leonie with the tears very near, "weally I've—I've dweamed lots about him, and—and—and—"

"Take her away, Sir—she makes me see red she does. No thank you. Sir—very much obliged, but it's part of my duty to see that people *don't* climb the barrier, and I kind of failed—p'raps the little girl what came and—"

They were outside by this time and the centre of an interested admiring crowd; it is only bleeding meat at three o'clock as a rule which can rouse the inhabitants of the lion house from their prison apathy.

Taking the dirty little paw Cuxson, crumpling up a note, put it into the dirty little palm and closed the fingers tightly over it. Whereupon Gertrude Ellen blushed furiously, and went to her mother with her clenched fist behind her back, where she kept it stiffly until tea-time, when she held out the bit of paper without a word, to the tune of "Lawks a mercy me!" from her mother, who immediately ordered more buns on the strength of it.

"Lor' bless yer, lovey!" said Mrs. Higgins, whose bonnet was bobbing on the nape of her neck, leaving the wisps of hair to straggle unrestrainedly in the honest grey eyes, as she knelt on the ground and tugged Leonie's short skirts into place. "Yer did give us a turn, dearie; yer might 'av 'ad yer 'and nipped orf by that there brute. Come '*ere*, Lil and 'Erb—I'll 'ave yer eaten by the camuls next!"

The bow-legged twins, with their spirit of adventure quashed, rolled back to mother, and stood wide-eyed as she ran her work-worn hand through the stranger's luxuriant curls.

"Give us a kiss, lovey, an' go an' get some tea!"

For the second time that day Leonie moved to obey the same command, but this time there was no hesitation as she put her thin arms round the woman's neck and kissed her sweetly once and again.

And the woman, who sensed something amiss in the quivering little body, held her firmly, patting her gently with the same hand which dealt out indiscriminately such resounding and often well-earned smacks among her own; and Leonie sighed and leant confidingly against the stout, badly corseted figure.

"How comfy," she whispered shyly. "How soft you are. Auntie never holds me in her arms, and when Nannie does she's always full of bits of things that stick *out*."

And then with a little scream of delight she was away, speeding over the gravel in the wake of a lumbering great form wending its way in and out of the crowd.

"Cut along, Sir, or you'll find her 'obnobbing with the gorilla next! I've never *seen* such a child for downright mischievousness."

Cuxson cut along as bidden and for all he was worth, pulling Leonie up in front of the ticket office for elephant rides, and after purchasing tickets sidetracked her to a tea-table.

* * * * * * * *

"Mind you bring Jingles when you come to stay!"

"Pwomise," called back Leonie from her Nannie's arms as she opened the door to them and lifted the tired happy child from the taxi.

But she didn't because she never went.

CHAPTER VIII

"And make my seated heart knock at my ribs
Against the use of nature. Present fears
Are less than horrible imaginings."

—Shakespeare.

Big Ben announced the approaching hour of midnight, throwing the sonorous notes to the soft spring wind which wafted them up to Harley Street.

Save for the light thrown by the dancing flames of a log fire, and the orange disc made on the desk by the light of a heavily shaded lamp, the room was dark; the silence broken only by the occasional crackle of the wood fire and the faint rustle as Sir Jonathan turned a page.

"Notes" was written in letters of brass across the thick book heavily bound in leather, and of which the small key to the massive Bramah lock was kept in a pocket especially made in every waistcoat Sir Jonathan possessed.

Slowly he read through the page he had just written, crossing a t, dotting an i, adding or scratching out a word of the writing which was in no way more legible than that of any other surgeon; and when he had read he ran his hand through the mass of snow-white hair, sighed, and pushed the book further back on to the desk.

It is an eerie sound that of someone speaking aloud to himself, and still more eerie when it occurs in the middle of the night when the only part of the speaker to be clearly seen is the strong white hands moving in the orange disc thrown on the desk by the heavily shaded lamp.

And it is a strange habit this talking aloud of the solitary soul.

Mad?

Not a bit.

Dumb in the babel and din of chaotic midday, unresponsive to the uncongenial matter around, it will talk on subjects gay and grave, and even laugh with the silent sympathetic shades of midnight.

Nevertheless it is mighty eerie to hear it unawares.

For the twentieth time the famous specialist picked up a letter and read it from beginning to end.

"Strange, Jim, old fellow," said he as he laid it down, "strange how I think of you to-night. Seeing your little one, I suppose. But somehow to-night more than ever I feel the blank you made in my life when you left. How you'd have loved the kiddie, Jim. Strange wee soul with a shadow already on her life—a big black shadow, Jim, which I—I am going—!"

He turned his head and looked over his shoulder.

"Ugh!" he said, as he turned back to the desk and drew the book towards him.

"Leonie Hetth—age seven—walks in her sleep and dreams—dreams are evidently of India—things that walk softly and purr—a small light—and wet red which may mean blood—green eyes and a black woman who—who—"

Once more he ran his hand through his hair, but time irritably, then shook his head from side to side rubbed his hand across his eyes.

"I've been sitting up too late these last few nights over that opium case. Don't seem to be able to collect or hold my thoughts. Jim, old fellow, I wonder what made you leave Leonie in the care of that damn silly, shallow woman, and I wonder how you could ever have produced anything so highly strung and temperamental as your little daughter. I sup—"

He stopped quite suddenly and rose, standing with his head bent forward.

There was not a sound!

Feeling for the arm of his chair with his face still turned to the curtained window he sank back, only to spring upright with a bound.

Noiselessly, swiftly he crossed to the window, and pulling back the curtain an inch or two peered out into the small garden with its one tree and border of shrubs.

There was no sound and nothing moved.

"Strange!" he muttered, "I could have sworn some-one knocked."

He jerked back the curtains so that they rasped on the brass rod, letting in the almost blinding glare of the full moon which drew a nimbus from the silvery head and threw shadows which danced and gibbered by the aid of the log fire over the walls and ceiling, and in and out of the open safe.

He turned, but stopped abruptly when half-way across the room, standing stock still with his back to the window.

There was a faint distinct tapping as though slender fingers were beating a ghastly, distant drum.

It stopped—it continued—it stopped.

Then fell one little solitary rap like a drop of water falling on a metal plate, and it died away into silence.

And Sir Jonathan threw up his fine old head and laughed.

"Surely I've got India on the brain to-night, and as surely I want a good long holiday," he said, as he sat down at his desk and picked up his pen. "And I must remember to tell the gardener to clip that tree to-morrow. How Jan will laugh when I tell him that I was absolutely scared by a branch rubbing against the window."

For five long minutes he sat frowning down at the pen in his hand. Three times he commenced to write, and three times he stopped; twice he lit a cigarette and let it go out, and deeper grew the lines between the brows and round the mouth, until he shivered and turned quickly in his chair.

"That felt just like a sea-fog creeping up behind; stupid to keep the window open even in spring," he said as he picked up a log from a basket by his side and threw it deftly into the wide-open grate, leant sideways to separate two brass ornaments on a table which had jangled one against the other, and sighing turned restlessly in his chair.

"Confound those great market lorries," he muttered, looking round the room with its cabinets and shelves filled with the strange and weird, beautiful and unsightly curios he had brought back from every corner of the globe. "They shake the house enough to bring it down about one's ears."

The moon was slowly shifting as he leant back and settled himself comfortably in the high leather chair; the room was getting darker and there had fallen that intense almost palpable stillness which envelops most great cities after midnight, and against which his thoughts stood out like steel points upon a velvet curtain.

Clear and sharp as steel they shot indeed, this way and that through his mind; but hold them he could not, analyse or arrange them he could not, neither would his hand move towards the pen a few inches from the finger-tips.

"God!" he suddenly thundered, striking the arm of the chair with his fist. "The answer is just there on the tip of my tongue—before my very eyes—within reach of my fingers, and yet I cannot grasp it—ah! why! could it *possibly* be—"

He rose as he spoke and crossed to a massive bookcase packed to overflowing with books, switched on a light hanging near, opened the glass door and ran his hand lovingly over the leather volumes.

Then he very gently laid his hand on his left shoulder and turned with a smile lighting up his face, which abruptly went blank in astonishment.

"Upon my word," he said, "whatever made me think that Jan had come in and had put his hand upon my shoulder. Old fool that I am to-night."

For a moment he stood looking into the shadowy corners, then turned again to the case, ran his finger along a row of books until he came to one with the title "India," pulled it out and opened it under the light.

The book opened quite suddenly and wide, and his eyes fell on the first few lines. Without a movement he stood staring down at the printed words, reading to the end of the page, then he violently closed the book, thrust it back into the case, and closing the doors, pressed against them with both hands as though in an endeavour to keep back something which was trying to get out.

"No! my God! No! never! not that—not *that* as an end—not for *that* baby—and yet—"

He moved across to the desk, sank heavily like a very old man into his chair and covered his face with his hands.

Then very slowly and as though against his will he uncovered his face, and leaning forward stared across to the bookcase whilst he groped for the pen beside the book.

"And the cure," he muttered, "the remedy—I *must* find it—I—I—"

His heart was thudding heavily with the merest suspicion of a complete pause between the beats, his hand trembled almost imperceptibly, whilst his eyes glanced questioningly this way and that.

"I don't understand, I don't understand!" he whispered, just like a frightened child as he plucked at his collar and moved his head quickly from side to side as though trying to loosen some stranglehold about his neck.

He turned and stared unseeingly into the fire with the look of perplexity deepening on his face, then slowly he raised his eyes, first to the delicate tracings of the Adams mantelpiece, then to the varied ornaments on the shelf.

"Tish!" he said impatiently as they roved from the central figure of benign undisturbed Buddha, to a snake of brass holding a candle, and on to a blatant and grotesque dragon from China.

For a second he stared uncomprehendingly, then raised his head.

Inch by inch his eyes moved until they reached the top shelf of the overmantel and stopped. A shiver shook him as he lay back in his chair, his widespread fingers clutched at the chair arms, a

Joan Conquest

tiny bead of perspiration showed upon the broad forehead.

Staring down at him, shining evilly in the moonlight, was a glistening, unwavering eye.

Just a slanting mother-o'-pearl eye in the battered head of a god or goddess of India, with features almost obliterated by the passage of centuries.

For a full minute Sir Jonathan sat staring up at the eye which stared back; then moving with a convulsive jerk, ran both hands through the mane of silvery hair as though to lift some crushing load from about his head; and turning sideways in his chair stretched out one hand between the eye above and his own as he clumsily seized the pen in the shaking fingers.

"Ah! my God!" he muttered, "the answer is still there, on the tip of my tongue, before my eyes, within reach of my fingers, and I cannot grasp it—ah!—yes—"

Slowly and with infinite pain he wrote, printing the letters in thick and crooked capitals, whilst his breath whistled through the dilated nostrils and one foot beat unceasingly against the desk.

"The answer to the problem concerning Leonie Hetth is in the third volume upon—"

His hand stopped suddenly when the fingers involuntarily spread wide apart, letting fall the pen which rolled across the book; and the silvery head turned inch by inch until the grey eyes had lifted to the one shining in the shadows.

And there commenced a desperate, a bitter struggle for a child's reason, perhaps for a child's life, as the moon gently withdrew her light.

Like the clammy wraiths of fog upon the moor, like the searching tentacles of some blind monster of the sea, fear crept upon the splendid old man in this still hour of the night.

It held his hands, it was folded about his mouth, it pounded violently upon his gallant heart, whilst the eye looked him between the eyes, so that his brain was seared as strive he might to turn away his head he kept his face turned piteously upward.

"What is it," he muttered thickly, as though his tongue clove to the roof of the mouth, "what is it that is pulling me, pressing upon me, choking me! I have no body, no—no hands—I—have—no power to move—I—"

And then he screamed, though but a whisper fell, as with a spasmodic jump of his whole body he flung himself round in his chair, and cowering low against the arm, peered into the deepening shadows.

"All round about me," he whispered, "all about me those hands are pulling, and yet—and—and—"

He laughed until his face, a white cameo against a grey velvet pall, grinned like a mask of mirthless death, as slowly he raised one clenched fist and shook it weakly until it fell back with a dull thud, useless, against the chair.

"I thought I was afraid—I—I thought I saw—I saw death behind—but I—I shall not die until—until I have written—written—what is it I am to write—ah! yes!"

Searching sideways with his left hand he groped and found the pen, then very carefully, very slowly turned towards the desk.

He drove the pen in fiercely, making a thick black mark; he pushed it until the nib stuck, spluttered, and broke as he flung out both hands as if grasping at something which evaded him.

"Gone!" he mouthed, though there was no sound of speech in the room. "Gone—gone!" and he suddenly tore at his collar and his cuffs as though to break some bond which held him, as he glanced furtively about the room.

For one long moment he sat leaning forward, staring far beyond the Indian screen upon which his eyes were fixed, and then slowly, almost imperceptibly, his head moved.

The drawn white face had the hunted look of some animal at bay, the agonised eyes moved as the head moved; slowly, slowly, inch by inch, the breath coming stertorously as the mouth tried vainly to frame some word.

The moon had gathered the last fold of her silvery raiment about her and was creeping away through the open window just as Sir Jonathan looked straight up into the eye gleaming malevolently through the gloom.

And as he looked the head moved gently so that the eye leered cunningly into the distorted face beneath; it, hovered for a fraction of time on the edge of the shelf and fell, just as the old man, with a blinding flash of understanding sweeping his face, sprang to his feet, stood upright, swayed forward, and fell back sideways, dead, across his chair, staring across the room into eternity with eyes full of knowledge and infinite horror.

CHAPTER IX

"How have I hated instruction, and my heart
despised reproof!"

—The Bible.

"Oh! dear!"

The plaintive ejaculation fell on the drowsy noonday air, and
the speaker fished a chocolate out of the box, offered her in
heartfelt sympathy by her companion.

"Buck up, old thing!" said the latter. "These very same old
exam rods were laid up in pickle for our forbears, and they
survived the ordeal. The summer's here and the holidays are
due, so let's grin and bear it, and what *does* it matter if you *do*
mix your futures and conditionals? As long as it's French and
you don't split your infinitives you're all right, the splitting, I
believe, *is* a mortal sin in some cases, though I don't quite
understand how, or exactly what it means."

Seaview House is an establishment for the finishing of young
ladies, which process includes the rounding of their anatomical
angles by means of dancing and physical culture, and the
polishing of the facets of their intelligence by the gentle manipulation of three or four foreign governesses and professors of
music, singing, drawing, etc. These latter smile suavely
through the excruciating half-hours they allot to each unfinished damsel, and tear their hair in private at the memory of the

Joan Conquest

daily and hourly murderous executions of the old masters at which they must perforce assist.

And as much, and even more, attention is paid to the repousse work on the outside of the platter.

The hirsute covering is brushed and burnished until the heads of the two score damsels bob about in the sun like globes of ebony, or straw, or Dutch cheese, or ginger; finger nails shine like old cut glass, just enough and not too much; figures are repressed or augmented until they look more like figures and less like sacks of barley, or wood planks. They are taught to sit down and stand up, and to cross, enter or leave a room like humans instead of colts, to pitch the voice in a low and gracious key, and to look upon slang as a luxury only to be enjoyed in the absence of those in temporary power. In fact the establishment is quite old-fashioned but infinitely charming, and has the reputation of having more old pupils to a score of years happily or advantageously married, and fewer ditto employed in a useful capacity than any other school in Eastbourne.

Which is all as it should be!

"Yes! but," continued, let's call her Annie Smith; she does not appear in the book again so that it really does not matter about her nomenclature. "I could just see Leonie from my desk and she was smiling all over her face and romping, simply *romping* through the French papers."

"Oh! but," sympathised, let us call her Susan Brown for the same reason that we christened Annie Smith, "*she* has a brain!"

Nice Susan Brown hadn't, but balanced the lack by a wealthy parentage.

"Yes! of course she has! And *isn't* she beautiful!"

Nice Annie Smith was as plain as a bun, but balanced her

defect by a heart of gold, and found her ultimate and perfect joy in an overworked curate and seven children by him, all of whom were destined to sit round the festive board like seven plain little currantless buns on a plate.

"Yes! isn't she! She's wonderful, I think, and oh! so very different to all of us."

"I found the very word to suit her in the dictionary," rather importantly added Susan Brown, "*bizarre*—"

"Whatever does it mean?" inquired Annie Smith, who was destined never again to run up against the word or its meaning during the rest of her neutral life.

"Er—a kind of a—er—*je ne sais quoi* in the temperament—not exactly a nonconformist, you know; but just a little—well, not *quite* like *us*!"

"I see!" contentedly replied mystified Annie Smith. "But I *do* love her; she's such a dear. So gentle and so ready to help everybody, and so *splendid* at sports. What tremendous friends she and Jessica have become, haven't they, since the night of the scare? I often wonder what made her walk in her sleep like that; she's never done it since."

"Indigestion, I've always thought. Cookie was away on her holidays, if you remember, and her *locum tenens*, understudy, you know, made pastry like cement; I always thought, too, that Principal gave her that lovely little room right away from the rest of us on account of it—the sleep-walking, I mean. I'm sure I should have *died* if I'd found her standing over me in the moonlight in the middle of the night. It must be awfully jolly though having someone in India who writes to you every three months. *Isn't* she lucky to have been *born* in India, and to have had an ayah, a kind of native nurse, you know, who *still* worships her, and writes to her, and sends *real* Indian presents, and to have had a V.C. for a father—Leonie, I mean?"

Annie Smith laughed that happy laugh which is the outcome of a perfectly contented mind. "She deserves all the luck she gets, and what luck for *us* having her as head next term. What a favourite she is with everyone, even old Signer Valenti! Oh, dear, I wish to-morrow's exams were over; my fingers feel just like blanc-mange when I think of that nocturne."

"Never say die, Ann! *Have* you heard Leonie play the Moonlight?"

"No! What's it like?"

"Simply *awful*, just like Mam'zel when she thumps downstairs in her felt slippers."

There fell a space of drowsy silence in which the girls lay back on the grass incline, and solemnly munched chocolates with youth's delightful dissociation from anything more perplexing than the passing of the actual hour.

"No!" murmured Annie Smith, breaking the drowsy spell. "She's *not* like us—couldn't be with a V.C. father and India as a birthright. But isn't it all *wonderfully* mysterious?"

Dear unsophisticated soul, whose *wanderlust* was yearly arrested, or rather satisfied, with the summer holiday by the sea, and whose rector father acted as a weekly soporific to his congregation.

"I wonder who gave her that perfectly *horrible* charm?" she added sleepily.

"The ayah, I *think*," came an equally sleepy answer. "Did I tell you that I found it in the bath-room the other night? It's an eye—a cat's-eye, you know—a perfect beast of a thing; I would swear it winked at me when I dropped it on the floor. Anyway I left it there and simply *flew* out of the room to tell Leonie, and Jessica pinched, I beg Principal's pardon, took my bath. Ugh! and she wears it night and day—oh! look, here she comes—"

"Oh!" sighed plain Annie Smith, "isn't she *beautiful*!"

She was!

Unaware that anyone was watching, Leonie stopped in front of a bush of red roses. She neither touched or sniffed them; she just flung out her arms, lifted her face to the blazing sun and laughed.

The simple school frock showed the wonder of her figure, with the beautiful rounded bust, the slender waist, and the moulded limbs; the sun drew red and yellow lights out of the heavy russet hair, gold flecks out of the green eyes, and a flash of crimson from the rather full clear-cut mouth with its turned-up corners.

Her skin was like ivory with the faintest tinge of pink just on the very tip of the rather pronounced cheek-bones; her hands were small and fine, and the fingers were like pea-pods, long and slender and slightly dimpled.

And when she moved away towards the summer-house where she could see the sea, she moved not at all from her waist upwards. She held her head and shoulders as though she had carried baskets of fruit or washing upon the crown of her pate since her youth; her glorious bosom was like a bed of lotus buds in the southern wind; she moved like a deer, or a snake, or a bacchanalian dancer, as you will; but in any case in a way which in the present tense caused the Principal to mourn in secret, and in the future brought the condemnation of women and the eyes of men full upon her.

And behind the summer-house she leant against the wall.

"One more term," she said, "only one more term, and then I shall be free—free to go—free to wander—free to follow the voice which is calling, calling! Only one more little term!"

And Fate, grinning, pinched that one more little term between her knotted old thumb and finger so that it was stillborn.

CHAPTER X

"And hath gone and served other gods."

—The Bible.

Shriek upon shriek tore the peaceful stillness of the night, and in one second the sleeping house was transformed from a place of rest and quiet to the semblance of a disturbed rookery.

Deathly silence followed the horrible screams of fear and the sound of the girls calling one to the other, during which mistresses extricated themselves from the encumbering bed-clothes to rush on to their respective landings; elder girls peered in terror from their bedroom doors, and younger ones clung to each other or the bed-post, or the door-knob, any-thing in fact which would help to support their quaking little knees.

Once again the terrible screams rent the air, whipping every-one out of the stunned apathy which great fear brings to some folk, just as the Principal came out on to her landing and looked up to the second storey.

"Miss Primstinn," she called, and her voice showed no sign of the thudding of her heart.

Pushed by one of those willing hands always so eager to thrust someone else to the forefront of the battle, Miss Primstinn, clutching her courage and a drab dressing-gown in both hands,

Joan Conquest

half ran, half slipped down the stairs.

"*We* will investigate, Miss Primstinn, and the young ladies will retire to their rooms and shut the doors."

In days long past the house had been well built after the excellent design of a wealthy old architect who had fled the place when Eastbourne had become a centre for girls' schools and summer trippers.

The full moon flooded the hall round which ran the galleries belonging to the successive storeys, each crowded with girls in various designs of night attire who hung over the oak balustrades to watch developments.

But they all leapt in unison, as though spurred into action by an electric shock, when a deep voice boomed from the shadows round a green baize door in the hall which led to the servants' quarters.

Then a distinct sigh of relief whistled softly through the entire house when the electric lights suddenly blazed and the speaker was discovered to be cook.

Cookie in an emerald green moirette petticoat and a somewhat *declasse* bedjacket, a tight knot of hair playing bob-cherry with her kindly right blue eye, and a rolling-pin clutched truculently in her red right hand.

Dear old Cookie who scolded and complained unceasingly, but who loved the entire school with a love which took the substantial form of delicious cakes, and buns, and jellies.

"H'I've come to h'investigate, Mum!" she called up. "Berglers or worse got into Miss Jessica's room through them dratted French windies, I'll be bound. Now just you stay where you are, Mum, an' I'll go an' see, an' if I screams then come along. And I think a policeman might come in handy, there may be one on the beat."

She waddled away to another green door always left open o' nights, and which led to the wing reserved entirely for the girls of the Upper Sixth; and where each one revelled in her own dainty separate bedroom.

"The young ladies will retire to their bedrooms and close their doors. Mademoiselle, I depend upon you!" With one hand on the banisters and one foot poised for descent, the Principal pitted her will against overwhelming curiosity and won.

Backing like a flock of sheep before the sheep-dog, they slowly retired and shut the doors, only to fling them wide open and rush to the balustrade in time to see the Principal, followed by Miss Primstinn, hurrying down the stairs to meet Cookie, who had run back into the hall shouting at the top of her voice.

"Come along, Mum! Quick! Miss Jessica's dead and Miss Gertrude dying. And where's Miss Lee-onny—fetch her some-one—it's 'er friend, little Miss Jessica, wots—wots—"

The Principal, whose face looked suddenly livid and old, laid a hand on Cookie's shoulder.

"Run and fetch the doctor, Cook, please, it will be quicker than the telephone! I can trust you to keep your head. Dr. Mumford is too far away, fetch the new one at the end of the road."

"Please to send Brown, Mum, she's younger an' quicker at runnin' than me. An' I think I can 'elp you, Mum," said Cookie quietly, unconsciously responding to the strength of her mistress's character. "An' I'd like to fetch Miss Lee-onny, Mum, she's that to be depended h'on an' clear'eaded."

The Principal sighed under the sudden inrush of relief which had come to her at the mention of her favourite pupil.

She loved Leonie with a love quite separate from her affection for all the young souls in her charge, and secretly admired the strength of will which more than once had been pitted against her own; moreover, accustomed to the quiet monotonous passage of time, she suddenly realised that she needed someone young and energetic in this emergency.

And the girl she needed in her distress was kneeling on her bed with arms upraised above her head.

The dying moon was slowly withdrawing her waning silvery light from the billowing mass of tawny hair, tumbling in lavender-scented masses around the girl; lingering for a moment on the eyes staring from under the unblinking eyelids, and for a second upon the glint of even teeth showing through the lips moving in prayer.

And then she spoke, in the eerie tones of those who talk in their sleep; and the words were even those of India's most holy writ, sonorous and full of a surpassing dignity, rising and falling as she knelt motionless, her eyelids slowly closing upon the terrible staring eyes.

"The sacrifice . . ." she chanted monotonously, "with voice, hearing, mind, I make oblation. To this sacrifice . . . let the gods come well willing!"

And as the moon sank to rest there was no sound save for a little sigh as Leonie, with closed eyes and white hands clasped upon her breast, stretched herself upon the bed, then with a violent movement sat up, and wide awake stared about the room.

"Yes?" she whispered. "Yes?"

And her strange eyes, with pin-point pupils in a yellow green circle, seemed to follow something which crept slowly round the bare walls as far as the chintz window-curtain moving softly in the breeze of the coming dawn. The room was full of shadows thrown by a creeper festooned outside the wide-open window; soft whisperings brought from the distant corners of the earth by the restless ocean filled the air, as she hastily twisted her hair into two great plaits with steady hands.

Then she slipped quietly to the edge of the bed and searched with her bare feet for the crimson slippers; searched fearfully as though afraid of what they might touch whilst her eyes glanced this way and that through the shadowed room.

"Who is calling me?" she whispered. "Who wants me?"

But there was no sound save for the whispering of the distant sea.

She bent her head sideways as though to listen, rose to her feet, and standing back against the bed, looked down at the shadows which danced about the hem of her garment. A swift furtive glance over her shoulder and her hand stole to the crimson kimono hanging on the brass rail, whilst a jewelled cat's-eye winked cunningly among the embroidery of her night-robe.

"Come in," she said suddenly and sharply, "don't stand outside the door, come in."

And when there came no answer she thrust her arms swiftly into the sleeves of the crimson kimono, and running across the room flung open the door, and finding the corridor empty passed hurriedly on, leaving the door wide so that the shadows skipped freakishly about the room in tune to the rhythmical whisperings which the sea bore from the distant corners of the earth.

CHAPTER XI

"Thy brother Death came, and cried,
'Wouldst thou me?'
And I replied,
'No, not thee!'"

—Shelley.

The electric lights gave out a kind of fictitious radiance against the dull grey of the hall windows through which the dawn was struggling.

The place was packed with girls. Some clustered near the baize door, standing nervously on tip-toe and with the intent of retiring precipitately if there should be any sign of the Principal; others hung over the stair or gallery banisters; the domestic staff stood round their own particular door, their white faces shining dully like Chinese lanterns; no one spoke or moved. In fact they might have been posing for a photographer until those above suddenly swayed and bent this way and that, and those in the hall parted to give way to Leonie.

Clad in crimson satin kimono, with feet thrust into crimson satin slippers and her hastily plaited hair hanging in two great ropes, she passed through them like a flame, emanating strength and resolve and a tremendous power of will. Although she looked neither to the right nor left as she ran swiftly and disappeared into the wing where lay her little friend, there was something very pleasing in the way the girls put out their hands to touch her as she passed; and something distinctly encouraging in the whispered remarks that followed her, and which might be summarised in the "*Now* it's all right," which under the high pressure of intense excitement almost burst from the lips of Annie Smith.

Like an arrow she sped to the bed, unconsciously pushing aside the women who, almost frantic with fear and quite out of their bearings, were doing their best to grapple with the problem of life or death so suddenly placed before them.

Kneeling, she turned the girl's livid little face towards her, vainly feeling for the pulse in the wrist and bruised neck; then sprang to her feet, faced the Principal and took the situation into her strong, capable young hands.

"What happened? And have you sent for the doctor?"

Her usually sweet, clear voice was like the dull sound of a cracked earthenware pot when flipped by thumb and finger.

"Yes, dear!" was the quick reply. "The doctor will be here any moment—and hot bottles and blankets are being prepared. Gertrude could not sleep and crept into Jessica's room to look for a German grammar for the examination to-morrow—to-day, and found Jessica in—in this—faint."

And the elder woman suddenly laid a hand on the girl's arm and looked up at her with the confidence she always inspired. "Help me, dear!" she whispered, with the dread of disgrace and an untimely ending to an honourable career in her old grey eyes.

And Leonie smiled, answering with the superb confidence of youth, and a slight ray of hope pierced the suffocating fog of fear, and brought Cookie from the head of the bed where she had been standing in the shade of a screen.

"Can I 'elp, Miss Lee-onny?"

"Cookie, *dear*—you and Miss Primstinn, Miss Leanto and—yes, and Ellen—none of the girls—and quickly—there's not a moment to lose."

"The doctor's coming, Mum," said a voice from the half-open door.

"The doctor is coming, dear," repeated the Principal.

Leonie answered with a strange authority in her words.

"We will not wait for the doctor!" She passed the tips of her fingers slowly across her forehead and down her cheek to the back of her neck, as was her habit when trying to solve some problem. "No, we will not wait, because—because *I* know!"

Ten minutes later the door opened to let in a young man, who stood for a moment outlined against a sea of faces, and then turned and shut the door most decisively and locked it.

"Who thought of that, I wonder," he said to himself, as he watched the four women kneeling round Jessica stretched out upon the floor.

They were going through the movements used in resuscitating the drowned, and he, too, knelt at a nod by the side of the fat old woman in an emerald green moirette petticoat and a somewhat *declasse* bedjacket, who was breathing heavily through the unaccustomed exercise.

"Let us be—a bit, Sir!" she panted. "She don't some'ow feel—quite—as dead—like! Give us a—a chance. One—two—three—four. It's the—reg'lar—as does—it. Miss Lee—onny's orders—Sir—bless er—"

She jerked her head in the direction of Leonie, and the doctor looked.

Behind her friend's head she knelt, her plaited hair twining like snakes to the ground, her eyes closed, her mouth slightly open, and the fingers of both hands pressing the temples of the child upon the floor, whilst to and fro, lifeless, dull, swung the great cat's-eye from a gold chain about the neck.

"Good God!" muttered the young doctor who, having travelled the world as ship's surgeon, knew that the scalpel and soda-cum-gentian do not constitute the whole of the art of healing.

As he looked a great bead of perspiration dropped from Leonie's forehead, between the taut arms, on to her knees; and a sudden shiver shook her from head to foot, and he heaved his overcoat into a chair, and edged very quietly until he knelt between her and Cookie.

"It's 'orrible, Sir!" the latter whispered, as she glanced at the pupil she loved most.

And it was.

By now the perspiration was pouring in streams from the girl's face, whilst the slim body shook and shook like a young tree in a storm; her teeth chattered like castanets, her closed eyes were sunk in purple black orbits, the cheeks were drawn and grey, and the nostrils were dilating like those of a far-spent horse.

"For Gawd's sake stop 'er. Sir—she's a-killing of 'erself."

The doctor shook his head, took out a brandy flask and a metal box from a leather case beside him on the floor. He held up the ready-filled glass syringe to the light and sent a squirt of what looked like water through the gleaming needle.

"If the young lady shows signs of life I want you to get this brandy down her throat *at once*, and begin to massage her heart."

"Massige! that's same as kneading dough, ain't it, Sir!"

"That's it! Miss—Miss—oh! Leonie will want the most attention, she is only just alive. I will give her another two minutes, and if nothing has happened by then I'll stop her, though it'll be an awful risk!"

"What's she a-doin' of, Sir?"

"She's forcing her own life, her vitality into her friend; she's practically raising the dead!"

"*Lor*, Sir!"

He had just raised his hand to touch Leonie, praying to heaven for the girl's reason, when she suddenly flung back her head.

Up through the house-top, to the stars, the heavens, rushed the terrible cry, wailing as wails the wolf who has lost its mate, insisting as insists one who has staked his all on one final throw, imploring as implores the mother in the last dire throes of childbirth.

What the language was, what the words meant, to whom the prayer was addressed, no one knew.

But at the third terrible appeal to God, or Fate, or Death, or Life, and even as those who listened outside and those who ceased their labours in the room stuffed their ears with their fingers and sobbed, little Jessica opened her eyes, and smiled just as Leonie, flinging up her arms, crashed face downwards on the floor.

CHAPTER XII

"The fix'd events of Fate's remote decrees."
—*Pope.*

Vultures drowsed in the shade thrown by the crumbling, sun-cracked, heat-stricken mud walls and houses which lined the meandering unpaved streets, or rather passages, of a certain village in northern India; crows were packed everywhere, taking no notice for the nonce of the feast of filth and garbage spread invitingly around them, and in which sprawled the disgusting, distorted bodies of somnolent water buffaloes; inside the houses hags, matrons, maidens, and little maids slept through the terrific heat of the noonday hours; in the distance the Himalayas, supreme and distressing, like a ridge across eternity, lay behind the turrets and minarets of the town which, thanks to the Indian atmosphere and the long distance, shone white, fretted, and—well, exactly as you can see it any day in paint at the Academy or in Bond Street.

Perfectly motionless upon the high khaki-coloured wall, which entirely surrounds the village, with dust upon his aged feet and raiment and once white turban, oblivious of the heat, the flies, and everything that slept, sat a man with age written upon every gnarled joint, and in every crack and fissure of the parchment-like skin.

So old, and *yet* with life, and hope, and youth eternal in the dark hawk eye which gazed unseeingly through the outer world straight towards the mountains.

And the old body made no sign of life, even when the vultures without sound soared majestically heavenwards, whilst the crows rose in shrieking disordered squads, and a kite whistling melodiously swooped from nowhere downwards across his head to the filth of the streets.

Neither did he turn his head or his eyes when a coal-black stallion, guided only by the pressure of its rider's knees, came to a stand directly beneath him in the shadow of the wall, having scrambled and slithered, jumping like a deer, climbing like a goat down the rock-strewn road which leads to the village from the great house at its rear; one of those abominable roads allotted to the calloused native foot, honoured for the first time in this instance by the passage of the prince's son and heir.

An arresting picture the rider and his horse made as the man bent low in the saddle and salaamed, then raised his turbaned head and sat motionless, gazing at the holy man.

Minutes passed before, with arms filled with offerings and garlands of marigolds and jasmin swinging from his wrists, he slid from the saddle to the ground, and took his way up the narrow tortuous path which Fate had marked out for him through all time.

High caste, high born, as slender and delicate and as pressed with life as a budding branch in spring, Madhu Krishnaghar stood beside the priest in the incongruous setting of the mud walls.

A coat of fine white linen with broad orange waistband came to just below the knees; white trousers fastened tight about the ankle fitted almost like a stocking from ankle to knee; the slender, narrow feet were shod in native slippers, the white turban with its regulation folds outlined the pale bronze face with the sign of the man's religion traced between the eyebrows; diamond solitaires sparkled in the ears, and one necklace of great pearls hung about his neck.

"Usual large gentle eye, hawk nose, mobile mouth and small-boned oval face" would doubtlessly have been the flippant comment of any occidental passer-by; "meet 'em everywhere, gambling at the street corner, or squatting in the bazaar, or riding elephants."

Yes! but—is not India's future history writ large upon that small-boned oval face for those who, having the vision, read as they walk warily.

For those who run hastily past life's signposts cannot and will not see that, like the fresh green grass which hides the dug pit, those gentle luminous eyes draw attention from the subtle cruelty of the mouth, through which gleam the pitiless perfect teeth.

Glorying in his bull-neck and massive chin, and blinded by his insular, inherited upbringing, the European will exclaim "Pah!" at sight of the thin cheek and delicate oval face, failing utterly to notice the set of the ears on the head; just as, muscle bound through worship at the shrine of Sport, he will mistake the eastern courtesy and poetry of movement for obsequiousness and humility, ignoring the terrible root from which these delicate flowers spring; the root of patience; with its tentacles ever twining and twisting through the eastern mind, causing the very old to die placidly with a smile on their shrivelled lips, and the young to envisage plague, pestilence, and famine with a mere lifting of the shoulder. Patience! the card which India does not hold up her sleeve in the game of life she is playing; the dull-coloured drab little bit of cardboard which she throws on the table openly, but which we ignore amongst the highly coloured, bejewelled pictures she places before us, smiling with the tender luminous eyes so that we shall forget the subtle cruelty of the mouth.

Placing his offerings at the holy man's feet, and laying the garlands gently about the bowed shoulders, Madhu Krishnaghar, the son of princes, stooped and lifting the hem of the dust-covered garment, laid it against his forehead, then quietly sat down a pace removed from the ancient who took no notice whatever of his proceedings.

And time passed, linking one hour of noon to its neighbour and the next, until the hags, matrons, maidens, and little maids awoke to the freshness of the evening and the monotony of its tasks.

Kites called, crows screamed, men gambled in the shadows of the evening and the upstanding, distorted, disgusting water buffalo; while the two men, master and pupil in the religion of death, sat hour after hour without movement, staring at the mountains, the dwelling-place of Siva the terrible, and the birthplace of Kali his bride.

Far into the night they sat, until the last quarter of the moon had sunk to rest, when, with one single movement, the old man sprang to his feet, flung out his arms, and bent in utter humility and cast dust upon his once white turban.

His voice was but a shrill cracked whisper when he called upon his god from the crumbling top of the sunbaked, moon-drenched wall, and turning, lifted his travel-stained mantle and laid it on the young shoulders beside him.

An hour had passed, and more, before the holy man's tale, which ran back through the past seventeen years, was finished. And when it had been told the high caste youth trembled in the ecstasy of his religion, amazed at the enlightenment thrown upon his own enigmatical life, uplifted at the task before him. Yea! he trembled in the ecstasy of his religion, forgetting that love and passion and life ran just as riotously in his supple perfect body.

He leapt to his feet, smiting his forehead with clenched hand.

"Give me a sign, O Kali! Show me that thou art pleased!"

And he rent his garments in joy, showing the bronze breast with the blood-red marks of his terrible religion traced upon it; then thrusting his fingers in his ears sank to the ground and buried his head between his knees.

A black kid, the happiest of all good omens, bleating with hunger, tripped and stumbled from a courtyard; yet even as it found its mother and buried its little head in the warmth of the soft side, there had come across the plains a weird, long-drawn-out sound, fraught with disaster to those who believe in signs.

Long and shrill it sounded and ceased; and once again—to be lost in peals of indecent, discordant laughter.

Uncontrolled, uncontrollable, loathesome sound which tears India's nights to shreds.

The jackals had found at dawn.

CHAPTER XIII

"A continual dripping in a very rainy day
and a contentious woman are alike."

—The Bible.

In the late spring Leonie stood at a cottage window watching the rush of the incoming water as she listened to her aunt's ceaseless lament, idly wondering if both would reach high tide together, and if there would be any chance of slipping out for a swim before bedtime.

She loved her aunt with the protective love of the very strong for the very weak, and smilingly found excuses for the daily tirade against fate, or ill-luck, or whatever it is weak people blame for the hopeless knots they tie in their own particular bit of string by their haphazard bursts of energy, or apathetic resignation to every little stumbling-block they find in their path.

Daily, almost hourly, through the splendid North Devon winter the aunt had wailed, and bemoaned, and fretted, driving the girl out on the tramp for hours in the wind, and the wet, and the sun, only to return hurriedly at the thought of the weak, hapless, helpless woman in the cottage at Lee.

Susan Hetth complained about everything, from the lack of society to the smallness of her income, plus a few scathing comments upon her niece's weather-browned face and the hopeless outlook for her matrimonial future.

Her own bid in the matrimonial market *en secondes noces* had failed, and though Hope had not taken it lying down, the passage of the years had not been lightened by what seemed to be a daily addition of silver threads to the jaded ash gold of her hair, and the necessity of a still more flagrant distribution upon her face of the substances she employed to camouflage the passage of old Time.

Ah, me! that moment before the stimulating advent of the early cup of tea, when divested of our motley we see ourselves in the mirror as, thanks be, others do not, and laying eager hands upon that offspring of charity, the boudoir cap, wonder if it has been in hobnailed boots that the old Father has tramped across our face during the night hours, dragging his scythe behind him.

Leonie's school-days had ended abruptly.

Nothing definite had or could have been said, but it was not likely that the parents would see exactly eye to eye with their daughters, who wrote reams and whispered volumes of the delightful mystery which surrounded the girl who next term would be head of the school.

Long and excited had been the conclaves with the Principal, persuasive or threatening the arguments used, according to the parental temperament, and the upshot of it all was that Leonie had been asked to go; and proud, hurt Leonie had left, with a valiant smile on her lovely mouth, and a strange little questioning look that had only quite lately crept into the beautiful eyes, and which neither the outpourings of Jessica's love, a demonstration of affection from the entire school in the shape of numerous and weird presents, or the broken-hearted kiss of both the Principal and Cookie had been able to eradicate.

The girl felt that she had left under a cloud, which a slight attack of what the doctor had diagnosed as brain fever had not served to line with silver.

He had insisted upon complete change and rest, and had called twice a day when Leonie was really ill, and four times when she was convalescent; so upon fair Devon had they decided, Leonie cajoling and smiling until she had obtained a year's lease, at an absurdly low rent, of the little cottage on the left of Lee harbour as you face the sea.

It is a place of charm if you are willing to do most of the work yourself with the aid of a daily help.

It is certainly rather like a band-box with the lid on, and the ocean at high tide is only prevented by the harbour wall from invading your front garden, which is the size of a handkerchief.

But if you sit at the window you can feel the spray on your face, and if you lie a-bed the tang of the air sweeping across the Atlantic will get you out at the double; and the smell of the pines, and the hum of the bees in summer, and the rush of the storm, and the crash of the waves in winter, are of God's own fashioning.

What with shopping expeditions to that crime in brick and mortar called Ilfracombe, visits here and visits there, croquet, bridge, and picnics, the summer and early autumn months had not dragged unduly for Susan Hetth.

But when the last visitor had gone, and the first real storm had broken a window, then she had sunk like a lump of lead in a bucket of cold water out of which she refused to be lifted.

Leonie was youth incarnate, causing even the courteous folk of Devon to turn and stare as she swung past with a cheery greeting in a skirt and hob-nailed boots ending at her knees.

For the first month, as one always does in Devon, she had walked herself to the verge of scragginess, then had gradually put on weight, as is the correct method. Her whistle could be heard in the woods and fields, and on the beach from Lee to Hartland way; all the country folk loved her, and scolded her for the risks she took in swimming, and she seemingly had no care in the world.

But the great heat of summer, the shriek of the wind, and the scream of the birds in autumn would bring a little pucker between her brows; the storm would drive her spirits up to breaking point, the calm would leave her eyes full of trouble; in the woods she would stop and turn to listen, then frown and trudge along between the trees.

She was not at rest, for an unconfessed fear, a spook without name or shape, was plucking at her will-power and her heart, a phantom of which she would rather have died than have said one word.

So she stood twisting the blind cord and watching the rocks as they gradually disappeared under the swirling waters.

Susan Hetth sat near the fire, which is oft-times necessary in the spring at Lee, and tapped in irritation, and most irritatingly, with her foot against the low fender.

She was worried.

She was not by birth or heredity a bad-tempered woman, merely one of straw, who after the first two months of every quarter invariably found herself in a corner which one injudicious move might render uncomfortably tight.

Her financial situation, in fact, had become so critical, and the bank manager's demeanour so unpropitious, that in the previous year more than once the dawn had found her trying to decide between the Scylla of the thankless post of lady companion to some wealthy parvenu on the Riviera, and the Charybdis of raising money enough to allow her to harbour paying guests in the no-man's-land of Earls Court.

Then Fate crossed her knees, and out of her lap had tumbled a widower possessed of a substantial banking account and four children.

A few more days, a little more encouragement, and he would most certainly have offered her his name and the half of his worldly goods in return for her help in quelling the riotous behaviour of his motherless brood.

But there had supervened the crisis at school.

And grasping for once in her life the necessity of immediate action if she wished to prevent an embellished account of her niece's untoward behaviour from reaching the man's ears, she had fled to Devon, leaving behind a trail of dainty scented notes explaining that it was all on account of a slight nervous breakdown from overstudy on the part of her niece "who," she added casually, "as I think I told you, is the only daughter of my dear brother, Colonel Hetth, V.C."

Snobbish, but quite effective as bait for a person who has not complete control over the eighth letter of the alphabet.

That very morning, quite unheedful of the beauties of the little witch village, she had gone to collect her mail lying at the post office, which in summer is almost hidden in its garden of flowers; and amongst an assortment of spring sale catalogues from emporiums, mostly situated in South Kensington, had found a letter from the widower, begging to be allowed to come down for a change of air, and an opportunity of laying a proposition before her.

She had wandered up the side of the hill, unmindful of the birds and buds almost bursting with the intoxication of spring; had pitched the catalogues anywhere on the grass, as is the wont of the untidy who have no bond with nature, and had tried to solve the problem as she scraped the mud, with the aid of a twig, from her Louis-Quinze heels.

But she was harassed, poor, hapless creature, for more than one reason.

The words of alarm from the nurse, the innuendoes from departing maid-servants, and the direct warning from the old specialist which had long since faded from her mind, had been forcibly revived by the happenings at the school; and being one of those who invariably plump for the worst, and without giving the slightest thought to the criminality of the proceeding, she had definitely decided, if she could coerce the girl into falling in with her plans, to marry her to the highest bidder before worse could happen.

But she was downright afraid of her niece. Afraid of her moral strength which dominated everything and everybody; ill at ease with the straightforward way she had of speaking her mind on occasions, and following up her speech with action. Never an untruth had she known to pass the girl's lips, not once had she heard her say one belittling thing about a living soul, and only twice had she seen the sweetness and gentleness swept with anger.

Cruelty to anything small or weak could transform the girl into a flame of wrath, and her weakest spot was her overpowering sympathy with anyone in distress, without any inquiries into the direct cause of the adversity, which spot caused her to be considerably taken in by many of those who had discerned it.

An almost abnormal moral strength, allied to great gentleness and pity, combined to make a character extraordinary in one so young, and which her aunt summed up and summarily dismissed from her mind in the trite sentence that "she certainly did not take after her parents."

She was considered slow by the youths, and perplexing and therefore to be avoided by the girls of her own age, and dull or frightfully conceited by the men who had fluttered round her almost exotic beauty until they had come up against the icy barrier of her supreme indifference.

To those who knew her intimately, such as the fisherfolk and the farmers, and the tramps with whom she would sit and converse by the wayside and share her lunch, she was the most lovable, cheery soul in the world, which, of course, meant the county of Devon.

"Damn standoffish, what!"

Such had been the verdict passed by someone married who hailed from London town, when Leonie had refused to sit out a dance in a secluded shady nook.

"Just a bit of heaven!" had said the tramp as he turned the corner in the lane, leaving Leonie sitting on the milestone pondering upon the man whose ragged clothes were out of keeping with the shape of his nails, and the timbre of his voice with his unkempt hair.

But leaving all that aside, and in all conscience it was bad enough, the biggest worry hung as heavy and as threatening upon the horizon as does at times the monsoon over the Indian Ocean.

Once upon a time Susan Hetth had committed an indiscretion, nothing *really* wrong—she hadn't the nerve. But the nuisance of it was, that, in addition to the indiscretion, she had broken the eleventh commandment and had very nearly got hanged for her lamb.

In the second year of her widowhood in the month of November, whilst her hair was still golden and her colouring unpurchased, she had dined *a deux* in one of those delectable, ghost-ridden, low-ceilinged sets of chambers which are tucked away in a certain Inn within the Fleet Street boundary.

Which is a silly thing to do if you do not own a car and a long-suffering discreet chauffeur.

The *diner a deux* and a bit of a play had been the honest programme; but the inevitable had happened in an all-enveloping blanket of a fog, on account of which everything in the shape of a hackney carriage had gone home, and an excursion on foot to the nearest tube rendered hopeless by the simple fact that you could not see your hand before your face.

Which would not have mattered a bit if only, as the fog lifted and the clock of St Dunstan's chimed the hour of three a.m., she had emerged from the narrow opening into Fleet Street with the aplomb or *savoir-faire*, which are almost twins, necessary to the occasion.

She would then have beckoned to and smiled sweetly upon the young ruffian into whom she bumped as he lounged on his way to Covent Garden Market, and promised him just enough to bring her a taxi or something on wheels, into which she would have got if it had materialised, and been whirled away to safety and bed after adieux to her host uttered with the nonchalance necessary to allay the young ruffian's suspicions.

Instead of this she had slunk from the opening with her host close behind, had bumped into the young ruffian and with an exclamation of dismay had shrunk back into the shadows and her host's arms.

In consequence of which action the bare-footed ruffian had shadowed them until they had met a four-wheeler, had held the lady's dress from the wheel and overheard the address given to the driver for which he had received tuppence, and had disappeared into a doorway where he had spat on his unearned increment and made his plans.

The upshot of it all being the admittance a fortnight later of young Wal. Hickle, attired in his best and primed with her family history, into the presence of the terrified woman.

He had simply asked for twenty pounds on the nail in return for his silence.

And she, scared out of her wits, instead of threatening him with the law, had given him a cheque—yes! a cheque—and he, with a flash of that cunning which was to lead him eventually to a seat amongst the plutocrats, had pocketed it and grinned.

"I doan' wan' mor' 'en twenty uv the best, lidy, jus' to mike a start—an' I doan' wanter part wiv yer 'and-writin' niver. So jes' yer send two rustlers, wot means notes, of ten pun each, rigistered, to W. 'ickle spelt wiv a haitch, 2 H'apple Blossom Row, Coving Gardin, afore this toime ter-morrer. An' jes yer remember that h'as long as yer lives I've got yer bit of 'andwritin.' I ain't goin' ter use it, but some dye it might come in 'andy. 'Ardly loikly as 'ow yer'd buy twenty pun wurf of veg from Wal 'ickle eh, lidy?—it 'ud want *some* h'explanation."

Then this soul made in the image and likeness of his God and found good, but hidden under the civilising process of the twentieth century which had given him the morals of a jackal and the status of a pariah dog, sighed as he looked round the dainty room.

"S'welp me," he said, as he touched a satin cushion with his coarse, broken-nailed finger-tips, "h'if oi h'understand wye a woman the loikes uv *you*, wiv h'everyfink she wants, cawn't run *strite!*"

"Oh! but," whimpered the woman, "it was all the fault of the fog, *really* it was!"

"Garn!" replied the young ruffian as he opened the door and slammed it behind him.

CHAPTER XIV

"Surely I am more brutish than any man!"
                                    —*The Bible.*

And just about midsummer Fate tweaked the string to which was hobbled Susan Hetth.

A vulgar but resplendent bachelor middle-aged millionaire, sterling, not dollars, in order to set his gastronomic house in order, had taken a notion for the simple life for just as long as the notion should last, and a perfect bijou of a thatched cottage t'other side of Clovelly for a year.

With a notion of buying the cottage at Lee in which had dwelt the three historic maids, he had swept one day through the village in the latest thing in cars.

Baulked in his intent, and with time upon his podgy hands, he had rolled, minus the car, along the village path over the strippet of water and the sunbaked grass to the harbour.

There he had bent, with ardour and misgivings, to pick up Leonie's towel, just as the soft wind caught her bathing cloak as she stretched out her hand with a smile of thanks.

She had grabbed at the cloak and missed it by a bit, so that it had swept behind her, hanging from one shoulder like some Grecian drapery, and the rotund little man had trotted round

Joan Conquest

her draped side, picked up the cloak by the big button, and completed his trot, covering her up as he moved.

And as he trotted his little porcine eyes had glistened as they lingered upon the perfect figure, from the slim ankles to the confused face, and Leonie had blushed, though you could not have discerned it through the tan, pulled the cloak tighter and hurried across the road to the cottage gate.

But with the clumsy swiftness of the elephantine, the man had run after her and opened the cottage gate just as Susan Hetth opened the cottage door with the welcoming announcement that tea was ready.

"Ha!" he had snorted as he almost ran up the path, leaving Leonie to stand still and stare in amazement at the little scene. "And I'll have some tea, too, Lady Susan Hetth, and how d'you do. Long time since we met, eh?"

Diamonds sparkled in the sun as the man stretched out an effusive hand, and a flame of anger sparkled in the small eyes as Lady Susan drew back frigidly.

Not being of them herself she set all the greater store on knowing those she considered exactly the right people.

"I don't think I have—" she commenced in her most primpsy voice, when she was interrupted with a perfectly odious familiarity.

"Now you're not going to say that you don't remember our little meetings in Earls Court *and* Fleet Street and"—the man spoke with an extreme slowness as though keeping guard over each letter of each word—"*and* our little correspondence, come now."

Leonie frowned and moved a step forward protectingly as her aunt caught suddenly at the door handle, and then jerked herself forward with outstretched hand.

"Auntie, dear—"

But her aunt was speaking in the falsetto of forced levity, and Leonie held her peace and waited for an opportunity to slip past and into the house.

"Why, I do believe," said Susan Hetth, suddenly metamorphosed by a certain tone in the man's voice into the terrified woman of years ago, "Yes! I do believe it is Mr. Walter Hickle—"

"*Sir* Walter, *if* you please."

"Indeed, in-deed—how *very* delightful, and after *all* these years! Leonie, this is—is—er—"

"I'm one of your aunt's friends, Miss Leonie, bobbed up out of the past. Glad to meet you, hope we shall be friends, too."

Leonie, who had gained the door, looked back over her aunt's shoulder and spoke with a gentle courtesy very much her own.

"I always like to meet Auntie's friends!"

Not knowing the man from Adam she spoke no untruth, but in spite of reiterated calls to come down to tea she remained in her bedroom until the loud-voiced guest had taken his departure.

While the two women were having yet another cup of tea Sir Walter Hickle, millionaire, tradesman, and knight, sat down gingerly upon a rock and made his plans.

He had made his plans as a bull-necked, offensive youth the first day he had pulled out from Covent Garden with a barrow piled with walnuts bought out of two rustlers, value of ten pun each.

"I'll *get there*!" he had informed the nuts as he tweaked his cap over one eye, and his red neckerchief into place; and had sworn a mighty and quite unprintable oath as he struck a huge fist into a horny palm at the corner of Ludgate Circus and New Bridge Street.

"I'll *get there*!" he informed the seaweed as he lifted the soft grey hat from his bald head and adjusted the enormous pearl pin in the pale pink satin tie; and he sighed stertorously as he complacently patted his knee with a podgy hand, upon the manicured plebeian fingers of which shone two magnificent diamond rings.

And if you cannot penetrate the strongholds of Devon county, it is not difficult to make acquaintance with her visitors, especially if your visiting card is a gilt edge security for future excursions and diversions done in top-hole style.

Unsuspecting Leonie, who never kept a grudge, after a week or so of astonishment and aversion, thinking in her innocence of heart that she perceived the trend of events, made up her mind to meet the rotund old knight with the simple graciousness due to her aunt's would-be husband.

True, the elasticity of her graciousness did not stretch enough to allow her to accept the never-ending invitations which poured into the cottage; but she would tuck her remonstrating aunt into the car which was ever at the gate, and smile delightfully upon the infatuated old fellow who put her aloofness down to mere girlish waywardness.

Although the corporeal part of the old vulgarian grated on her susceptibilities, she was quite willing to believe that if one chose to dig deep enough it would prove to be only the rough earth covering a positive mine of rare temperamental gems; and in her blindness whistled cheerily as she thought of the joy her aunt would feel at not having to drop her title when she changed her name, and at being able to retain the same initials for her monogram.

CHAPTER XV

"To sell a bargain well is as cunning
as fast and loose."
                                    —*Shakespeare.*

"Now I want you to listen to me, Leonie!"

"I am, Auntie!"

"I mean *seriously*! I want to talk about myself for one thing,
and our very straitened means, which do not permit us to go
on living even like this; and oh! lots of other things."

"Right, darling!" said her niece, moving across the room to sit
on a broad stool at her relation's feet, but twisting her head to
one side with a quick movement when her aunt laid her hand
dramatically upon the tawny hair.

"Please, Auntie, don't! I can't bear to have my head touched!"

"Just what I want to talk about!" vaguely said Susan Hetth as
she tried to disentangle an old-fashioned ring which had unfor-
tunately caught a few shining hairs in its loose setting.

"Please don't touch my *head*, Auntie!" repeated Leonie as she
sat back. "Let my hair *go*, please!"

"I'm not touching your hair, child," impatiently replied the

Joan Conquest

elder woman. "It's got caught in one of my rings!"

Leonie's eyes were almost closed in a strange kind of psychological agony; then just as though she acted unconsciously she seized her aunt's hands and pulled them quickly from her head, tearing out the hair entangled in the ring by the roots.

"I can't stand it, Auntie. I have never been able to bear anyone touching my head," she said very quietly.

"I think you're insane at times, Leonie, *really* I do!"

The terrible words were out, and for one long moment the two women stared into each other's eyes.

"You think I am insane at times," whispered Leonie. "*You*— Auntie, *you* think I am *insane!*"

And the elder woman, floundering in dismay at the awful effect of her unconsidered words, sank to her neck in a bog of explanation.

"No! Leonie—no, of course not—I wasn't thinking—of *course* you're not mad—insane I mean. What an idea! only I am worried about you, you know that, don't you, dear! *Do* be sensible, dear. Of course your brain is not *quite* normal. It can't be with all that sleep-walking, can it, and all your abnormally brilliant exams!"

Susan Hetth's disjointed remarks sounded like the clatter of a pair of runaway mules, while Leonie clasped her hands tight as she sat crouched on her stool.

"Of course people *will* talk, you know, dear! They did when you were quite a baby and began walking in your sleep. And they did, you know, at school after that unfortunate child nearly got strangled by her sheets—I always do think that school fare is *most* indigestible—and *so* likely to cause blemishes on the skin!"

Leonie bowed her head.

"Most unfortunate that you should have snubbed young Mr—what's-his-name—so severely—and that his sister should have been at school with you. Out of revenge *she* has been talking about you and your sleep-walking. People are most unkind and *most* unjust—and you are *far* too pretty to receive any consideration from your *own* sex, how*ever* much attention you may receive from the opposition—I mean sex—opposite sex, I mean—"

Leonie sat absolutely still.

"Anyway, my child, we need not worry—there is a way out of our little difficulties."

Sensing that something was coming Leonie sat back with the light of the oil lamp full on her face as she stared at the clutter on the mantelpiece.

"I *do* so want you to do something for me, darling."

The tone of Susan Hetth's voice and the touch of her hand on the girl's arm were as wheedling as if she were about to ask her to tramp into Ilfracombe on some trifling midnight errand.

Leonie answered quite mechanically.

"What is it, dear!" she said. "Say the word and I'll do it!"

"Is that a promise?"

"Ra-ther! Anything to please you, Auntiekins!"

Susan Hetth took her fence in a rush!

"I want you to get married," she said abruptly out of pure fright, and wrenched at her bead chain when Leonie leapt to her feet.

The girl stood quite still, outlined in her simple low-cut, short-sleeved dress by the wall, her hands pressed back against it.

There was no sound except the soft gurgle and murmur of the water until she spoke, quietly, but with a world of horror in her low-pitched voice.

"You want me to marry—*you*—when a moment ago you said that you thought I was mad—you want me to marry some honest, unsuspecting man, and bear him children!"

Susan Hetth, shocked to the limit of her Pecksniffian soul, made a nerveless fluttering gesture of protest with her hands.

"Don't speak," said Leonie quickly, "please don't speak until I have done. Marriage! I will tell you what I have thought about it while I have been waiting for my mate."

"Oh!" exploded Susan Hetth vehemently. "*My dear!* Surely you have not been corresponding with anyone!"

Leonie hesitated.

How was she to make her aunt, this shallow, unbalanced being, understand the joyous expectancy with which she had awaited the moment when she should meet the man born for her?

How was she to take the exquisite longings, the veiled desires, the beautiful virgin thoughts, from her heart and lay them before this woman who had taught her nothing but the twenty-third Psalm without its real interpretation, plus the correct Sunday collect and daily prayers.

How explain that to her the little golden ring would not represent a key opening the door to the so-called freedom from which fifty per cent of women descend, via the shallow flight of steps marked a good time, to the plain of discontent; or that to her the word love was sufficient, in that for her it included those of honour and obey, without any separate declaration in public.

When she spoke she spoke hurriedly, flushing from chin to brow.

"Auntie—I correspond with no man—but my—my mate is waiting for me somewhere—calling me all the time ever since—oh! ever since I can remember—and—and I should have married him when I had met him if—if—"

In anger at this fresh complication, piled upon her appalling want of tact of a few moments ago, Susan Hetth struck her hands on the arms of her chair.

"I think you absolutely *indecent*, Leonie, to go on like this about someone you have never even seen. Now listen to me, and don't be so theatrical. I have had an offer of marriage for you by someone who knows all about you, and who, after my assurance that there is nothing hereditary in your family on either side to account for the strangeness of your actions at times, is perfectly willing, even anxious, to marry you."

"To take the risk, you mean," broke in Leonie. "Oh!—well, go on."

Aunt Susan, somewhat out of breath from the rapidity and unaccustomed lucidity of her words, inhaled deeply and continued.

"He will make you an astounding marriage settlement, give you everything you want, and swears to make you per-fect-ly happy!"

"And his name?"

"Oh! don't be stupid, Leonie, of course you know whom I mean!"

Leonie leant forward, stretching out her hands, her face dead white in the light of the lamp.

"Tell me *his name* and don't drive me beyond breaking point, Aunt Susan!"

"Tosh!" contemptuously remarked her aunt. "Don't be so childish—I mean Sir Walter Hickle, of course!"

Expecting some violent words of protest the elder woman half rose from her chair, but appalled by the deathly silence and the look on the girl's face, sank back, cowering in her seat, and stared in the direction her niece's hand was pointing.

"Look, Auntie, look!"

Leonie stood with one hand pointing at the mantelpiece and the other pressed against her throat as she tried to speak coherently.

The pupils of her eyes were pin-points as she gazed at a wooden frame which, adorned with edelweiss and the Lucerne Lion, held the snapshot of a complaisant individual leaning over the harbour wall, attired in a well-fitting but ill-placed yachting suit.

"Old Pickled Walnuts! You want me to marry him—when—when—oh! when I thought *he* wanted to marry *you!*"

She laughed, a laugh which sounded like the jangling of broken glass, and died almost before it was born; and her aunt, terrified at the sound and the expression on the girl's face, seized the outstretched arm and shook it violently.

"What *are* you talking about, Leonie!"

Leonie freed her arm with a shudder.

"Please don't touch me!" Then making a desperate effort she

continued quietly, so quietly indeed that Susan Hetth looked anxiously over her shoulder towards the door.

"Don't you know that's his nickname? Oh! of *course* you do! You *know* he made his fortune by pickling walnuts too rotten to sell. Sir Walter Hickle—twist the name a bit and it's all in a nutshell—a—a pickled walnut shell"—the little unnatural laugh broke across the words—"and you want *me* to marry him—Auntie! Auntie! he's awful enough, heaven knows, but not bad enough, nobody could be, to have a—a mad wife foisted on him—no! never—I'll go out and work!"

There was something very decisive in the last words, but Susan Hetth, like most weak people, found her strength suddenly in a mulish obstinacy, which is a quite good equivalent for, and often more efficacious than mere strength of will.

This obstinacy, backed by the knowledge that people were beginning to gossip about the girl's aloofness and love of solitude; that the cashing of another cheque would see her overdrawn at the bank; and that until the girl was settled and off her hands she would not be able to solve her own matrimonial problem, drove her to a show of mental energy of which she would not have been capable in an everyday argument.

"Work!" she cried, "work! What can you do? *Nothing*—except go out as a companion or nursery governess!—and who would take you without a reference—and who would give *you* one? Tell me!"

Leonie remained silent—stunned.

"As I have told you, we simply cannot afford to live even like *this*! I'm overdrawn as it is, and—"

"But," broke in Leonie with a gleam of hope, "but I have father's money coming to me. I'm not quite sure how much it is, but you can have it—*all*!"

"It's two thousand pounds down for yourself, and two hundred and fifty a year in trust for your children—to be given you on your *wedding* day."

"Oh!"

It was just a little pitiful exclamation as the girl realised the net which was closing about her feet, but from the meshes of which she made a last desperate effort to extricate herself.

"I think I—see—a way," she said slowly. "Yes—listen—this terrible mystery that surrounds me, this—this curse which seems to bring disaster or pain to everyone I love, simply makes life not worth living—so if—if I make a will in your favour, Auntie, dear, and go for a swim at Morte Point where the cross currents are—it will—"

But Susan Hetth interrupted violently, horror-stricken at the suggestion made indifferently by the girl she loved as far as she was capable of loving.

"How is suicide going to help?" she demanded shrilly. "There would be an inquest, every bit of gossip, everything you had ever done would be brought to light; the verdict would be insanity—"

"Oh, *Auntie!*"

Driven to desperation and without finesse Susan Hetth flung down her trump card.

"But—I—I haven't told you the—the *worst*," she stammered, dabbing her eyes with her handkerchief, and peering from behind it at Leonie who, wearily pushing the hair off her forehead, stood apathetically waiting.

"That—that man"—she jerked her head at the mantelpiece—"has—has a hold on me!"

"What—do you mean Sir Walter—do you owe him *money*?" Leonie stared in amazement as she spoke.

"Oh, no—it's worse!" came the reply, followed by a curtailed but sufficiently dramatic recital of the past indiscretion, to which Leonie listened spellbound.

"And you *do* believe that it was just a bit of bad luck, and that there was nothing *really* wrong in it all, don't you, dear," insisted the woman who, like ninety-nine per cent of humans, forgot the real tragedy of the moment in the recital of her own pettifogging escapade.

"Absolutely," replied Leonie flatly.

"And you *do* see the necessity of giving in, now that he has threatened me with exposure if you refuse him when he proposes, *don't* you, dear?"

"Absolutely," replied Leonie for the second time.

There followed long minutes of silence which the swirl of the waters alone dared to break, and then the girl spoke.

"My life," she said very softly to herself; "my lovely, beautiful free life done. The wind, and the birds, and the sea—Auntie—oh, Auntie—*Auntie*!"

And she turned and flung herself against the wall with her face crushed into her upstretched arms. "Think of it," she whispered hoarsely, "think of it, my youth, my spirit, my body given into that old man's keeping. I who have kept my thoughts, my lips, my eyes for my mate that was to be; I who have longed for his love, for the hours and the days, and the months, and the years, even unto death, with him. How could—"

There was a click of the gate, and she flung round from the wall, dry-eyed, dry-lipped, desperate, as her aunt hurriedly rose.

"It's him—Sir Walter, Leonie—are you going to accept him?"

"Of course," came the steady reply, and Leonie looked the elder woman straight in the eyes, which darted this, that, and every way. "Will you go upstairs, please."

* * * * * * * *

Just before dawn Leonie slid in through the window, and the water, trickling from the bathing dress which clung to the wonderful figure, formed little pools on the faded carpet.

"Nothing will ever make me clean," she whispered, "nothing—nothing—nothing. There is no ocean big or wide or deep enough for that, oh! God—my God!"

For five long minutes she stood absolutely still, looking straight and unseeingly at the mantelpiece.

Then as a rooster somewhere shrilly heralded the coming day she awoke to her surroundings and moved.

Like a beaten dog she crept to her bedroom, and stood staring at the reflection of her haggard face in the mirror. A bird suddenly burst into a song of welcome to the dawn which was dyeing the sky rose pink, and she crossed to the window-seat, dropped to her knees, and buried her lovely head in her outstretched arms, amid the ruins of her beautiful Castle of Dreams.

CHAPTER XVI

"For Fate has wove the thread of life with pain!"
—*Pope.*

When *empty* Rockham is a haven of delight, whether the little connecting coves be awash with the tide, or the limpets, in an unglued state, are airing themselves awaiting the return of the water.

You can wander at will, if you have the right boots on, over the never-ending sharp ridges of the rocks; you can pass hours gathering *laver*, though it is not at its best just there; and you can find sea-anemones and such treasure-trove as pit props, and boxes of butter, yea! and even casks of wine after a storm if the gods be kind to you.

Also you can don your bathing dress in comfort behind the wreck, one of many, which has remained as witness to the force of the terrific gales and the ripping propensities of the saw-teethed rocks.

Walk in from Lee or Mortehoe, Woolacombe or Croyde, over fields in which lambs stand on their front feet in exuberance of youth, or caper on their back ones until called to order by their maternal parent; or through lanes lined with primroses and violets, or roses, or nuts, or berries, according to the season, whilst on the top twig of the high hedges yellow-hammers, chaffinches, robins and the like gossip to you about the hawk hovering in the distance.

Arrived there, pause on the edge of the incline. *Don't* go down if you see a paper bag fluttering in the breeze, because a paper bag is but a forerunner of lanky locks dripping on a towel-covered shoulder, and bare and uncomely feet fiddling in the warm sand, whilst adjacent is the rock over which the faded blue bathing dress hangs out to dry.

Wait for the empty hour and then fly into the second cove, and the next, and the next, but—*don't forget the tide!*

The sand-covered rough-haired terrier stood with his head cocked on one side, looking at the wonderful, waving, glistening mass in front of him.

It certainly looked like seaweed, but it didn't smell like it, and long bits of it floated in the air just like golden threads; besides, there was something uncanny about it which sent thrills into the roots of his rough hair, causing it to rise in clumps along his spine.

It looked as if there were something dead underneath, too, and yet it didn't; anyway it certainly did not look as though it were meant to be played with or barked at; and he hastened back along the treacherous narrow passage, which connects the two last coves, in search of him-who-knew-all and was never afraid.

"No, old fellow!" was the only response he got to his invitation to "come and see." "I've already been fooled over anemones, and rooks, and passing cloud shadows, and very dead starfish—nothing' doin', so calm yourself!"

But the dog backed into a pool, emitting barks which were strangled at birth, snapped at a bit of rock which caught him unawares upon his unprotected flank, trotted forward, backed again into the pool, and turning, ran down the passage, came back and did it all over again.

Talk about water-drops wearing away a stone, why they are simply not in it when compared with a dog's method of wearing down your resistance. After the fifth repetition of the above tactics the man rose, stretched, put his pipe in his pocket, and hurling a pebble at the delighted quadruped, followed in its wake.

"Just look at that, and don't say I've brought you here for nothing," said the terrier, as plainly as he could with eyes and quivering body and tail.

The man looked and held up a finger, which caused the dog to sit up and beg, and walked as softly as possible up to Leonie who, tired out with worry, heartache, and a long swim, was sitting fast asleep on that one slanting, delightfully comfortable rock seat, with her hair spread out over her face, and down to her knees, mantle wise, to dry.

It is a somewhat ticklish job to lift an unknown lady's hair and tell her abruptly that you think the tide is on the turn, and the man stood in perplexity, while his brain refused obstinately to register anything more practical than an overwhelming admiration for the picture before him.

However, with the attempt to unravel the problem, his hand went instinctively to the pocket which held his pipe, and the slight movement simultaneously upset his balance and solved the problem.

He slipped with a rasp of nails on rock, waved his arms in a manner likely to cause envy in any mere flag-wagger, and recovered himself with all the clatter and confusion insepa-rable, under such circumstances, from the saving of self-respect and the knees of skirt or breeches.

Quite unconscious that her stockings and high boots were upon another rock, her skirt only reached just below the knee and her legs and beautiful feet were bare, Leonie sat up as straight as she could and peered from between her masses of

hair; upon which the dog, thinking that he alone was responsible for the discovery of this wild beast, yelped and barked and
growled as he slid in and out of the pools.

Pushing her hair back, and shielding her eyes from the sun and
her face from the man, she flashed one swift glance from his
shoes to his hair; that non-looking, all-seeing glance of woman
which leaves fork lightning at the post, and causes you to wish
you had spent a little more time upon your toilet.

Although she had barely looked at him, Leonie could have
described the man before her down to the minutest detail.

No doubt about it he was good to look upon, with his steady
eyes, the straight ultra-refined nose with slightly-distended
nostrils, and a jaw which, in shape and strength, belied the
almost feminine beauty of the mouth.

He stood well over six feet, though you would hardly have
thought so because of the massive shoulders which seemed to
have been created to carry the troubles of the entire world.

His hands, the outward, visible and infallible sign of the inner
man, were perfect male hands, long and thin with square-
tipped sensitive fingers, and a certain look of steel about the
back and wrists.

But although he had been looking at her steadily for quite a
minute, owing to some inexplicable overpowering sensation
which had seized upon him, he would most certainly not have
been able to tell you the colour of her hair or that her feet were
bare.

"I beg your pardon," he said quite suddenly and a little
hoarsely, "but my dog brought me to you—and as I think the
tide is on the turn, I thought—"

But any further description of his thoughts was cut short in
most unseemly fashion as, with an ear-splitting bark, the terrier

hurled himself into the girl's lap, standing up to put its fore-paws round her neck, wriggling and squirming until the four feet, collar, and head were thoroughly knotted in the beautiful hair.

Leonie held on to her scalp to lessen the pain as stray hairs were literally dragged out by the roots, whilst tears of agony streamed down her face on to the man's hands as he held the squirming animal and endeavoured to loosen its bonds.

"Cut it!"

"What! All that!"

"Oh! I can spare it, but I can't stand the pain much longer, and I can't bear having my head touched. Look, I'll hold the dog firmly on my lap and bend my head, it won't hurt quite as much then, only do be quick!"

She put both hands on the shivering dog, who seemed to have sensed that something had gone agley, and pressing him down upon her knees bent her head, and her hair fell in waves about the man's feet as he unclasped a pocket-knife.

What there was in the attitude, whether it was the humility of the bent head or the utter abandon of the waving hair about his knees, the man never knew, but he suddenly began to hack savagely and ruthlessly at the great strands until the dog was freed and flung far on to the sands.

Then he bent and took hold of Leonie, lifting her bodily from her seat into his arms, crushing her desperately against his breast.

Just for one moment he stared down with blazing eyes, the nostrils quivering slightly, and the lips drawn back enough to show the white even teeth, whilst the rough tweed of his coat marked her cheek, and the strength of his arms and hands bruised her body even through her clothes; then he frowned, pushed her hair almost roughly right off her face, and looked at her with the dawn of recognition in his eyes.

And for just as long Leonie lay quite still, her eyes half closed, her scarlet mouth opened slightly, enough to show the small white teeth.

And then, she was standing on her feet with her hands clenched in his against his breast.

"*You*!"

"And *you*!" she replied, striving gently to release her hands.

"Forgive me! For God's sake forgive me! I—I have no excuse!"

A seagull perched itself on the point of a jagged rock, uttered its raucous cry and was gone towards Bull Point Lighthouse shining in the sun; a flock of rooks suddenly swirled from the cliffs, screaming battle upon their opponents as Leonie answered.

"There is nothing to forgive! Some things are beyond our ken. Will you get me my boots and stockings?"

Her hands shook ever so slightly under the strain of the control she was forcing upon herself, and the pupils of her eyes were strangely dilated, looking like bits of night sky set in a moon circle; but she spoke and moved quickly as the man, having brought the foot-gear and unwound the cut hair from the abject dog, leant down and picked up a tough seaweed root.

"No!" she said sharply, laying her hand on his. "No! It's too late to beat him!"

"I *must*!"

"I say *no*!"

"But you don't understand!"

Her lashes lay like a fringe on the cheek over which swept a flood of colour as she whispered so softly that the lap of the water almost drowned the word.

"*Please*!"

Save for the murmur of the water there was no sound whatever in the rock-strewn empty spot; and save for the swaying of the seaweed in the pools there was no movement as those two stood close to each other and Fate counted time.

Then Leonie smiled radiantly and sat down upon a rock with a stocking in each hand.

"Come and lunch in the next cove!" her companion said in a matter-of-fact voice, carefully winding the cut strands of hair and slipping them, without asking permission, into his breast pocket. "It's not so sunny in there, and I've cold soup and cold chicken, salad, jelly and cream—will you?"

"Ra-ther!" said she, beginning to lace her boots. And picnicking *is* fun in the last cove at Rockham. The air smells so heavenly, the wind is so soft, the clouds so lumpy and white; and there are little caves in which to dress and undress for the purpose of bathing, to boil the kettle, or hunt for those little bits of over-dried wood which go off with the report of a pistol and plop out to singe your garments.

And so *very* few get as far!

Somehow the tide is generally on the turn, and if by chance it is not, the tortuous and narrow passages between the coves, with their rocking rocks and hidden pools, are enough to twist the ankles and temper of anyone who is not Devon born or bred.

"Yes! I am due to sail for India about this day month," said

Jonathan Cuxson, Jan for short, a little later, as he drove the cold drumstick of a Devon chicken into the paper bag containing salt, while Leonie, holding the fellow leg in both hands, or at least the fingers of both hands, gnawed right heartily at the middle thereof, and the pardoned dog sat quivering with hope deferred.

"Isn't this perfectly wonderful," he went on, and Leonie mumbled "whum-whum" as interestedly and politely as her bone would allow. "I mean our meeting like this!"

She smiled and sat forward, resting one hand upon the rocks, and the puppy, with a lamentable slump in manners, crawled up from behind and gently relieved her of the bone which still had luscious scraps of white flesh adhering to it, and a dream of a shining gristly knob at the end.

"Your idea of picnicing is somewhat luxurious," she said, taking a cardboard plate full of jelly which he had smothered in cream. "Tell me what you are going to make of your life!"

"You must blame or thank Mrs. Pugsley for the luxury. I'm at Woolacombe, perched on the top of the hill, and she simply spoils me. Will you have a cigarette?"

Leonie shook her head, and the two great, hastily twisted plaits wriggled like shining snakes, causing the dog to lay one paw on his bone and snarl.

"I don't smoke!"

"How delightful!" said Jan Cuxson. "I was sure you didn't—I love women who smell of lavender."

"Won't you smoke—your pipe—and tell me what you are going to make of your life."

"They—the plans—have all been fogged up this morning!" he said slowly after a moment's pause. "How strange it all is. Do you know that I was going up to town next week to hunt up *you*, of all people? Do you remember anything of my father's death?"

"We don't talk about it," said Leonie quietly, and the man looked at her with a sudden questioning in the steady eyes.

"I am taking on his work, you know, specialising in the brain. I have got through all my exams quite decently, thanks, I think, to his wonderful notes, have travelled a bit in the east, and before settling down intended to go to India—what for do you think?"

Leonie shook her head. "Holiday?"

"Er—yes, almost. You know I simply *loved* my father, and his very last entry in his book of notes was about *you*. One line was this: 'Most interesting—shall go to India and find the ayah.' He died of heart failure, you know, and he must have written the last line before he died—it is: 'The answer to the problem concerning Leonie Hetth is in the third volume upon—' There was nothing after that—I thought he would be awfully pleased if I carried out his last wishes, and meant to hunt you up and see if you were still—er—bothered with dreams and then—"

He stopped short as Leonie leapt to her feet and ran back from a wave which had most unexpectedly swirled upon her from behind a rock.

"Quick!" she laughed, "quick—the tide will be in. Where's the dog?"

The dog was cavorting with a crab in a pool.

"Jingles!" sternly admonished his master, who was heaving everything pell-mell into his haversack. "By the way, what became of Jingles the first?"

A shadow crept into Leonie's eyes as she thought of the pain and disaster she invariably seemed to bring to those she loved most.

"He—he was run over—it was my fault, I whistled him across the road and a car caught him. If we hurry," she continued, "we shall be in time for tea—Auntie will love to see you again!"

"Oh! of course—I'd almost forgotten her—will she?"

CHAPTER XVII

"He that rebuketh a wicked man getteth
himself a blot!"
                    —*The Bible.*

By all the ill-luck in the world Sir Walter Hickle was sitting in
the patch called the garden, turning a small parcel elatedly over
and over in his pocket, as Leonie, and her companion, and the
dog came sliding down the hill towards the cottage.

For the time being Leonie had totally forgotten the proceedings of the night before, which had metamorphosed her
radiant self from a free into a bond woman.

"Oh!" she said, putting one hand unexpectedly on Jan
Cuxson's arm and digging her stick fiercely into the ground, as
the man in the garden half rose from his chair and sank back
with a frown.

"Oh!" she repeated.

"Tired, dear?"

Neither of them noticed the little endearing word which had
slipped out so naturally, but Leonie's face was wan and her
eyes were dead as she dragged herself down the last few yards,
while her aunt fluttered down to the gate to meet them, with
her mind and skirts in a whirl.

"Jan Cuxson!" she exclaimed, offering a limp hand, and "How *very* nice," she continued, lying quite successfully. "I should have known you anywhere. *Do* come in and have tea!"

And in the same breath, and with that strange cruel cunning of the shallow mind, which is the abortive twin of decent feminine intuition, she leapt at the difficulty she saw threatening, and tried to dispel it.

"Let me introduce you to Sir Walter Hickle, my niece's fiance."

Sir Walter ambled forward with outstretched hand as Cuxson, nodding curtly, bent to pick up Leonie's stick, which had clattered to the floor.

A malicious gleam shone in the elder man's little eyes as he looked at the splendid young fellow who had seemed, physically anyway, so fit a match for Leonie as they tramped down the hill together; and though there was no sign of his inward perplexity and repulsion in Jan Cuxson's face as his eyes swept the obese figure of the notorious old knight, his jaw took a sudden, almost ugly, outward thrust with the birth of a mighty resolution.

Leonie walked to the gate with him when he took his departure, having refused tea from a certain undefined feeling that he could not even sit in the same room as the man whom he intended to do out of the odd trick.

He crushed Leonie's hand as he looked straight into her eyes, so desperate and ashamed, and spoke very gently and deliberately as he slipped his hand to her wrist and pulled her a little closer.

"I shall be in the last cove to-morrow at eleven, waiting for you."

And naturally Leonie had responded to the mastery in the

voice, as all women do respond when the voice is the right one; and a soft wave of colour swept from chin to brow as she turned from the gate, and walked through the doorway straight to her bedroom; while her future lord pranced furiously among the bric-a-brac, and her aunt's beads and bracelets clashed against the china as she wrung her hands over the tea things, and portending disaster.

Leonie sat down on her bed with her eyes shining like stars.

The lid of her life's casket had opened wide, and from under a hideous heap of fear, disgust, lost illusions, and despair, hope had sprung, spreading her iridescent wings in the warmth of love.

She sat until the shadows crept about her, then got up from her bed with a little laugh, and descended to give battle for her life and freedom.

Think of every synonym connected with the word tumult and you will get a vague idea of the storm which crashed about the girl's defenceless head as she stood with her back to the door of the tiny sitting-room, with a perfectly gorgeous diamond ring sparkling and flashing in front of her upon a table.

"I cannot marry you, Sir Walter, I simply cannot do it," she was saying, slowly and distinctly. "You must let me go. So please give the ring to somebody else, there are heaps of girls ever—oh, ever so much nicer than me!"

She smiled sweetly as she picked up the ring and held it out to the man, who snatched it from her as he sprang to his feet, and hurled it through the window.

Then he moved to the other side of the table and leant both clenched fists upon it as he looked Leonie up and down.

"You needn't wear the ring, my girl," he said slowly, "but no one picks Walter Hickle up one day and throws him down the next. You're going to marry me this day month, you take that straight from me. Let's hear why you've changed your mind so sudden; willing to marry last night, unwilling to marry to-day.

"Come on, now, out with it!" he suddenly shouted, bringing his hand with a crash on the table as Leonie hesitated, blushing divinely.

"Only—be-cause I—I don't love you, Sir Walter, and it's—it's *not* right to marry without love!"

"Posh! There wasn't so much of this 'ere right to marry last night. Fallen in love with that young feller-me-lad, I suppose. Where did you meet him? What were you doing? How—how—"

Leonie turned the handle of the door, but shrank back as the man, with a bound, flung himself at her and wrenched her hand free; and Susan Hetth clashed her bracelets and bits as she put her hands tightly over her face, in her fright forgetting the mixture of colours she heaped on it daily in the hope of stemming the neap tide of old age.

"Get out, you there!" snarled the man, lashed to fury by the whip of jealousy. "Get out, go away, wash your face—you look like a—a—like a damned fut'rist, get *out*!"

And not daring to pass the two near the door, she prepared to get, with a great loss of dignity, through the bow window; in fact, one foot was just over the sill when the man called her back.

"Come back," he bellowed, "I want you as witness to what I'm goin' to say to your niece, the young lady what plays fast and loose with honest men. Fast and loose, I *don't* fink!"

Leonie shuddered as the veneer of refinement cracked under the strain of the man's rage, showing the brutality and grossness immediately underneath.

She pulled her hand free, and backed towards the mantelpiece, against which she leant, staring at him.

"I am not going to marry you!"

The voice was low but positive, and the quiet in the room was intense as Sir Walter bounced up within a foot of her and shook a fat forefinger in her face.

"Aren't you," he said, "aren't you! And I'll just tell you three things what'll make you change your tune, my girl.

"One," he placed the fat forefinger on the ill-bred thumb, "an' the least important, you'll marry me 'cos you're an 'etth, daughter of Colonel Bob Hetth, V.C., an' your fut'rist aunt ain't—hasn't half rubbed it in about the Hetths never breaking their word, I give you mine!"

"Please leave my father's name out of this," quietly replied Leonie, her face dead white from the sickening thudding of her heart.

"Well, if you don't keep your word, Miss tiger cat, I'll run you in for breach of promise, an' bring your father's name into court!"

"You couldn't!"

"*Couldn't!*—couldn't what?" stormed the man.

"Run," said Leonie gently, and added sweetly, and with great vulgarity, "you're too fat!"

"Two!" continued Sir Walter, purple in the face, but wisely ignoring the insult to his person. "You'll marry me 'cos no one else'll have you. You're batty, my gel—gone in the top storey—can't even go out to work for your living 'cause you ain't always to be trusted. I know all about yer, but I'm willin' to take the risk. There won't be any trapersin' round the 'ouse after dark once yer married to me, I give you my word. Course, if you like to go on spungin' on your aunt, obligin' her to live in a 'ole like this, well, that's your look h'out—'ardly up to mark tho', being an 'etth, daughter of a V.C."

His small eyes gleamed as they rested on Leonie's stricken face.

"Stop, please," she said hurriedly, "I can't stand any more just now. I—I couldn't really. Will you give me a week to think it over?"

The man laughed contemptuously.

"A few days, a few hours, then?"

There was something horrible in the humiliation of the girl's pleading, but it made not the slightest impression on the ex-costermonger, who had at one time been accustomed to enforcing his commands with the buckle end of his waist-belt.

"Not a minute, not a second," he chortled, seeing the end of the chase in sight. "Think of the 'old I have on yer aunt. Lady Susan Hetth, sister of Colonel Bob 'etth, V.C., creeping out h'of a gentleman's rooms at three h'o'clock of the mornin' an' payin' me 'ush money—think of h'it. *Now* what 'ev you got to say. Why don't you be sensible an' quiet, gal? I've *got* yer, it ain't no use kickin'. Be sensible an' I'll smother you in di'monds, give yer two Rolls-Royce, yacht, Monty Carlo any time, Park Lane—make every other woman want ter scratch yer eyes out—what more *could* yer want? Now what have yer got to say!"

What was there to say?

Aunt Susan tried to obliterate herself behind the window curtain; Sir Walter, thumbs in armholes, tilted himself backwards and forwards on toe and heel as Leonie came forward and leant with both hands the table, as she looked from one to the other without speaking.

In fact the silence became intolerable to Sir Walter, who had expected, and would have thoroughly enjoyed a heated altercation, in which he would have known exactly where he was.

"Well, what 'ev yer got to say, my gel?"

Leonie looked from one to the other.

"I will marry you this day month, Sir Walter." She threw up her hand as he laughed triumphantly. "Wait one moment! But until that day I will have nothing to do with you, *nothing*. I will not meet you nor go out with you, nor bother about a trousseau, nor the future in any way. I shall go out and come in when I like, and go where and how I like. I shall meet whom I like. I won't deceive you, I shall meet Jan Cuxson just as often as I like. And I should advise you not to interfere with me in any way. He is young and strong, and, as an old friend of the family, might resent it. You can trust him, he is a gentleman—which means—oh, well!—you will find the exact meaning in a French dictionary."

She crossed to the door, turned, and looked, slowly from one to the other.

"Is the bargain concluded?"

"Yes!—I'll take yer on those terms—but you'll pay a 'undred per cent interest on the month, I've lent yer—an' *then* some I give yer *my* word!"

The door shut quietly as the man sank into a chair.

"Batty!" he said as he mopped his bald head, "absolutely balmy. But it's worth while—it's worth while—let her have 'er month—let 'er—I shall have a whole lifetime to break 'er in."

CHAPTER XVIII

"Why fret about them if to-day be sweet!"
—*Omar Khayyam.*

The great grey breakers heaved themselves skywards, paused for half a second, split and crashed down upon the rocks the next morning as Leonie and Jan Cuxson sat on the sands under the lowering sky.

They had argued, analysed, plotted, and planned, only to find that each road they launched out upon full of hope, terminated in the blind alley of the old man's power over the girl.

"I've just got to go through with it," said Leonie, "there is simply no way out."

The man caught both hands in his.

"Dear heaven, how I love you, child! How I long to pick you up, as I did all those years ago, and carry you out of all this to happiness. Leonie! Leonie! You must marry me, I love you so."

And she had sat quite still, not daring to move for fear of the mighty passion which surged about her.

Yes! Quite true! They had only met twice; but there is a certain kind of love, exceeding rare it's true in Europe, which from an infinitesimal seed is capable in one second of blossoming into a tree, fruit and all, in the shade of which you can sit content until your life's end.

It simply sprouts all over the East.

Wishing to prevent a conflagration Leonie spoke quite calmly as she withdrew her hands.

"And I couldn't marry you, even if I were free, because—at times—as I have just told you—they say that I—I—am not responsible for my actions? I'm—I'm supposed to be—"

"Be quiet!"

Cuxson pulled her fiercely into his arms, crushing her cheek against his.

"Tell me all, every detail."

They sat there as the tide went out, and the man registered the facts of the tragic tale in his mind, eager to be out on the trail of the mystery overshadowing the girl he loved.

"Mad!" he laughed when she had finished, "*mad*—no more than I am, and I'm sane enough in all conscience except in my love for you. I shall go to India, and wring or bribe the truth out of that ayah. But we needn't worry about the date of starting yet a while, and between then and now we shall have found a way out of this seeming impasse. What is it?"

Leonie had twisted herself suddenly out of his arms, looked over her shoulders and shivered.

"It is what I was telling you about, a sensation of someone standing close behind me."

"It's nothing, Leonie, just imagination," said Jan Cuxson.

For how could he see a certain high caste native of India

walking slowly down the gangway from the great ship just docked at Tilbury, and smiling inscrutably as he placed his foot in the country which held the white woman he sought?

Leonie turned her head quickly, and shivered again, violently.

"It was just as though someone had called me," she said, speaking just above a whisper.

"Look at me, dear!"

Leonie looked straight into the honest grey eyes, and the fear died out of her own as she met the steady gaze.

"I'm slow, dear, dead slow, plodding I suppose they'd call me, but once I'm on to something I never let go until I've won. Things are black, sweetheart, but something is telling me that I shall find a way out. When—when is—"

Leonie lied.

It was beyond her power of will to place a limit to her sudden newborn happiness; she would not give a definite date, and relying on the certainty that the man would never allow anyone to gossip to him about the wedding, she lied—deliberately.

"Oh! there's *plenty* of time, don't let's talk about it."

She sprang to her feet and flung out her arms to the sea.

"Let's forget, Jan, let's forget! Let's steal something from Fate and be happy. Let's be friends, pals; we can't be anything else, because I am in honour bound. And—and—I'm *so* hungry "—she turned her radiant, laughing face to him—"I'll race you to Barricane for tea."

She was off as she spoke, with Cuxson close behind. They jumped from rock to rock, they slipped, they slithered, they splashed up to their knees in pools and out again.

The man did not break the compact when he caught her in the shadow of the wreck and drew her into the shelter of his arms.

"Pal!" he whispered. "Little pal!"

And she lay quite still until the thud of their hearts, caused by the strenuous exercise, had given place to the stronger, steadier beat of steadfast love; then she slipped down, ducked under his arms and was away, and her laugh was caught by the wind and blown back to him as he ran in hot pursuit.

CHAPTER XIX

"Write them upon the table of thine heart!"
                                        —*The Bible.*

Leonie's wrist watch very softly chimed midnight, announcing in gentle tones the birth of her wedding-day, as she sat with her chin in her hands staring out to sea.

She frowned and pulled savagely at the band until it broke; there was a faint crash, and a faint splash, as the watch, hurtling through the air, ricocheted from a rock into a pool as the girl stretched her arms above her head, leant back, and closed her eyes.

Her last midnight swim, the last time she would slip the bathing dress over her beautiful virgin body, the last time she would revel in freedom, oh! the last time of anything decent, and pure, and sweet.

She had not lost her heart or her head, in fact she had gone through none of those amorous gymnastics which seem necessary to the cardiac state of being in love.

She *loved*, and she knew it, and confessed it on her knees at night, and when she walked, or swam, or rode, or carried her food on her back, or braided her hair in the day. She was loved and she knew it, and thanked her God when she lay down to sleep at night, and when she shopped, or placated her petulant relation, or played bridge or the piano equally badly, or got wet through in the storm, and tanned by the wind.

Many times Sir Walter had almost been on the verge of giving her her desire.

Almost! Because it only needed two things to make him toe the line of sensual infatuation; the first being the graciousness of every line of her beautiful person when she met him by chance; and the second, the ungraciousness of her distinctly unpleasant manner upon the same occasion, over both of which he promised himself as he inwardly raged at her frequent, prolonged and unexplained absences, he would shortly have full control.

The month had slipped by so quickly, the month in which she had indifferently left to her aunt and fiance the choosing of her trousseau, and the arrangement of the ceremony; also the honeymoon, that subsequent insight into purgatory which she was to endure as best she could in an isolated, thatched cottage t'other side of Hartland Point.

A month during which she had walked, and talked, and walked again with Jan Cuxson, who caused her heart to thud heavily even though he did not touch her hand in greeting, or parting, or at any other time.

They had gathered *laver*—that most delectable vegetable-seaweed—at the base of the Woolacombe rocks; dug and scratched for the elusive cowrie shell in the sands of Barricane Beach; devoured Mrs. Parker's teas of bread and butter and cream, jam and cake, laid on snow-white cloth upon trestle table; and watched their flat-pebbled ducks and drakes skip more or less successfully across the waters.

They had tramped to Croyde, George Ham, Saunton, and all the other lovely spots, and whistled over the lighthouse wall at Bull Point to be regaled by tea on a tray, handed over by one of the perfectly charming family of Howgego, which comprises the lighthouse keeper, his wife, and his bonny daughter.

All this had been done by stealth.

Creeping about the cottage in stockinged feet at dawn, polishing the high boots before retiring to bed until they shone again; packing the haversack, creeping out of the cottage, vaulting the wall to the left to evade the gate which either jammed or creaked, and away up the steep incline, also to the left, and to wherever love listed.

Upbraidings at night are quite bearable when the heart is aglow, and the future dimmed by present happiness; but upbraidings in the early morning are quite intolerable when the outlook into the future shows a black abyss through the medium of an empty stomach.

She had seized upon every passing moment, wringing the uttermost out of it that she might have something put by with which to fill in the blanks of the drear future, the vacuum where should have been a tumultuously throbbing heart of love, and a pulse of life and passion.

Also did she glean and garner, so as to be tucked in stray corners, memories of a flower in a hedgerow, a boat on the wing, a look in a dog's eyes, and the indescribable smell of a mixture of tobacco, sea air, and leather; and all the other little genuine antique, and ever new odds-and-ends of the collection labelled Love in the heart museum.

Not a word had she said about the wedding.

Cowardly? Yes, indeed! But if a prisoner were given a bottle of champagne to drink just before his death by hanging, it's odds on that instead of merely tasting a few drops he would drink the whole bottle, and go to his doom with the exultant thought of something nice, anyway, having happened to cheer him on his final exit.

She simply radiated love, and allowed neither the frequent upbraidings of her distracted aunt, nor the hourly approach of the fatal day to dim the sunlight of the hour in hand.

"Never you worry," she said one day, when her aunt had waylaid and implored her to have her wedding-dress fitted, "We'll pin it with safety-pins if it doesn't hang right, and as long as I'm at the church door on time, nothing else really matters. And I've given you my word on that."

And she had vaulted the wall and taken a short cut through the golf course until she had come up behind the man who loved her; and he, reading the trouble in her strange eyes, had drawn her hands to his heart and held them tight.

How often had they stood in the shade of the fir trees in the heat of the day, with the intoxicating smell of the pines in their nostrils, and the soothing sound of the humming of many bees in their ears.

They had stood so still, so close, and so very much alone.

Oh! he loved her and her ways!

Loved the rarity of her beauty, and the vitality of her body, loved the extreme care she took not to allow her fingers to touch his when passing a cup or a hefty sandwich.

Revelled in the surge of colour which swept her face when sometimes he caught and steadied her on a rock; and the way in which, when sitting on the sand, she would suddenly scrunch up her knees with her arms for no apparent reason, and bury her scarlet mouth, and the eyes which betrayed her, in the rough tweed of her skirt.

He exulted in the little half-catch of her breath, the little happy laugh, the extra polish he knew she put on her boots just for his sake; and, above all, that perfect sense of virgin woman which emanated from her, allied to the promise of a passion which most inhabitants of a northern clime would have utterly misconstrued and misunderstood.

Yes! He revelled and he exulted in every minute of every hour spent with her; blinded with love, led astray by the thought of months ahead in which he felt that Fate surely would find a way out for them, he let the time slip by, up to the moment when Leonie said good-bye quite gravely, shaking her head without a smile at the usual invitation to meet on the morrow.

CHAPTER XX

"Working spells
Upon a mind o'erwrought!"
                        —*Thomas Hardy.*

Secure in the solitude of her last few hours of freedom; oblivious of the fact that her aunt, enraged and alarmed at the unseemly and most untimely absence of the morrow's bride, was idiotically wringing her hands as she ran up and down in front of the cottage; worn out and weary with despair, Leonie, in her bathing dress, had gone to sleep with the full moon shining down upon the small, pale face, full of shadows.

Jan Cuxson, uneasy at the girl's curt refusal to meet him during the last twenty-four hours, had started to walk to Woolacombe from Ilfracombe where he had spent a wretched, restless, futile day.

He had tramped through the sleeping village of Lee without a look at the historic cottage once inhabited by the Three Old Maids, and along to the other little cottage on the sea front where the absence of light in Leonie's room caused him to guess that she was abroad. He passed as quietly and quickly as possible, having determined to avoid the place for fear of meeting the aunt, or old Hickle, and losing his self-control.

As long as you know exactly where to lay your hand on them you don't worry overmuch about your gold cigarette case, or your favourite pipe, or the diamond brooch you pin haphazard into your laces; but mislay them for a moment and see what a turmoil of inquietude you will be in!

Never doubting the honesty of his beloved, tricked as it were by her happy, care-free attitude, the man had drifted contentedly in the sun of love, and the month of June; but to-night a bank of clouds was rising to meet the moon half-way upon her celestial journey, and the winds of doubt and uneasiness were lifting the corners of that warm, comforting mantle of serenity which we seldom have a chance to take down from its peg in the wardrobe of life.

Yesterday she had left him with a flat refusal to meet him, and her eyes had been like the eyes of the dead, and her hands had been like ice, and her voice had been most uncompromisingly final.

All day he had argued with himself, surmised and made excuses, sunned himself in the cove at Rapparree, assuring himself stubbornly that everything was quite all right; and at last, dinnerless, desperate, and afraid, had started off hot foot to find her; intending to crush the resistance out of her with the outpourings of his love, and force her to risk everything for the sake of a life-long happiness.

It was just about one o'clock when he scrunched past the rusty old wreck and clambered up and over the rocks and through the opening to the second cove; and his heart leapt as he steadied himself when his eyes found that which they had eagerly sought; then missed a beat as, for some unknown reason, he stood stock still, and drew back into the shadows.

Leonie was standing knee deep in a pool.

The saw-edged rocks rose behind her, shining like steel in the moonlight; great strands of seaweed swirled about her, for all the world like snakes, weaving in and out of the burnished hair which spread itself fanwise on the water about her knees.

Save for the thinnest, finest silk bathing dress which clung to the perfect body, as does the soft fragrant skin to the peach, she was nude, and so unaware of eyes upon her that the man held his breath, fearing she might spy him in the shade.

He knew, as everyone knows, that through the criminal teaching of the girl-child in Europe, she would have had it instilled into her mind as soon as it was capable of understanding, that the slightly draped *tout ensemble* of her glorious body was something to be thoroughly well ashamed of, though on other occasions, by means of slit skirts and excessive decolletage, she could expose in sections just as much as she liked to the eyes of any alien waiter who hung over her with the sauce, or any chauffeur who helped her into a car.

Her eyes were wide and staring straight in his direction, and that she was asleep he had not the faintest idea.

So clearly was she outlined against the rock that every line of the lovely limbs, every exquisite curve of the beautiful bosom showed as plainly as if she had been standing in the broad light of noon as she stepped out of the pool.

With face upturned, and arms outstretched to the moon, she stood undulating slightly with the exquisite movements of the nautch girl, which has nothing to do with the *danse de ventre* and other such disgusting muscular exhibitions.

Watch a spider's thread floating in the air at dawn, then you will get some idea of the gentle, supple, alluring movement.

The wind, blowing up before the storm, blew against her hair, and it streamed out in front of her; her arms, twining and twisting, slid in and out of the silky mass until she appeared to have at least four; her exquisite feet seemed to beat upon a human figure which was really nothing but the shadow of the rock behind her, and Jan Cuxson, in the shadows, suddenly smote his forehead as she lifted up her voice and cried:

"Kali! Kali! Kali!"

The word thrice repeated rose softly on the night air, but struck like a hammer upon the ears of the man who, in studying the brain, had found himself often and inextricably entangled in the religions and mysteries of the East.

"My God!" he whispered, "My God, she is asleep and—"

But he never moved as Leonie suddenly showed that she was aware of his presence.

It was not that she saw him, or that she knew him; she was simply aware that a man was watching her.

Not once did the eyelids close over the glaring eyes shining like two green phosphorescent stones; not a sign of recognition showed in her face as she laughed the sweetest little laugh in the world and moved towards him.

Jan Cuxson had travelled pretty widely in the last few years, and had seen almost every kind of dance in the various ports at which he had called, and the towns he had visited in the East, but for absolute voluptuousness, and the portrayal of physical passions, he had never seen anything to compare with this which he watched horror-stricken by the sea.

"What have they done to her? What have they done to her? What spell has been cast? What cruel thing have they done to her?"

Over and over again the questions raced unanswered through his brain.

For at the thrice repeated cry he had understood in a flash that fastidious, pure, innocent Leonie was unconsciously perforning the preliminary rites customary to the worship of Kali, the goddess of death, the wife of Siva, the daughter of the Himalayas; which rights might best be described as a prolonged and terrible orgy of every passion known to man.

And well was it for Leonie Hetth that Jan Cuxson was straight and thoroughbred, and that his love was pure, else might it have gone badly with her, bringing her perchance to the door of the madhouse; for there is but a hair's breadth between those who are wakened roughly from the sleep in which they walk, and act, and speak, and those who rave in padded cells.

She held out her beautiful, bare arms in invitation, and as he remained quite motionless, glided ever so swiftly to him, so close that he felt the sweetness of her breath upon his cheek.

"Behold!" she cried softly in perfect Hindustani, "Behold! O my beloved! has the Sweet One! the Gentle One! the most blessed Mother looked with graciousness upon her children! May our lips cling in worship, yea! and our bodies in worship! She looketh with soft eyes upon our love, blessed is she, O! Durga! most terrible, most fierce, most cruel!"

Jan Cuxson hesitated.

If he put his arms about her she might waken at any moment, and then the shame and horror of it all.

If he did not respond might she not hurt herself in her wrath as do those who worship the Black One, and of whom he had heard in his travels in India.

What on earth was he to do?

And where was he to find the strength to resist the overpowering appeal of the sweet passion she offered him.

He loved her, desired her, hungered for the touch of the sweet mouth, and there she stood in her youth, her innocence, her beauty, asking to be held against his heart, touching his hands gently with her finger-tips, desirous of his mouth, his hands, his love.

And even as he hesitated wild anger swept over the beautiful face, making it terrible to behold as she raised it to the moon with a laugh that made the man shudder to his soul, and gasp as she suddenly tore her bathing suit from her and held it towards him in both hands. He unconsciously took it from her, whereupon she shook from head to foot with wild unseemly laughter, and her glorious hair swept about her, hiding her completely from the desperate eyes that watched her.

"Behold, O Parvati! who steppeth lightly upon the mountains! Behold! has he chosen my raiment, therefore shalt thou be pleased! Yea! and even shall there be blood upon it!" [1]

And swinging her arm she struck it again and again against the rocks until the flesh was torn and the blood streamed, causing the man to move hurriedly with intent to waken the girl he loved, even at the risk of her reason and his ultimate happiness. But he stopped.

Leonie was standing still with uplifted arms, dripping blood upon her face whilst her sweet, clear voice rose sonorously in the *Vega* hymn known as the Love Spell.

Jan Cuxson had studied Hindustani in preparation for his travels in India, but he frowned as he listened, for he did not understand one syllable.

And then his eyes opened wide in astonishment as he caught the meaning of a word here and there, and "Sanskrit!" he muttered in amazement.

Pulling a piece of pale green seaweed from the rock, she twined it and whispered, "This plant is honey born; with honey we dig thee; forth from honey art thou engendered; do thou make us possessed of honey.

"At the tip of my tongue, honey; at the root of my tongue, honeyedness; mayest thou be altogether in my power, mayest thou come unto my intent.

"Honeyed is my in-stepping, honeyed my forthgoing, with my voice I speak what is honeyed, may I be of honey aspect.

"Than honey am I sweeter, than the honey plant more honeyed; of me, verily shalt thou be fond, as of a honeyed branch.

"About thee with an encompassing sugar-cane have I gone, in order to absence of mutual hatred; that thou mayest be one loving me, that thou mayest be one not going away from me!"

Leonie swayed slightly as the words passed faintly and yet more faintly, like a moan, from her lips; her eyes were closing slowly, very slowly; and she slipped to her knees, her bleeding arms held out towards the man before whom she knelt, as the breeze blew her glistening hair this way and that, exposing for a second, then hiding the glories of the exquisite white figure from the eyes which could not help but see.

Drooping lower and lower she stretched herself, face downwards, upon the sand, closed her eyes as the moon sank suddenly behind a dense mass of clouds, and peacefully went to sleep.

[1]In one of the rites concerning the worship of Kali, women's garments are thrown in a heap, from which men choose indiscriminately. The garment he chooses gives the man a right to the woman who owns it.

CHAPTER XXI

"And wilt thou leave me thus
That hath given thee my heart?—Say nay! Say nay!"
                                        —Sir T. Wyatt.

What in heaven's name was he to do now?

Touch her he would not; let her know that he had seen her in all her unhidden beauty he could not; yet the gurgling and rustling and whispering between the water and the stones told him that the tide was racing in, and that what he intended to do he must do right quickly.

All he wanted to do was to gather her up in his strong arms, and wakening her with kisses carry her to safety.

Safety from the sea, safety from the unknown spell which had been laid upon her, safety from the horrible future; a safety he felt which could only be found within the circumference of his arms folded about her in love.

But instead he looked round for the garments she must have left somewhere, and seeing them, stepped quietly across the widening pools and gathered up the soft, sweet-smelling heap of dainty raiment; clenching his hands tight upon them to prevent himself from burying his face in the perfumed delicate things which he had not the right even to touch.

A little knot of pale pink bebe ribbon came away in his hand, and he twisted it around the seaweed ring she had twined about his finger, then untwisted them both and slipped them into his pocket, and stooped to pick up something which had slipped from the garments and tinkled on the rocks.

"Oh, you beauty!" he said as he held the jewel out in his open hand, and "Oh, you brute!" he said again is the cat's-eye winked cunningly at him with the knowledge of all ages in its lustrous depths.

Then he went back, crushing his flimsy burden to his heart; and placing it upon a rock near the sleeping girl, strode off to the opening of the little connecting cove, where he stood in the shadows and called;

"Leonie! Are you there, Leonie?"

Leonie stirred, settled down again to sleep, and stirred each time the voice rang insistently.

Who knows if love would have brought her back to consciousness and the immediate necessity to rise and clothe herself, and flee for safety?

Anyway, the tide decided and sent a little wave that thoroughly drenched her and brought her to her knees shivering and bewildered.

"Tide in!"

She glanced round hurriedly and drew her hand across her eyes.

"Funny!" she said as she retreated before a wave which surged over the rocks and swirled up behind her. "But—why—I've nothing on! And my arm!—why, I'm simply cut to bits. And—and oh! I've been dreaming—and how dark it is; there must be a storm coming!"

As she spoke she hurriedly flung herself into her clothes, biting her lips as the lace and ribbons caught in the horrible gash in her arm, and was standing waiting for the water to recede before she jumped, just as a voice as from heaven itself called.

"Leonie! where are you? Leonie, the tide is coming in!"

She did not wait, she jumped clear, stumbling and falling on the other side, ripping her feet until they bled.

Then she got up and ran blindly, impelled by terror pursued by the fear of something far more terrible than death.

"Jan! Jan! help me!"

Without a word he caught her and lifted her, holding her closely.

Never a word he said as they raced through from one cove to the other, neither when the waters buffeted him nor when weeds twined about his feet, and rocks impeded him.

Swiftly he carried her up the slight incline and laid her on the grass, took off his coat, ripped out his shirt sleeve, and tearing it into strips, bound up the bleeding arm.

Then sitting down beside her he leant over sideways and picked her up bodily, clear from the ground into his arms; no mean feat with a toilet jug full of water, let alone with a hefty maiden weighted with grief.

He held her in that heavenly, comforting clasp known and practised by stout old nurses and some mothers, within which you feel that you can defy anything, even to the onslaughts of peevish Fortune.

His left arm was under and round her shoulders, his left hand gently pressed her head against his breast, his right arm was round her just above the knees, and he rocked her gently.

Oh! the heavenly, comforting bliss!

History was repeating itself, for Leonie, with great dry sobs shaking her from head to feet, was snuffling into Jan Cuxson's collar as she had snuffled into his father's years ago.

"Beloved!"

Sobs.

"Beloved! there is nothing to cry about—*nothing*! As I am holding you now, so shall I always hold you, and no harm can come to you from ocean, tempest or life. *Nothing* can hurt you because I love you!"

Sobs.

"*Leonie*!"

She lay absolutely still, unconsciously counting the beats of his heart which was thudding heavily against her right shoulder, and waiting for the moment when she would find the strength at last to turn down her "empty glass."

"Leonie! you've got to listen to me now, and I am not going to ask you to decide because Fate has decided for you. And oh! beloved, beloved, thank heaven that there is still time, that you are still free, that heaven instead of hell is waiting for you. Yes! dear heart. Fate has decided!"

He stroked her hair as he looked down into the little face crushed against his shoulder, and shifted her a wee bit that she might rest more comfortably. Leonie closed her eyes and trembled from head to foot as Fate pinched the decision between claw-like thumb and finger so that it was stillborn.

"Dear," continued Jan Cuxson as he gently patted her shoulder with his left hand, "dear, oh! my dear, just as I hold you now, so I shall always hold you. I am going to keep you, marry you, and take you right away to India next week; I'll telegraph that my things are not to be put on board to-morrow. You must have a nervous breakdown to-day, *you* darling, just to think of *that*," and his laugh rang out against the sullen stillness of the dawn, "then we will slip away, and get married, and—oh! Leonie, I *love* you."

Leonie said no word, but from her head to her feet swept a thrill which the man felt from his feet to his head.

He laughed again, laughed as a god might laugh with the world in his hand, and crushed her fiercely to him.

"Beloved! I love you! love you! love you! And you? Tell me you love me! Why, you dare not look me in the face and say no! You love me, dear! You are part of me; you are bone of my bone, flesh of my flesh! Sorrow shall not touch you when you are all mine, your joys shall be my joys! And—beloved, my children shall be your children!"

With a sudden movement Leonie wrenched herself from his arms and on to her feet, whilst a driving cloud surrounded them, and a growl of thunder came over from Lundy Island way.

"Love you!" cried the girl. "Yes! I love you, if that is the right word to describe what it is I have in my heart for you. No! don't touch me! Listen, I would live for you, *die* for you in love. Pain through you would be joy, joy through you would be heaven."

She clasped her hands to her breast, then threw them out towards him, palm uppermost, in a wonderful gesture of passionate surrender, but her face was terrible to see, with eyes like burned out fires, and great smears of blood across her mouth and cheek.

"All that I have for you and more—oh! much more—but—I—I cannot marry you!"

The glass went down with a little clatter upon the coldest of life's cold marble slabs as Jan Cuxson, grasping the girl's arms, pulled her roughly towards him.

That he had caught the arm right on the lacerated wound he had no idea as he stood looking down into the eyes which were on a level with the top button, of his coat.

"Beloved! beloved! You are tired, distraught! You don't know what you are saying! You are to go straight home and sleep, for *hours*, then come out refreshed and gloriously happy to meet me where and when you like! And we will fix everything down to the very smallest detail, oh! dear heart, think of it! and this day week we will sail for India!"

CHAPTER XXII

"That day is a day of wrath—a day of clouds
and thick darkness."

—The Bible.

"India!" repeated Leonie, "India!"

She flung round towards the sea, standing on the very edge of
the cliff, the violence of the wind against her the only barrier
between her and certain death.

"Tell me," she cried, pointing to the heaving, raging mass of
waters with a hand above which shone dully a blood-soaked
bandage. "Tell me what I did to myself down there just now. I
awoke in a different place from which I went to sleep. I had
no—I am cut and bruised. Terrible things happen wherever I
am—they follow me. I woke one night in a pitch dark room
and saw two green eyes staring at me from the wall. They were
my eyes—reflected in a looking-glass—*mine*—they shine at
night like a cat's—and there's a voice calling—often. Oh! I tell
you I'm haunted, bewitched, *cursed*!"

"Come to me, beloved."

She turned and went like a child into the outstretched arms,
and he, having wet his handkerchief on the mist-damped grass,
bent the weary head back against his shoulder, and wiped away
the blood-stains from the despairing face.

"You walk in your sleep, Leonie, by reason of the workings of an overwrought brain, that is all. India is the problem, and your ayah is the answer. *I* think she frightened you somehow, made some deep impression on you, on your baby brain, and we are going to India to find her. It's very simple, dear, once find the cause we can easily find the remedy, and it will be much better if you come with me. By the way, who gave you that cat's-eye?"

He had made a slip.

"When did you see it?" answered Leonie quickly, "I never showed it to you! Were—were you down *there* near me, *before* you called?"

"No," steadily lied the man, "but the thing slipped through your blouse one day—it's a brute. Who gave it to you?"

"My ayah! Do you know, I think you are quite wrong about her. Auntie says Mother told her that she nearly broke her heart when I left India, seventeen years ago, and she writes to me regularly every three months. Only last week I had a letter from—"

"Do you speak Hindustani?" interrupted Cuxson abruptly, with a frown on his face.

"Not a word!"

"Or Sanskrit?"

"Oh! no, neither, but the letters are in English, evidently written by one of those letter writers, who get so much for each letter they write for the illiterate poor. And in every one she says how she loves me and longs for my return, and although she is very happy in the service of some Ranee in the north of India, she wants to give it up and come to me."

There was a pause, broken by the nearing thunder and the

crash of the waves against the cliffs.

"Don't let's worry about that yet, dear, as everything is settled splendidly and—"

But Leonie pulled away and stood facing him with her hands in his against his heart.

"Do you really *love* me?"

The whisper was almost lost in the tumult of the breakers beneath.

"*Love* you, Leonie, *love* you!"

"What would you *forgive* me through love?"

"*Forgive* you! Everything! Dishonour could not touch you, and everything else I should forgive!"

Leonie tried to speak as she looked past him to the little green track between the downs which led to the world, and all it contained for her; and he, obtuse male, content in the plans he had mapped out entirely to his own satisfaction, and having blissfully taken the girl's consent to the programme for granted, failed to read the agony written across her face in capital letters.

"Tell me that you will be content, dear. I'm rich enough, but nothing compared with—oh! tell me, what do you like—what do you want—what do you *really* care for!"

She freed her hands and turned to look out to sea, where the day had been born in agony upon a bed of sullen, unbroken water.

Then she looked straight down at the waves flinging themselves against the cliffs, drenching her with spray, moaning, fretting at the barrier, retiring only to do the same thing over and over again.

"What do I want, O Man whom I love? I want a white house within high, white walls, on the edge of the sea. I want my arms full of children—yours and mine. I want love, oh! love and yet more love, that is what I want!"

The man twisted her round and held her at arms' length, her heels within an inch of the edge, her body bent back over the chasm, and her hair, spreading like a banner in the tearing wind, swept about his shoulders and across his face, intoxicating him with its perfume and silken caress.

Passion swept over him, he shook her like a reed, and her foot slipped off the earth into nothingness.

But not a word said she, though she prayed that he might suddenly let go his hold and send her crashing to sweet death on the rocks beneath.

You see what happens when you are decent and honest and have a mind to keep your word—just death rather than dishonour, and pain to others.

Whereas if only she had been dishonest, and therefore commonplace, she would either have chucked her given word to the devil, or the deep grey sea over which she stood, and cleared for her own happiness and a marriage licence; or kept her word in one sense while making deedy little plans of triangular pattern for future reference.

"Is that what you want, oh! heart of mine?" said Jan Cuxson, exulting in the sensation that his hands alone held her metaphorically and actually safe from the depths beneath. "And that is what I am going to give you, beloved, and more, much more in exchange for the treasure you will put into my hands. Oh! Leonie, my love—"

And yet he did not kiss her, but pulled her farther inland and let her go as she essayed to free herself, having come to the absolute breaking point.

What a wooing!

The copper coloured clouds were massed above and about them, the trees bent and straightened and bent again before the wind, the sea heaved in huge unbroken waves right to the horizon; Lundy Island, Hartland, and Baggy Point had disappeared in a driving sheet of rain.

How beautiful she looked as she stood in the storm, cut, bruised and dishevelled.

Just for one moment she looked into the eyes of the man she loved, whose hands were outstretched for the treasures she could not lay therein; and then she turned and fled as a great streak of lightning rent the clouds, and thunder like heavy artillery crashed about their heads.

She had not gone twenty yards when she stumbled and fell heavily.

Her boots were being hurled here and there by the waves in the cove where she had left them; her left foot was cut and bleeding badly, but a sudden desperate courage came to her when she felt herself raised and steadied.

"I shall carry you to the foot of the hill near your cottage!"

She struggled as he lifted her, struggled so violently that he put her on her feet.

"Don't touch me, Jan, don't come near me, because I—because—"

And the mantle of his satisfaction and content being suddenly rent into a thousand shreds by the knife edge of his intuition, he put both hands on her shoulders, looked down into the misery of her eyes, and very gently said one word.

"Because?"

"Because," and she began to laugh without making any sound, her mouth twitching, her shoulders shaking, "because I am to be married *to-day* at noon!"

"To-*day*! but you said—"

"I lied."

"You lied—to *me*!"

She made a little sound which reminded him of an animal agonising in a trap, whilst the fury of his own pain drove him to hurt her even more.

"Why—*lie*?"

"Why?" her eyes blazed as she defied the storm, her hell and fate. "Why?—because I love you, because I love you so much that I wanted to cheat life out of one month of happiness. And I have had it—I have had it—and I love you—"

She flung her hands up to the stormy skies and brought them down, clenched against her breast. "I love you, *God* hear me, I *love* you!"

And with a terrible cry that went wailing out to sea she fled away through the lash of the blinding storm.

CHAPTER XXIII

"The lighted end of a torch may be turned towards the
ground, but the flames still point upwards."
                                        —*The Satakas.*

 The church was simply packed!

The lucky ones, almost all women, wedged tight and fast,
crushed their beautiful clothes against their neighbours' lovely
raiment in the pews.

The unlucky ones stood in rows in the side aisles, just as their
commoner sisters stand in rows upon the pavement edge to
watch some passing show.

Some, less hindered by superfluous adipose tissue, had
managed to seat themselves upon the tomb of one Sir William
de Tracy, who had one time unduly concerned himself in the
murder of a certain Thomas a Becket.

Indeed he built this church in atonement for his unseemly
conduct, though something seems to have gone agley in the
architectural penance, as the ghost of Sir William is to be met
o' nights upon the sands of Woolacombe—so 'tis said.

Some of the still younger fry among the spectators, I mean
worshippers in this solemn ceremony, clasped the heads in
effigy of dead squire, or dame, or knight, in order to get the

necessary purchase for the task of pulling themselves up for just one second in the supreme attempt to catch a glimpse of the principals in the parade.

Except for the setting of this beautiful house of God it might have been an *entr'acte* at some theatrical first night; same comments upon actors and audience; same criticism upon dress and morals; same yawning and fidgeting.

What *had* they not suffered and sacrificed to flatter the vulgar old millionaire! Anyway they expected a good deal in return for the excruciating journey down by rail or car, the whole day lost out of the season in London town, *and* the wedding present.

Unless you own the genuine thing in rank or reputation, how *frightfully* difficult it is to send an astute vulgar old millionaire the one present which will open his doors to you.

If you do own the genuine thing, an electro-plated toast-rack will be all-sufficient. If you *don't*, well it's simply no good worrying around the bottom rung of the ladder which he has climbed, and from the top of which he sits making faces of derision at you.

The principal performers had just disappeared into the vestry as the old clock chimed twelve, and Jan Cuxson, swinging back the churchyard gate, strode up the narrow tomb-lined path to the church door.

Every woman turned to look at him as he passed.

"Look at 'e now, Mrs. Ovey! He be staying with me. Did 'ee iver zee sich a butivul face. Jist like a picture. Sit 'ee still, young Gracie, an' doan 'ee walk over thikee graves, now! I tell 'ee 'e'd make a proper bridegroom, 'e wud!"

"Iss, I reckon! 'Er 'av done mighty fine fer 'erself, 'er 'ave; Mrs. Tucker tol' me all 'bout 'un, but 'er be terr'ble young, b'ain't 'er, for the likes of thikee ol' man?"

The country women patted and pulled at their best clothes, and turned their sweet, slightly bronzed faces, with skins like satin, up to the blazing sun.

"Iss, vrai! that 'er be Mrs. Pugsley! But did 'ee iver zee the likes on they ther zatins an' laces an' juels they vine wimen be wearin'?"

"Iss! an' luk at th' ol' paint an' stuff ther be ol over ther vaces? Dear, dear now, ther lips be terr'ble raid, b'ain't 'un? Luks lik' they'd bin stealin' cherries! An' ther eyes be terr'ble black! Luks lik' the'd bin fightin' with ther 'usbands."

Silence fell, during which sweet music stole through the church windows to fall like a benison upon the charming simple folk who, by their courtesy and gentleness, make Devon such a blissful county to dwell in.

"Can't think, now," suddenly remarked Mrs. Ovey, "w'y thikee young lady 'av chose Mortehoe Church fer 'er weddin'!"

"I've year'd tell that 'er vather be related to zum lord 'oo 'elped kill some ol' parson, yers an' yers gone by! Gracie! now wat be th' ol' man's name now that taicher tol 'ee 'bout?"

"Tracey!"

"Iss, iss! I've year'd tell 'e be buried zumwher yer 'bouts, an' th' ol' bridegroom be proper zet to be married down yer!"

"After th' weddin'," continued Mrs. Ovey, supplying information, "all th' vine volks be goin' on to Lay Hotel vur summat t' ate. Arter that they tu be goin' vor 'oneymun over ta 'ardland in li'le ol' 'ouze. Poor li'le lady, an' th' 'ouze they be goin' to be so small ther b'ain't no room vur zervants nor nothin'!"

"My now, Mrs. Ovey, but that young feller be proper 'ansom, b'ain't 'e now? I reckon it be a pity that 'er 'adn't zeen 'im befor 'er vixed up with old 'un. I remember when Bill was courtin' me, 'ow—"

And so on and so forth, whilst inside the "vine wimen" from London Town made comments after their own kind.

"Some women have all the luck," remarked an enamelled dame, whose bridge and dressmakers' debts were on a par with those of her three daughters who had safely, oh! quite, but most unsuccessfully survived many seasons, "I wonder how Susie managed it? Gawky young miss, isn't she? Just out of school. Um—um—um!"

"*Really! is* she! Strange in her manner—you don't mean it—oh! of *course* not, dearest! *Fancy*! hates society, swims at night, walks ten miles a day—yes, of course! not quite cosmos, what d'you call it—um—um—um?"

"Miraud Soeurs, I believe—yes—did you like that draped effect? I suppose he did—poor old Susie's up to her eyes in debt! Didn't the happy bride look ghastly? Wonder how she came by the accident—and what it was—and means—um—um—um!"

"Yes! *very*, in a bizarre way. I'm damned sorry for her. Did you hear about the girl in the shop basement?—heavy! I should think so—put the screw on what?—hear the bride's settlement is simply enormous—um—um—um!"

And as they gossiped and criticised, tearing each other to pieces without zest, having already done it so often that their minds resembled rows of backyards piled with the rags and bones of their mutual enemies—or so-called friends—the organ played softly, and the sun through the stained glass flung dazzling lozenges of colour upon the tiles and pillars.

Then came that unmistakable rustle of anticipation, followed by the satisfied sigh of those who have patiently waited either for the hoisting of the black flag upon the prison wall, or the appearance of a popular bride in the doorway of the church.

There was a shimmer of white and silver, and a strenuous tussle in the pews and aisles as the stereotyped march from "Lohengrin" crashed through the little church.

Jan Cuxson made one step backwards, and stopped as his heel struck against the wall, then stepped forward and stood right in the path of the bridal party.

Straight down they came without a halt; gushing women who did not know her darted forward to shower the bride with their unwanted congratulations, hesitated and darted back with self-conscious giggles as they met the stony, unresponsive eyes in the death-white face.

Very slowly she passed, with the fingers of one hand resting on the arm of the corpulent, self-satisfied man beside her; the other arm, bandaged from elbow to wrist, was held in a sling across her breast, the fingers nearly touching the one jewel she wore, a sleepy cat's-eye hanging from a slender golden chain.

The happy bride was looking straight in front, down the road to Calvary, where stood a man outlined against the burst of light flooding through the door.

She neither slowed nor hastened as she passed through the lane of twitching mouths and popping eyes and approached him; then she stood quite still, a gleaming, living statue in shimmering satin and lace, and removing her hand from her husband's arm, laid it with a little gracious gesture on Jan Cuxson's, and he, bending low, gently kissed it.

An artist made the record lightning sketch of his life when in a few lines he drew the dignity, the despair, and the tenderness of the girl's face, upon whose brow and above whose heart rested weirdly two great crimson stains flung by the sun through the coloured windows.

For one brief second her moonlit eyes looked straight into the steady grey ones; then the heavy lids sank slowly, and the faintest rose colour swept from brow to chin, causing the artist to murmur to himself, "The ice floes are breaking!" as, like the gallant gentleman he was, he tore the sketch slowly across and across.

Two little words had been whispered loud enough to reach the ears beneath the orange blossom.

"I forgive!"

When he had said it Leonie once more laid her hand upon her irate husband's arm, and passed out into the sun to be met with the shrill cheers of the children who flung basketsful of wild flowers upon the bridal path, and the church was filled with a sound like a swarm of startled bees.

"Um—um—um!"

CHAPTER XXIV

"Many waters cannot quench love;
neither can floods drown it."
                                                    —*The Bible.*

The girl kicked aside the jumble of clothes littering the cabin
floor, and bending her head squatted upon the bunk, and inci-
dentally, and quite indifferently, upon a crepe-de-Chine blouse
which badly needed washing, and casually watched her mother
who was scrabbling through a cabin trunk in a manner remini-
scent of a terrier ratting in a hedge.

"Why on earth couldn't you stay on deck?" demanded the
mother angrily, as she lifted the transformation from her brow
and heaved it on to the upper berth, thereby unashamedly
exposing a head not unlike a gorse common devastated by fire.

"I can't find that—oh! here it is. What a state it's in. D'you
think the Chinese man could iron it?"

That was one of those hybrid negliges which can serve its turn
as a bath gown, a bedroom wrap, or, covered with a genuine
native-made tinsel shawl (bought at Teneriffe but made in
Birmingham), can pass as an evening gown in the tropics. The
cabin was on one of the liners which, calling at odd places like
Genoa, Naples, Algiers, etc., allows you to pick up letters
brought by the mail boat to Port Said. The inhabitants of the
inner, double berthed black hole, called by courtesy a cabin,

were the mother and her last unmarried daughter who lived in Surbiton.

The mother had successfully acquired a reputation as a world-wide traveller, and husbands for her numerous daughters amounting to a net total of six, by dint of travelling the latter backwards and forwards over those heartbreaking routes which suffer from two weeks or more of going without a break.

Try from Aden to Sydney with one break at Colombo, and the above long and somewhat involved paragraph will be easily understood.

"I say, mater, guess who gave me these—have one?"

Mater sat back on her heels, bumping her head against the washstand, plucked a Simon Artz from its cardboard nest, lit it, and emitted volumes of smoke from mouth, and nostrils, until the cabin resembled the smoking-room of any West End ladies' club.

"Oh! don't ask silly questions, it's too hot! Who?"

"The Grizzly Bear!"

"*No!*"

"He *did*! He'd been ashore!"

"*No!*"

"Yes! I'd been talking to him, and had just turned to say something to the Babe when he slipped down the gangway. I do wish we weren't so hard up. It's an awful rag going ashore. He came back an hour ago, found a letter, and has been sitting up and taking notice ever since. It was a man's handwriting, I saw the envelope!"

Mater flung everything pell-mell into the trunk, pushed it back with the aid of her daughter's heels under the berth, bent her head and sat down beside her.

"He looked so different that I actually asked him for a cigarette, and he gave me the box, and if it hadn't been for Mrs. Tomlinson-Tomlinson's hateful little brat—you know—Muriel—we should have had a good long talk. The little wretch actually sat on the arm of his chair; it's extraordinary how he lets children worry him."

"Yes! dear Lady de Smythe has christened him the wet nurse!"

Which leaves no doubt whatever that some time, somewhere the dear lady had been clawed by the grizzly.

"Why don't you get into your black sequin to-night! It'll be frightfully hot going down the Canal, and you can slip on the scarf if you go up on the boat deck, as everyone does the first time they go through the Suez."

"Yes! I might—the blue *does* want ironing!" replied the daughter, taking a hand in that weird game of "make-believe" which the majority of women play between themselves. For what ultimate benefit it is impossible to say, since from the moment the cards are shuffled they know, to a nicety, the tricks and manoeuvres of each player.

Anyway the sequin was fished out from somewhere, and shaken and pulled this way and that.

It consisted of a skirt of a kind, a waistbelt, two shoulder straps, and a big jet butterfly poised just where, for the sake of decency, it was necessary, and as a toilette allied with the boat deck would doubtless prove most attractive to the man who was not in search of a wife.

The man it was intended to subjugate, meanwhile, was lying full length on his deck chair intent upon a letter, oblivious of the noise of the harbour and the racket necessary to the boat's imminent departure.

Jan Cuxson had read the letter five times and was just starting on it for the sixth, subconsciously congratulating himself on his foresight, or horse sense, which you will.

His cabin was like nothing on earth, and in it, upon the outer edge of a dead maelstrom of his entire wardrobe, stood John Smith, cabin steward.

John Smith is not his name, but who does not know and bless him if they have ever travelled on this particular boat.

He has a big, very black mole on the extreme tip of his nose, and is the cheeriest, most optimistic soul on the ocean wave, yea! even those out-size waves in the Bay at its worst.

After the first lightning perusal of the God-sped letter, Jan Cuxson had given divers urgent orders for as much as possible of his gear in the hold to be thrown ashore.

Imagine it, and the boat almost due to sail!

He had then rushed to his cabin and initiated the maelstrom, until common sense had smitten him between the love-fogged eyes of his desire; whereupon he had heaved a huge sigh of utter contentment, propped himself against the door for the second perusal, rung the bell, countermanded all he had ordered, and left John Smith to it.

He had pulled the letter out of its envelope, growled at a vendor of Egyptian wares, and turned with a whole-hearted smile at the sound of a small voice.

"Is 'oo velly unhappy, Mr. Bear?"

The man did not know that he had become the object of that loathsome habit of nicknaming all and sundry which a certain clique on every boat consider so smart.

"I'm the happiest man on earth—water, I mean, little one. Yes! come along up—and why Mr. Bear?"

Followed a scramble, a gurgle, and arranging of infinitesimal frills.

"Mummie calls 'oo Mr. Grizzly Bear because you're cwoss! Mrs. Tom—Tom—li'son says Mummie's cwoss 'cos 'oo wouldn't take the buns she wanted 'oo too. Why didn't 'oo take the buns—buns nice, I fink!"

An agitated nurse swooped down at this crucial moment and recovered that which she had lost, leaving the man laughing aloud to the astonishment of all near him.

Laugh! Why he had not laughed since he had left Mortehoe Church, neither had he smiled at any time upon the boat, or upon anybody except the children; and now he laughed, all on account of an atrocious scrawl on many sheets of thin paper which he started once more to read.

"I hope," ran the scrawl of the man for whom Cuxson had fagged at Harrow, "that this catches you at Port Said, because"—followed a badly expressed bit of business. "London's had the shock of many seasons, by the way. You know that old brute, Pickled Walnuts, well I won't say anything about the old scallawag because he's dead. Well! he married the other day, you'd sailed I think, I didn't go to the wedding. Did you know Susan, old Hetth, V.C.'s sister by marriage—up to her eyes in debt—sold her niece to pay them, I suppose, to the old millionaire—wonder what hold she had on the girl.

"Anyway they went off somewhere in Devon for the honeymoon, God help her. It seems that she had had an accident the night before, or something, and fainted, or something, directly after dinner—the wedding dinner, I mean. Did you ever learn composition on the Hill? I *didn't*!

"The woman who looks after the cottage put Lady Hickle to bed and tucked her up; placed a bottle of port in—all came out at the inquest—old Hickle's room, and left the house. Next thing, about two o'clock in the morning, a shepherd or something saw a blaze and went to look. Cottage on fire, old Hickle burnt to a cinder, and the girl hauled out of bed just in time, gibbering in French or something in panic I suppose.

"The charwoman thinks the curtains caught fire in the candle, and that the port had made the old man sleep heavily and that he was suffocated by the smoke.

"Full moon, too. What a sight it must have been! Place burned to the ground.

"I believe Lady Hickle is quite a girl and very beautiful—and is starting on a tour round the world or something—she'll get most of his millions, I believe. By the way, who *do* you think have fixed it up. Dear old Bumble and Diana Lytham. Heaven be good to him. Your turn next, old boy! Well she'll be darned lucky who gets you, see how well I trained you, d'you remember, etc., etc."

The man sat still for some long time, then suddenly sprang to his feet and went aft.

The dressing bugle had sounded but he had not heard; the dinner bugle had sounded and still he had not heard, as he stood at the stern watching the swirling wash of the slow-moving boat.

"Full moon, too! She was hauled from her bed gibbering in French or something."

He quoted the words, and crushed the letter savagely in his hands, for even in the fullness of his joy he remembered Leonie's words, "Terrible things happen wherever I am—they follow me." But in the greatness of his love he figuratively shrugged his shoulders, gathered his beloved into the safe haven of his arms, and closed the moonlit eyes with kisses.

Whilst a jet butterfly fluttered in vain over a very decollete expanse which covered a heart agitated by rage and disappoint-ment on the boat deck.

CHAPTER XXV

"And thy life shall hang in doubt before thee."
—*The Bible.*

Leonie and her aunt were having tea at the Ladies' Union Club, of which the latter was almost an original member.

You know the place where, arriving on foot or with the trail of the omnibus upon you in the shape of a two-penny ticket grasped tightly in your right hand, you receive a stony stare as welcome from the hall porter, and one of dead fish glassiness from the rest of the staff.

There is a certain air of geniality diffused around a taxi arrival, but a *car!*—two or eight cylinder—owned, borrowed, or stolen, well! there you win in honours, no matter *what* kind of private address you camouflage with that of your club.

Having cleared a way across the tobacco-laden atmosphere, through which can be spied ladies, young and old, inhaling and exhaling with more vigour than grace, they had ensconced themselves in the seat for two which lies isolated from the jumble of chairs and couches.

That seat having the advantage of isolation, your conversation does not gladden the ears of your neighbour nor theirs yours.

You know what that is like—if you don't, well, it's the kind that if written would read in italics: *Ayah—kitmutgar—pukka—chotar hazri—syce*, with reference, ultra-distinct and emphatic, to *Government House, Simla,* and my dear old friend, *General Methuselah.*

Just those little British odds-and-ends which go to the ruling, more or less, of the land of the peacock. Add to that the general, what shall I say, touch-and-go attire of the majority of the members. You know what it is like.

Lace collars over reconstructed tailor-mades; pseudo-suede gloves, chiffon scarfs, generally ropey and heliotrope of hue; odd-coloured jerseys affiliated to odd-cut skirts, plus jangling oriental bracelets and chains, and mix that with a few puckered, leather-hued countenances and you get the club's principal ingredient.

Anglo-Indian.

Anyway the place is conveniently situated, and quite bearable if you can put up with the waiter or the somewhat over-decorated and ever-changing waitress telling you, in front of your guest, that you "can only 'ave cakes and bread-un-butter forrer shilling, every-think-else-is extra."

Cheery, when you may have been doing your best to make an impression!

Of course every member (if she ever gets as far as this) of every ladies' club will here draw her pharisaical skirts about her and edge nearer to her neighbour.

"*Did* you read this"—quotes—"*awfully* good, isn't it? Of course it's meant for the Imperatrix—the Toga—the Ninth Century—the Spook."

It *isn't!*

It's just typical.

Is there any one thing in any one ladies' club to differentiate it from its sister establishment—especially in the canteen?

I will pay one year's town subscription to any woman knowing, of course, the difference between husks and food, who will honestly declare that her heart has *not* plumped to her boots after a spur-on-the-moment invitation to a *man* to lunch or dine at her club.

By spur-on-the-moment I mean when she has not had the time to negotiate with the cook, via the head waiter.

You do not need the menu to tell you that plaice is here your portion; or a lightning glance to ascertain that the exact number of your prunes is six, and that of your guest half a dozen; or just a sip of your coffee—well! there you begin to talk feverishly and to press liqueurs and cigarettes upon the suffering guest.

But to come back to the club tea-room.

"My dear," Susan Hetth was saying, jangling with the best, and pitching her voice so that it literally, though slangily, beat the band, "I really think, considering your position and recent bereavement, that you *should* wear—"

"Please be quiet, Auntie," said Leonie, who in a grey and pale mauve confection looked like a field of statice against a pearl-grey sky. "I came here to talk about you, not clothes. You see I want to tell you how I have settled things before I sail."

Her aunt fretted with a teaspoon, and spoke in the absurd peevish way which had been so attractive at seventeen.

"For the last time, Leonie, I want you to listen to me!"

"Other way round, Auntie," said Leonie, who had chosen the club, of all places, for a last *tete-a-tete* with her relation, in the hope that the presence of others would serve as a dam to the flood of tears which had streamed almost unceasingly during the last month.

"But it's absurd, idiotic—"

"Auntie, dear, we've been through all that a hundred times, and a hundred million times more won't make me change. I will *not* touch a penny of Sir Walter's money—"

"Oh! Leonie, your *husband!*"

"Not my husband in any sense at all, except for the awful name. Why"—and she spoke with sweet intense enthusiasm— "do you know they are going to build a house in Devon for blind babies out of my marriage settlement, and endow it, and have resident teachers—think of it—"

Leonie broke off to manipulate the tea-things to the rhythm of a one-step.

"And all the rest of the money, Leonie, oh! it's scandalous!"

"Oh, that!" said Leonie, manoeuvring the milk out of a broken milk-jug. "Except for Sir Walter's special bequests, it all goes back to the family. They've almost all come to see me at the hotel, such honest, nice people; and oh! so grateful. Mrs. Sam Hickle is moving to Balham from the Waterloo Road to open a fruit shop, she brought me a huge basket of vegetables, carried it into my room herself; and a young Bert Hickle, who has a whelk-barrow in the Borough, brought me a whole turbot which had soaked through its newspaper wrapping. He gave it to the page-boy to carry, and I *do* wish you had seen their faces when the tail suddenly burst through, just as the page-boy was gingerly laying it down on a most appropriate resting-place, a marble consol."

Leonie laughed just as the music stopped, a ringing, happy laugh which caused people to stare and then nudge, or kick each other surreptitiously as they recognised her.

"It's all settled about you, Auntiekins. I'm paying your debts, which aren't so terrific, only foolish, and giving you five hundred pounds to go on with. That, with your own income, will be all right if only you will live in the country instead of hanging on to the edge of a society which doesn't want you. Still, you do exactly as you like, dear, only remember that I shall only have just enough to live on when I've got through the thousand pounds, and don't run up any more debts."

"Why not *invest* the thousand, Leonie, *sensibly*." Susan Hetth's voice was dull, choked doubtlessly by the dust of her castle ruins.

"I've got to go to India!"

"Why, for goodness sake?"

"I don't know, Auntie, I've simply got to go!"

"How silly," said Auntie, as she forced a cigarette inartistically into a holder, adding abruptly, as her commonplace mind jumped at a commonplace loop-hole, "Where is Jan Cuxson? I should think—"

Leonie answered quickly, breaking her aunt's words.

"I have no idea! I haven't heard from him since he left England."

"Huh!" said Susan Hetth, putting up an absolute smoke screen, "and what will you do after the money is spent, pray?"

Leonie stared wide-eyed into the tobacco haze. "That," she said slowly, "is on the knees of the gods!"

Talking being temporarily suspended by the band in the death throes of the overture to Zampa, the two women sat silent; one frantically trying to solve financial problems, the other with her head a little on one side as though trying to catch the thread of some conversation.

A strange thing happened as the band stopped.

Leonie rose quite suddenly, with a half-eaten cake half-way to her mouth.

"I must go!" she said quite flatly, placing the cake on a plate and looking at her aunt without seeing her.

"*Go!*" shrilled Susan Hetth, putting her fourth cup of tea down with an irritated slam. "Where on earth *to?*"

But Leonie turned and walked away with never a word of explanation, and her aunt, with the thrifty side of her plebeian soul uppermost, turned to the task of getting through as much as possible of what was left of the two teas for which two shillings had been paid.

The porter looked hard at Leonie when she asked for a taxi, hesitated for a moment, looked hard again, and refrained from putting the question hovering on his tongue.

"Seemed quite dazed like," he explained later to his wife in Camberwell as she juggled with sausages, "pale as death, with a kind of funny look round her eyes!"

"To the British Museum," Leonie said through the window as the taxi door closed, and the funny look round her eyes deepened into a line of perplexity between the eyebrows, as the cab bore her swiftly to her destination and her destiny.

She walked swiftly up the steps to the institution she was visiting for the first time, and through the glass swing doors, just as though she was hurrying to an appointment; she turned, without hesitating, sharply to the left up the long flight of stairs, passed through the rooms filled with relics of Rome found in Britain, and stopped.

Just for a second she put the palm of her ungloved hand against her forehead, sighed quickly, with her head bent forward, then passed through the doorway, turned to the left, stopped and said "Yes?"

And the man, in faultless western clothes save for the white turban which with its regulation folds outlined the pale bronze face, with a look of satisfaction in the dark eyes, salaamed before the beautiful woman who had looked at him questioningly.

"Allow me!" he said simply, bending to pick up the glove she had dropped, the smile of satisfaction deepening as he looked at her again.

She had turned from him, and stock-still was staring into the glass case which lined the wall.

Closer she pressed, until her nose, flattened against the glass looked like a white cherry.

"Kali," she read, "Kali, the Goddess of Death. I thought—I—"

Lower she leant to look at the square stone image numbered thirty-seven.

High breasted, squatting on her crossed legs, garlanded with skulls, with five hands, holding a sword, a thunderbolt, a skull, a snake, a cup, and the other two raised in blessing, the goddess leers at you like a very old woman from behind the glass.

Leonie turned swiftly to find herself alone; and the hunted look in her gold-flecked eyes deepened to horror as she gathered her skirts about her, and fled blindly through the rooms, and down the stairs, and out of the building.

Heading straight down Museum Street for Oxford Street, she ran across the road at the risk of her neck and the wrath of a taxi-driver; gave one terrified backward glance at a law-abiding student from India, who was going to his cheery lodgings in Bloomsbury; and fled into the tea-rooms which lure you outside with the pretty apple-painted ware in the window, and where inside, one beautiful little blonde head shines like a field of ripening wheat.

Safe, she crouched down behind the window curtain with her eyes fixed unseeingly on the distorted figures of the Java frieze.

BOOK II

THE EAST

CHAPTER XXVI

"But when the desire cometh,
it is a tree of life."
                    —*The Bible.*

The first-class passengers, leastways the passengers travelling
first class, lay stretched out side by side, one sex to starboard,
t'other to port, divided, however, more by the fear of the eyes
of the other sex, than by any hatch piled with chairs, or ship
rule pinned upon the notice-board, and signed by the chief.

Surely the hours of the tropical nights passed in sleep on deck
are those in which we should return thanks for lacking the gift
of seeing ourselves as the officer going on, or coming off
watch, the fugitive apprentice, or some stray passenger see us.

Human chrysalis, wrapt in the cocoon of sheet or unsightly
night attire, with starboard boudoir cap awry, exposing the
steel cracker or the lanky lock; unsightly pedal extremities
peeping from the unfeminine pyjama; ruby lips, uncarmined,
ajar; whilst to port like rocks from the ocean, unshaven chins
rise unrebuked from blanket billows, and pyjama button and
buttonhole play touch across the unseemly, unrestrained and
unconfined masculine torso.

It was one of those insufferably hot nights you get sometimes
as you turn into the Hoogli, when the smell of the land comes
in sickening wafts, and the enchantment of the East is

considerably lessened in your opinion by the oppression of the atmosphere.

You are going up the Hoogli! you are passing the Sunder-bunds! you can almost see the tigers squatting in rows at the water's edge! it is the East! it is India!—also it is infernally hot, and having retired to your cabin to disrobe, you anathemise your stable companion who has been likewise inspired; curse your overworked cabin steward who has heaved your bedding on to the wrong site; re-arrange everything and bed down.

Everyone was asleep when the light of the full moon caused a subdued lustre under the awnings, and a greenish light in Leonie's wide-open, staring eyes, as she suddenly swung herself over the side of her bunk and slid unhurt to the floor.

She made an arresting picture as she stood listening intently, her flimsy garment falling away from her shoulders, leaving the slender white back bare to the waist, while she held handfuls of the transparent stuff crushed against her breast, upon which lay a jewel hung from a gold chain.

Her feet were bare, her arms were bare, and her tawny mass of hair hung in two thick scented plaits to her dimpled knees; and she repeated some words over and over again like one insane or delirious.

"*Ham abhi ate hai—ham abhi ate hai.*"

Which being translated means "I come—I come."

Without the slightest hesitation she opened the door of No. 1 state-room, which she had had to herself after Port Said, and which, as anyone who has travelled on this particular boat will know, gives on to the dining saloon; passed swiftly along the narrow passage past the notice board and the head steward's cabin, and stood among the human cocoons on deck.

For a moment she paused irresolute, turned, and swiftly

mounted the companion-way to the bridge deck, her bare feet making no sound, her beautiful body shining like ivory through the flimsy garment she held gathered to her breast.

Oh! well for her was it that the ship slept, and that the awnings made it almost impossible for those on the bridge to see what took place on the deck.

Though a report of sleep-walking on board would only have served to broaden the lines of laughter in the chief officer's mercurial soul, and deepen the lines of cynicism around the second officer's cynical mouth when the one relieved the other on the bridge at the matutinal hour of four a.m.

And very well for Leonie was it that the captain had forbidden sleeping on his deck, and that the high caste native who had come aboard at Colombo was sitting on the port side as she approached.

Owing to his high caste, and the purity of his habits, the young native had passed the days apart from his fellow-passengers since he had come aboard; and the days left were too few for the white folk to show any curiosity concerning the handsome man.

You don't feel curious about anything after almost five weeks seafaring; you feel kind of stunned.

Leonie, therefore, had not noticed him particularly as he sat apart with his delicate oval face behind a book when she approached, or passed his chair; neither had she felt the gentle luminous eyes resting upon her from the nape of her sunkissed neck to her slim ankle.

Nor did he now, long after midnight, make any sign when, without touching the rails, she came swiftly up the companion-ladder, bending her bronze head to miss the edge of the awning; and he made no movement as she sped past him, crossed the deck to the starboard rail, and putting both hands upon it, swung her body back as you do when you are going to vault clear.

No movement of his body, but he gave a jerk of his will-power which brought the veins out like whipcord upon his forehead, and drove the nails deep into the palms of his hands.

And in response, Leonie's arms slackened. She stood quite still, staring out to where the Sunderbunds lay hidden under mist; then she put one bare foot upon the lower rail, and swinging herself up, sat sideways, leaning far over; in such a position that the slightest lurch of the ship would have sent her head-long into the water.

The native's eyes narrowed to slits, and his nostrils dilated strangely as he pitted his will against the force which was impelling her.

He dared not speak, he dared not touch her. For he knew that one moment of recognition, one breath of scandal touching himself and the woman he trailed, meant the crumbling of the altar he was building stone by stone to his god.

For that reason he had taken the mail instead of the slow boat she had chosen, and had thought long before deciding to come aboard, even at Colombo.

He was afraid because of the evening she had answered when he called her across London to his side, by the image of Kali the Terrible in a glass case; afraid that she might recognise him and be on her guard, undoing all that he had done in the last year in obedience to the mandate of the old priest.

Sleeping Leonie, having descended from her perilous seat, stood for a moment with outflung arms, looking across the waters; then turned and walked swiftly and softly like a cat, straight up to the man who rose. Sweetly she laughed up into his face as she laid one little hand upon the great white cloak which swung from his shoulders, unaware that in moving her hand her own garment had slipped, and that her beauty lay exposed like a lotus bud before his eyes.

She came so close that her bare shoulder touched the fine white linen, and the curves of her scarlet lips wet but a fraction of an inch from his own; and her whimpered words in the eastern tongue were as a flame to an oil well.

"This plant," she murmured, with the light of unholiness in her gleaming eyes, "this plant is honey born—at the tip of my tongue honey—mayest thou come unto my intent!"

He answered softly in the same sonorous tongue and she swayed towards him like a flower.

"About thee with an encompassing sugar-cane have I gone, in order to absence of mutual hatred; that thou mayest be one loving me, that thou mayest be one not going away from me!"

Where is the dividing line?

What is it that causes the saint suddenly to fling aside his holiness and hurl himself headlong to perdition? or the sinner to hurl aside his evilness and fling himself headlong into a monastery?

The jogging of memory, mostly, I think.

For what resolutions can not be conceived, and accomplished, or broken by the scent of a flower, the touch of a hand, or the feel of a piece of stuff.

Love, sudden, overpowering oriental love consumed the man, passion scorched his soul, and desire shook him from his dark head to the slender feet.

He was awake and the girl was asleep, and craving to set his seal upon her in her unconsciousness, he bent towards her until the fierceness of his breath disturbed the lacey frill about her breast, bringing to view the jewel suspended from a golden chain.

Instantly his joined hands were raised towards his face mechanically in prayer, his eyes burned with the fanaticism of his creed, and his face became old in knowledge.

The dividing line? the lifted veil? Nay! nothing but a jewel with the form and the colouring of a cat's-eye, which had cunningly winked up at him from the secret places of the girl's bosom; so that she returned to her cabin with her body unscathed, and her soul on the edge of the precipice.

And the most razor-tongued, detested colonel mem-sahib of the line in India thanked her stars that the mosquitoes had roused her frantically, but just in time, to see the trailing edge of Leonie's indecorous night attire disappear through the door.

Aloofness, allied to perfect shoes and silken hose, will find a woman more enemies on board than all the pretty faces and frocks in the world; and if, in addition, she *can* heap on such items as a seductive face and figure; and if gossip via the newspapers can and *does* supply information as to the contents of her pass-book, plus savoury rumours concerning mysterious incidents in her past; well! 'twere better for that woman to stop at home, bob her hair, and take to that field of literature which is not bound on any side by the hedge of convention.

So it came about that her friends, after stumbling up the gangway at the Kidderpore Docks, with handkerchiefs held against their noses to protect them from the effluvia wafted from Garden Reach, lifted their eyebrows slightly at the frostiness of the adieux between their guest and her fellow-passengers.

And no one in the scramble and flurry noticed the elderly pock-marked ayah who had been engaged as Leonie's body-woman as she lifted the hem of the mem-sahib's skirt and laid it against her forehead, and touched the instep of the high

Joan Conquest

caste native when he passed behind the girl and disappeared in the crowd of his countrymen which opened up a way before him.

An ayah, who, to the utter astonishment of her friends, had given up the high position of head body-woman to a Ranee of the North, in order to accept the humble post of ayah to a mem-sahib.

A post she had gained by the baffling methods of the East which bind each man's work to that of his neighbour with an unbreakable, untraceable chain; and gained too, over the sleek heads of many of her sister ayahs, who, armed with countless and phenomenally laudatory chits, had squatted patiently for hours in the servants' quarters of the bungalow at Alipore.

CHAPTER XXVII

"For lo! the winter is past,
and the rain is over and gone!"
—*The Bible.*

"That's Lady Hickle!"

The two men turned in their saddles as Leonie went by at a canter near the rails.

The raking great waler forging ahead like an engine of destruction was kept in check by Leonie, exuberant with health, the knowledge of a perfect seat and hands, and that uprush of spirits which an early ride on the Maidan brings—to some of us.

"Not *the* Lady Hickle?"

"The same!"

"Well, I'm damned! she's only a girl, and *what* a seat! Chucked the millions, too, didn't she? Having a good time?"

John Thorne frowned as he backed his horse before answering.

"We're great friends," he said shortly, and the other man tapped his teeth with his whip.

Thorne hadn't the slightest intention of implanting a snub, as the other man knew, knowing him and his most unfortunate manner.

Friends, yes! they were friends, two strong, super-sensitive characters drawn in sympathy one to the other; and John Thorne would have liked to have been a good deal more than a friend, but he had the sense to realise that the only kind of woman he could ever ask to share his rising fortune, bad manners, and worse temper, would be of the type designated in the short and unromantic word *cow*.

One of those slumbrous, sleek creatures who stand knee deep and content in a field of domestic trivialities; ruminate placidly upon the happy little events of the past hour; and always find a hedge under which to shelter at the first intimation of a storm.

Lucky, lucky cattle who do not know the temperamental ups and downs, the mental lights and shadows, the physical and psychological upheavals, or the intense joys and griefs of the more highly strung goat.

At that moment Leonie rode back slowly with some friends, and smiled at John Thorne.

"No!" Thorne went on meditatively, "no, she's *not* having a good time. I can't quite make it out. You see, although she was only married for a day, the defunct tradesman husband rather overshadows her father's splendid career—old Bob Hetth, V.C., you remember. It *would* in this caste-bound country. Caste amongst *us*, ye gods! Then her clothes are really lovely, oh! ripping! make Chowringhee confections look as though they'd come from the *durzi* or the Lal Bazaar. And it seems that she's living on her capital, and that her hair curls naturally—"

The other man laughed out loud.

"Oh! you needn't laugh. Wait until you've been stationed as

long as I have in Calcutta, then you'll—"

Leonie had turned and was coming up at a gentle trot.

"Gad! isn't she beautiful?" said the newcomer.

"Yes! I think that's *really* her trouble," replied Thorne as he moved to meet her.

"Good morning, and don't come too near the Devil. We were out in the fog this morning and it has made him as touchy as anything. Isn't it a simply perfect morning!"

For a moment she sat and looked at the funnels and masts swarming the placid Hoogli, turned her head as a far-away siren announced the arrival of a liner, gave a little sigh as she looked up at a kite sailing care-free overhead, and came back to earth with a smile.

"How d'you do," she smiled, upon the introduction of the other man. "And don't come too near the Devil, he's nervy; in fact I think he will burst with suppressed energy if I keep him standing longer. Shall we canter as far—oh!—"

"Hell!" finished Thorne after his kind, causing the corners of Leonie's beautiful mouth to lift as she raised a reproving finger.

The razor-tongued, most feared and detested colonel mem-sahib of the line, in the whole of India, rode up with a seat which would not have disgraced the sands of Margate.

Thinking that she might as well share the pig-skin, she had, upon her husband attaining his majority, taken a dozen riding lessons somewhere near Regent's Park; had hacked irregularly ever since, and still, when off her equine guard, talked about a horse's ankles.

"Don't come too near the Devil, Mrs. Hudson, he's *so* fidgety."

"Nonsense!" brusquely replied the lady as she nodded to the men. "It's you who are fidgety; comes of all your sleep-walking, brain fag or whatever you call it; you've—you've inoculated the poor darling," she added, clapping her hand on the Devil's hind-quarters.

Thorne made an ineffectual grab as the Devil reared so straight that Leonie's face was hidden in the mane, and backed his horse as the waler came down with a terrific clatter on the hard ground, scraping the colonel mem-sahib's foot as she wheeled about, emitting silly little cries, whilst men tore up from all sides with desire to help.

Up again he shot, pawing the air until it seemed that he surely must fall backwards, and men and women stared aghast until Leonie, raising her arm, brought her whip down between the silky ears.

"Damnation!" said John Thorne as Leonie patted the Devil's neck as he danced nervously on one spot.

"Time I took him home," she said. "The syce?—no! I daren't give him to anyone as he is—oh! good morning—

"Saw your *haute ecole* stunt, Lady Hickle," burst out a lad who rode a fallen star in the shape of a discarded discreditable polo pony. "Simply topping—but the Devil's a nervy demon, you *shouldn't* ride him—he'll get away with you one of these fine days. What happened?"

"He bumped into my horse, he's not safe to be out amongst us—indeed, he is *not*. Lady Hickle, I have been in Cat—"

The rest was lost in precipitate flight with the colonel mem-sahib's arms closely hugging her pony's neck, to the joy and the infinite delight of the rest of the spectators.

Unseen, uncouth John Thorne, furious at the scant courtesy shown to the lady of his dreams, had brought his whip down heftily, just above the mangy tail of the colonel mem's pony.

"I think I'll ride alone, if you don't mind," said Leonie with a ripple of suppressed laughter in her voice.

"All the way to Alipore?"

"Oh! it's not far, and I daren't trust the syce, the Devil would simply *eat* him."

The boy sidled in between her and Thorne, to the latter's infinite annoyance.

"Are you still keen on the *shikar* stunt, Lady Hickle?"

He gazed at her adoringly, and she smiled back into the honest, merry eyes.

"*Shikar* stunt?"

"Yes! you remember—Sunderbunds—dak bungalows—*shikari*—wild animals in bunches—discomfort and all the rest. Say yes! Oh! *do*!" as Leonie slowly shook her head, "It'll be such a rag! Major and Mrs. Talbot—she's a fine shot—you and me, and we've got to get another fe—woman 'cos a simply top-hole fellow walked into the club last night, who's wonderfully keen on it; we're kind of related, his father was my mother's second cousin."

"And the higher the fewer," interposed Thorne, as Leonie laughed. "And what's the top-hole fellow's name?"

The youngster eyed the elder man with disapproval.

"Name—coming brain specialist—setting the old fossils in Harley Street by the ears—forgotten more than they've ever learned—name—why, Jan Cuxson. Won't you come, Lady Hickle?"

Leonie had suddenly bent to adjust her stirrup leather.

Her face was dead white, her eyes like stars, her mouth like a gate to heaven.

Almost a year and not a word, not a sign!

Tortured by doubt, racked with love, she had gone her way silently; blaming herself one moment for the ease with which she had shown her love; staking her all the next on the honesty of the man who had kissed her hand in forgiveness in the old Devon church.

Making excuses, heaping the blame upon herself, wearying, wondering—and now!

She lifted her face, which shone like the Taj at noon, and the worshipful company of men looked at her, almost stunned by its incomprehensible radiance.

"Yes," she said softly, without thought of the Devil's nerve-storm. "Yes, I will surely come!"

As she spoke there was a terrific report as the hind tyre of a passing car burst with due violence, a sudden convulsive bound as the Devil leapt with all four feet off the ground, and a thunder of hoofs as, with the bit between his teeth, he cleared for the open just as a man on a sixteen-hand bay turned in at the race-stand opening.

CHAPTER XXVIII

"To turn and wind a fiery Pegasus
And witch the world with noble horsemanship!"

—Shakespeare.

The onlookers behaved in the orthodox runaway-horse manner.

Women screamed, or took the opportunity to manipulate a surreptitious powder-puff.

Men shouted and waved their topees, or shouted and performed equestrian gymnastics, and the jockeys *en masse* cursed their masters' presence, and the more or less mythical value of their respective mounts.

Just for that one moment in which anything occurring out of your ordinary rut leaves you practically stunned into inertia.

Then things began to shape themselves, and for one unbelievable second caste was thrown to the soft wind which was sweeping up the last rags of mist.

Military mingled with commerce, the I.C.S. which, written in full, means God's Anointed, looked *at* instead of *through* the railway; jute condescended to the tourist, and white ejaculated to kaffyolay as they all sat gazing after the retreating form of the Devil and the pursuing shapes of one or two, who, fairly decently mounted, were pegging away stout-heartedly in a perfectly vain, but praiseworthy effort to save Leonie from certain death.

And then a sigh of relief went up.

A bay, stretched out, was flying like the wind, hoofs thundering on the hard ground, tail streaming, as, urged by his master's heel and voice, he strove to get to the tank before the runaway.

The distance and the speed were too great, the horse and kit were not sufficiently familiar to allow the spectators to identify the one man who seemed to have a plan in his head, and a horse under him.

The women strained their eyes in an endeavour to distinguish him, men kept theirs glued to Leonie who was riding straight and apparently making no effort to check the Devil, and policemen, forgetful of their dignity, their status, and their red turbans, hung over the rails near the grand-stand entrance with a riff-raff of taxi chauffeurs, pukka chauffeurs and syce.

For the first two hundred yards across the brown grass of the Maidan, Leonie thoroughly enjoyed the tearing gallop, having failed to grasp the fact that the Devil was bolting; but after having spoken soothingly, and pulled firmly without making any impression, somewhere about the middle of the polo ground she awoke to the fact that something had to be done.

"They're in it! No! missed, by Jove!"

The jockey bunched himself in an ecstasy of relief, and his mare danced with a fellow-electrical feeling as the Devil, wheeling sharply from the sparkling water in the tank, missed the lone tree by a foot; then gathering fresh impetus from the ever-nearing sound of thudding hoofs, tore towards the rails enclosing the two tracks.

They are not high, but they are fairly close together, and four in all, and a horse, blind from fear or temper, is quite as likely to let you down at the first as at the fourth.

But Jan Cuxson saw a gleam of hope.

Surely the runaway would slacken, surely no horse could possibly take four fences at that terrific speed; and if he did slacken, then the bay, as nimble as a cat in spite of his weight, would catch up, and something would be done before they dashed headlong across the tram-threaded, crowded Kidderpore Road.

Except for admiring her seat and seeming calm acceptance of her inevitable and horrible end, he had not bothered about the girl as a human being; but he frowned suddenly in a vague effort of recollection when she stretched out her hand in a beckoning gesture for help to the man she heard racing to her rescue.

"By Jove!" he cried, and "*By* Jove!" repeated the others behind, and "By *Jove*!" echoed the distant on-lookers as, without hesitation or click of hoof on wood, the Devil rose to the first, the second, the third and the fourth rail, skimming them like a bird, while the bay, just two rails behind, crashed over them with nothing to spare.

Inky words take a long time to write, but Leonie's perilous career towards the river was merely the matter of a few cyclonic minutes, leaving the drivers of bullock and water-buffalo carts, *gharries* and trams no time in which to make an opening for her tempestuous passage.

"Wah! Wah!" shouted a group of natives, draped in gaily coloured shawls, who watched admiringly the woman's perfect seat, caring not an *anna* that she might be thrown and break her neck or be crushed to death. In fact, the halo of death encircling the woman's head lent enchantment to the sport, causing some of the more wealthy to bet upon her end.

A woman, white or brown, more or less in India of what account? though it were a different matter in the case of the sahib who rode in pursuit, with a mouth like a steel trap and eyes of fire.

Two women, with babes astraddle on the hip, turned to watch Leonie, then stuffing more betel nut into their already crimson mouths, moved lightly through the dust towards the bazaar. Crouched at the foot of a tree, inhaling the smoke from the bowl of his rude native pipe, an old man under the benign influence of the drug, lost in dreams, took no notice whatever of the disturbance around him.

But the drivers, with raucous cries, twisted the tails of their kine to port or starboard, or beat them forcibly, and the tram driver, roused from the lethargy engendered by the cool of the early morning, by the shouts and cries, put on his brake, bringing his tram to a stand-still just as, with a terrific clatter of hoofs, Leonie dashed past the front of it with Cuxson at her heels.

There was a moment's uproar when, wishing for a better view, the driver of a tawdry *ekka* urged his half-starved pony forward.

The bay caught the side of the pony's bleeding mouth, causing the wretched animal to rear from pain and twist sideways into a bullock cart.

In its usual leisurely way the bullock swung itself also sideways, and almost under the bay's feet, causing him to lose a precious second, for which Cuxson made up by a ruthless use of his spurs, whilst before Leonie's eyes, quite close, through the trees, appeared the funnels and masts of the river craft.

"Oh!" she said involuntarily, having retained no impression during her motor drives of the road to Kidderpore; as the Devil tore with her across the old polo ground and the old Ellenborough course, straight to the crowded Strand Road.

And then she sighed a little sigh of relief, for the bay heaved alongside and a hand stretched for her bridle.

Side by side they clattered across the Strand towards the Prinseps Ghat, standing just as ostracised and white as the Marble Arch.

Would the two horses crash headlong into the columns, or would the Devil yield in time to the strong hand pulling on the bit?

Neither.

Terrified by the shouts of the populace, and the shrill whistling from the river, he raced along so close to the left side of the monument that Cuxson's boot scratched against the stone.

But as they crashed across the Strand and the sharp incline on the other side of the railway lines appeared, Cuxson, knowing that the moment had arrived, dropped his reins, and gripping the bay with his knees, leant over towards Leonie as she dropped her reins, and loosening her grip on the pommel, prepared to break her neck or her back or both as she slipped from the saddle.

Then she felt an arm round her waist.

She knew intuitively her rescuer's intention, *but*—!

Would a man's left arm be strong enough to lift her across her horse's hind-quarters at the terrific speed they were going, combined with her weight?

Would he be able to hold her until his horse slackened speed, or would they both overbalance and hurtle to the ground together? Would there be time to stop the horse, or would they all be hurled into the water?

The questions had hardly flashed through her mind when she

Joan Conquest

felt herself lifted and swung.

For one petrifying moment the bay, pulled savagely until blood stained the bit, reared with its double weight within a yard of the steep incline, then, yanked cruelly by its master, swung sideways and came down; just as the Devil, striving at the last moment to check his wild career, hesitated for one half-second, then, pushed by his own terrific impetus, slid over the incline, and turning a complete somersault backwards, crashed into the water.

* * * * * * *

Leonie's scarlet mouth trembled, and her yellow-green eyes gleamed as the man she loved pressed both her hands in his against his coat, until the high relief of the button was marked upon her skin, even through her glove.

"You," she said, so softly that the one note sounded like the chime of a temple bell.

"You!" he said, giving her arms a little savage wrench, then letting her go as the sound of approaching hoofs heralded the arrival of the first of the hunt to be in at the averted death.

A score or more of natives in their vivid colours, which seem so atune with all that has to do with love, mattered not at all; but Leonie turned and pointed casually to the Devil, enjoying his matutinal bath, as the boy flung himself from the discredited polo pony on which he had done his best.

He seized both her hands and held them very tightly, then catching sight of Cuxson, let them go suddenly.

"Of course!" he said, "of course you would—you lucky beggar!" Then added triumphantly, "But anyway, *I* told her so!"

CHAPTER XXIX

"A merry heart doeth good like a medicine!"
                                    —*The Bible.*

Guy Dean, the cheery optimistic lad who worshipped openly at Leonie's beautiful feet, and who was seeing the world at the behest of his wealthy old father, had been as good as his word.

Bursting with excitement, he hurled himself into his racing-car one Sunday morning, about a fortnight after Leonie's hasty ride riverwards, and passed like a whirlwind through the fairly empty streets of Calcutta and the suburb of Ballygunge to the Jodhpur Club.

She was waiting for breakfast under the trees with some friends, discussing the four-some they had just finished, and watching the arrival of various cars which were parked, with some difficulty, with the others which had arrived earlier.

"Sounds all right," said Cuxson, as he looked with disfavour upon the club's breakfast *piece de resistance*, namely fatty sausages and mashed of all things. "I am beginning to feel quite thrilled. Let's see, it will take us about a day to get to Tiger's Point by launch from Kulna, and there we find monkeys, adjutant birds, spotted deer, and tigers all ready."

"Don't rot!" said young Dean. "I've bribed the finest *shikari* in the whole of Bengal to stage-manage the whole thing; he did seem rather contemptuous over the *chotar shikar*, as he called it, I must say, until I began to juggle with backsheesch, and then he bucked up considerably and said he would do his very best to provide sport for the mems. The programme includes a ruined temple but not a tiger, 'cause he says it would be too risky a job at such short notice; also, and the real reason *I* should say, there hasn't been a tiger seen, anyway killed, since one was wounded and caught near that same Hindu temple umpteen years ago."

Leonie wrinkled her forehead at the last sentence, and looking up caught Jan Cuxson's eyes upon her.

"That sounds *so* familiar," she said perplexedly, "I—"

"The tiger at the Zoo which we knew all those years ago was trapped near a ruined Hindu temple in the Sunderbunds, Lady Hickle," he said quietly, watching the curious dilation of the pupils in the greenish eyes as he spoke.

"The very one!" broke in young Dean, as he suspiciously eyed a proffered curry.

"How did you come to think of the stunt?"

"I ran up against a perfectly top-hole native prince at polo last month. Amongst other things we started talking elephant and *bagh*—tiger, you know," laughed the lad, who always seemed to be on the point of bursting with high infectious spirits. "No, take it away, I will *not* eat a cold *chupattie* of the consistency of a bicycle tyre—as I was saying, we talked tiger, and somehow or other he suggested a few days' pursuit, through the Sunderbunds, of the spotted deer, muntjak or sambur—"

"Neither."

"Well, they're *spotted*."

"Dogs, perhaps."

Ignoring the execrable repartee, the boy turned completely round to Leonie.

"By the way, Lady Hickle, if you ever go to Benares, don't forget to get off *en route* and visit the tomb of what's-its-name, it's quite near—oh! I forget—but it's on one of this fellow's father's estates. They don't let many people go and see it— afraid, I expect, of paper bags but if you *do* go you'll find an elephant or two hanging about to take you to the place in state. He's, the native prince, got some of the finest elephants in the whole of this mosquito-ridden land—makes a hobby of them."

"What happened to the original tiger?"

"Noah pushed him into the ark."

The lad grinned, and offered his cigarette to Leonie, who shook her head.

"Oh! stop fooling, Dean. Did a sahib manage to trap the brute, or what?"

"Yes! and sent it across to Blighty and shoved it into the Zoo. They're frightfully sick about that tiger being in a cage; they wouldn't have minded a sahib killing it for the good of mankind it seems, but putting it behind bars is an insult to some god, or something like that. Are you any good as a gun, dear lady?"

Leonie smiled at the tardiness of such an important question.

"Fair," she said, refusing an unkempt pot of marmalade as she turned to Cuxson. "I used to pass most of my holidays with the Wetherbournes, you know them, don't you? They were awfully keen on sports, and had a rifle-range, but I could beat them any day with a revolver."

"That doesn't matter, Lady Hickle," said the lad blithely. "All you'll have to do'll be to bob up and down in the tiger-grass in the approved style; keep your trigger away from the bush, and so as to feel thoroughly creepy, your eye out for pugs; which, in case some of you don't know, means tiger-tracks, not the dog with the beastly curly tail—and—oh, jolly!—here come the Talbots—just in time for the *khubber* which means tiger-news for those whose Hindustani is not as perfect as mine. Mrs. Talbot, don't pass us by, we have plenty of room and some superb sausages."

Edna Talbot laughingly sank into a chair next Leonie whom she liked, and immediately became enthralled in the discussion.

Honest, sweet little woman, with an honest plodding husband in a native regiment, inhabiting the dreary crumbling fort, without a murmur, whilst living in hopes of better things to come. Soft-voiced, considerate towards her native servants who worshipped her, one of the finest shots in India, and a true upholder of the British Raj in word, action, and clothes.

A perfect oasis, in fact, among the desert of her sisters, who storm in season and out at their native staff, before whom they likewise show themselves in ill-considered neglige, with their unbrushed hair down their backs, and their bare feet thrust into the evening shoes of last night's dance.

So it came about without any undue fuss that, after surviving the excruciating heat of the railway journey, three sahibs, two mem-sahibs, and their servants steamed out of Kulna in two launches to Tiger's Point, where awaited them the finest *shikari* in all Bengal, with an adequate retinue in which was included a *chukler* or skin dresser.

And who would notice the look in an ayah's eyes as she wiped her beloved mem-sahib's ant-ridden bunk with cotton-waste soaked in kerosene, and who on earth would connect the jungle guide with the British Museum.

CHAPTER XXX

"A mighty hunter, and his prey was man!"

—Pope.

It was the second evening and they were nearing the ruined temple.

Walking silently and in single file along a faintly discernible track is an eerie proceeding if you are not used to the Sunderbunds.

True, in this jungle there are no serpent-like creepers festooned from tree to tree to impede your progress, or luxuriant and rank vegetation to hide snakes and other poisonous reptiles; neither is there a canopy of thick dark leaves above to obliterate the light of day, or the stars at night.

But the space between the crowding sundri trees which predominate, is packed with an undergrowth of light shrubs through which you have to force and tear your way if you lose the track; and you trip and twist your ankle at every step on the abominable sundri breathers which thrust themselves through the soil at every inch, and vary in thickness from a stick of vermicelli to a good stout bough.

"Look," will whisper your *shikari* as he sinks silently to the ground; and look you do with all your eye-power, and yet fail to see the spotted deer gazing at you, motionless from sheer

Joan Conquest

fright, only a few yards away in the undergrowth, so at one is the animal's colouring with the dappled shadows on the leaves.

What depths of humiliation you plumb when the deer flees to safety through the trees and your *shikari* sighs.

Leonie as a gun had proved a dire, undiluted failure.

As a companion no one could beat her. Nothing tired her, nothing dismayed her. The terrific heat, the untoward hours and meals, the sting of mosquito, and the rip of the thorn left her unmoved.

She and Edna Talbot had gleefully climbed the ladder up to one of the two *suapattah* huts, which are a kind of shelter of leaves built for the sundri wood collector upon high platforms near the water, and in which they had passed their first vermin-stricken night. They had climbed cheerfully down the next morning without a word of complaint about the hours of torture they had endured as they sat at the hut door in the light of the moon, whiling away the time until the jungle cocks should crow by watching various shapes come down to the creek to drink.

But the first time a deer, hypnotised by fear or curiosity, had stood stock-still before her, simply asking for death, Leonie put her gun down and shook her head.

"I can't," she said sturdily. "I simply *could not* kill except in self-defence."

And although young Dean sighed lugubriously over his lady's defalcation, Jan Cuxson adored her utterly for her woman-liness, and translated the remark the head *shikari* made as he handed back to the mem-sahib the rifle he had examined.

"He says he knows that in time of need you would be brave, and would have no fear even of a man-eater, but he says that you *must* carry your rifle because you can never tell in the jungle what may be awaiting you round the next corner."

As none of the party knew that the temple stood well hidden but quite close to the edge of one of the smallest creeks, open only to the narrowest native craft, they had no idea they were being taken there by a most circuitous route; and the *shikari* who did know thought that the silent guide was doing it purposely in order to give the sahibs an opportunity to add yet more to the ever-increasing bag of odds-and-ends, also to his backsheesch later on.

They were all longing to get to the ruins; more than desirous for their evening meal; aching to remove their boots, and the dust, and other evidence of a hard day's tramp.

"We are almost there, mem-sahib," said the very fine old *shikari* who, by the way, is a real personage, as he noticed a certain lack of elasticity in Leonie's movements. "Let us hasten, because at the fall of the shadows, all that is evil will come down to the waters, and behold! as this jungle is cut across and yet across with water-ways, the evil ones may even cross the sahibs' path."

"How much farther is it?"

"Another half-mile of this path, sahib, then through a glade without trees, then another mile and we find the outer wall of the temple."

The perfect English came from a small knot of natives difficult to distinguish in the shadows.

Leonie swung round and stared, and turning to Jan Cuxson put her hand on his arm.

"Funny, isn't it?" she said softly. "But do you know I am sure I have heard that voice before, and all this"—and she waved a hand vaguely—"seems so very, very familiar."

The head-man halted them once more at the edge of the clearing.

Strange bare spots these clearings which occur now and again in the Sunderbunds, looking for all the world as though they *had* been cleared by man some time or another for building purposes. Well, who knows if that doughty adventurer, Khan Jehan, did not prospect thereabouts centuries back.

"We will now place the mem-sahibs in the centre of a widening circle," said the *shikari* patiently, showing no sign of the detestation in which he held all sports-women, and the amount of trouble and anxiety their presence always entailed in a *shikar*, however insignificant.

To lose a sahib would be bad enough, but to see a mem-sahib seized and carried off before your very eyes, well, by the power of all the gods, that would mean ruin if not death; for, being a very wise old man, however good the news, he always prepared for the worst.

"I dislike these clearings at the setting of the sun, O defender of the poor!" he explained to the major, who kept his wife close and was beginning to wish he had not brought her, even if she were far and away the better shot of the two. "The trouble is upon one without even the warning of a cracking twig. Neither have I any love for the temple, for behold! one, even a great *guru* up to within a few moons of this day, lived there in worship, making sacrifice to the Black One. Yet is he not there to welcome us. Maybe he has fallen victim to the *bhoot* of the great cat whom he once fed."

Luckily for their peace of mind the sahib log only understood a quarter of a man's lament, and did not trouble their heads about ghosts.

"Aye, verily am I bewitched to allow of such tarrying, likewise to let such fear enter my head," he muttered to himself, and as a cloak to his misgivings sharply ordered ten men to proceed to the centre of the clearing in a semi-circle, and there await further orders.

They did as they were ordered, and were standing motionless when suddenly without a sound a great striped body leapt straight from the shadows of the surrounding trees upon a boy who had out-distanced his companions.

The instant double report of Jan Cuxson's rifle deadened the lad's horrible screaming and the growling of the wounded beast as it crouched flat, almost hidden behind the human body in the undergrowth, with tail lashing, and great claws tearing the boy's shoulder, as the rest of the terrified coolies ran shouting back to the party.

"Fire, sahib," commanded the *shikari*.

"Can't," tersely replied Major Talbot. "I shall kill the boy if I do; the brute's making a shield of his body. I'll creep round to the flank and—"

"Fire, sahib," urged the native. "Better to kill the lad as he is badly wounded," then added, "Tesch," as Talbot shook his head. "Stay here, sahib, to protect the mem-sahibs, I will creep to—"

"*God!*"

The word simultaneously escaped the three men as they and Edna Talbot raised their rifles.

Leonie was walking across the space, neither hastening nor hesitating, towards the tiger which crouched, growling softly, with its tail sweeping the ground.

Did she hypnotise the brute, or did her supreme courage build an invisible barrier between the two?

Who knows!

Joan Conquest

Anyway she calmly approached within five yards, raised her rifle, took deliberate aim, and fired just as, with a hoarse-coughing roar, the tiger sprang.

There was the dull thud of a bullet, a snarl, and the animal fell back across the boy's body, twitching convulsively.

Without one moment's hesitation, while the rest of the party stood helpless owing to her position, Leonie, letting fall her rifle and drawing her revolver, walked right up to the writhing brute and fired straight into the terrible mouth.

With one supreme effort the tiger reared itself on its hind legs, gave a choking, strangled cough ending in a spurt of blood and froth which drenched Leonie, and fell back dead; and the entire native staff, shouting in wonder and joy, tore across the clearing and prostrated themselves, in grateful layers around the girl's heavily booted feet.

CHAPTER XXXI

"For her house inclineth unto death!"
—*The Bible.*

We lie beneath the mosquito net, we undress behind the purdah, we sit on the verandah, or stroll in the compound; we dance, we ride, we eat, we sleep, ever heedless of the eyes watching, and of the hidden form; but above all of that relentless will which causes some of us uncontrollably to do odd things at odd moments under the Indian stars, to our subsequent disgust and wonderment.

Leonie, with Jan Cuxson behind her, stopped outside the temple door, which, hanging upon one hinge, moved slowly to and fro in the night breeze.

And at the side of the altar, in the black shadows of the doorway which led to the secret places of the temple, a pock-marked native woman, draped in an orange coloured *sari* embroidered in silver, laid one hand upon the priest's arm and pointed with the other.

"Behold the Sahib," she whispered with a snarl of hate at the corners of her mouth, stained crimson with betel juice. "He who seeks her in wife," she continued, pushing the *sari* back from about her head so that the thirteen silver rings she wore in her crumpled left ear tinkled faintly, and her nose-ring of gold set with small but real turquoise gleamed dully, "and once wedded she will return across the Black Water. O father of the people, O wise one, I love her and thou didst promise."

She suddenly beat her breast, and the heavy silver bracelets jingled faintly, then shrank back against the painted wall as a young man, even the jungle guide, and beautiful to the verge of unseemliness, stealing from the shadows, smote her fiercely across the mouth, and pulled the *sari* roughly over her head.

"Hold thy peace and watch," he whispered, with a swift movement of the arm, most suggestive of a cobra uncoiling itself with intent to strike, as Leonie turned away from the doorway with a shudder.

She took two steps and stopped irresolute, with the rays of the full moon shining upon her upturned perplexed face.

Then she stared down at the myriad things which crawled and hopped in and out of the gleaming bones which lay about in little heaps, or scattered in ones and twos, even up to the door and into the dim interior.

Too absorbed, neither Jan nor Leonie noticed the murmur of voices from the far end of the court, nor the reek of the tiger's blood which came from her stained dress and the carcase of the dead beast which was in the process of being skinned, and around which hovered the native staff awaiting the distribution of the coveted tiger's fat.

Which more by faith, than any medicinal property it contains, is supposed to work miracles in stressful times of rheumatism, and cattle sickness.

Jan Cuxson, trying to grasp and knot together the tag ends of a dawning knowledge, stood behind his beloved, patiently awaiting her next desire, instead of picking her up in his arms as he should have done, and carrying her off to safety, a good wash and a better dinner at the other end of the court.

He was surprised when she spoke quickly and below her breath.

"Take me away," she whispered hoarsely as he caught her outstretched hands and pulled her fiercely into his arms. "Take me away, the place is evil—evil I tell you—and"—she raised her hand and passed it across his face, laughing softly, "I think I am bewitched—something is—is—pulling—is—"

She looked back over her shoulder, stared hard for a moment, and then, tearing herself free, ran like a hunted deer through the crumbling doorway into the blackness of the temple.

"Who fears, O Woman?" whispered the man, whose beauty touched the unseemly as he sank to the ground. "Who fears?"

Half-way up the temple Leonie stopped, standing in a silver pool of moonshine which blazed like the blade of a knife through a hole in the roof; lighting up the ruined altar, the grass-grown stones, and the image of a female deity carved in bas-relief upon a huge block of granite.

Nude was the woman carved out of stone, and of so dark a blue as to be almost black; with tongue protruding and hair in waving masses, through which were thrust four arms; garlanded with skulls she danced wantonly upon the body of a man, with two hands raised in blessing, in the third a knife, in the fourth a bleeding head.

Kali! Kali! Kali!

If only Jan Cuxson had been able to do something, anything, what a mint of trouble he would have saved himself and others, but instead, he stood rooted to a spot just inside the door, incapable of moving hand or foot, held by a force he did not even guess at, and therefore could not fight, watching Leonie as she moved slowly forward, as though she were walking in her sleep towards the blood-stained altar.

"So will she always come," murmured the old priest as he laid his hand caressingly upon his well-beloved pupil. "So will she always come. Love? Pah! who fears the love of man in the Black One's temple? Who?"

And there was no answer from the shrouded future.

Leonie stood still, quite still, unconscious of the eyes about her, and everything save the terrible problem she was trying to solve.

Then suddenly she cried aloud, and the words, like wings, beat against the roof and walls.

"I know!" she cried, "I know! I know!"

And whirling round towards the spell-bound man, she turned her hands, palm downwards, with a wonderful eastern gesture of renunciation, and crumpled into a heap before the altar, and the three watching figures stole noiselessly back into the secret places of the temple as Cuxson, freed, strode hastily up to his beloved.

He gathered up the unconscious girl as tenderly as a woman, oh! a good deal more so, and turning her face to his shoulder, carried her out of the temple; stopping for a second to hold her more securely in his left arm as he bent to pick up something which glittered in the moonlight: a piece of orange silk heavily embroidered in silver, for which Leonie had ransacked the Old, the New, and the Lal Bazaars; a bit of her ayah's *sari* torn and caught in a sundri breather. "And she stayed behind on the boat," said Jan to himself, with a flash of inspiration as he turned the thing over in his hand, and slipped it into his pocket.

And though his heart ached over his beloved's mental and physical distress, he inwardly rejoiced at the untoward occurrences of the day which had supplied his solid, trustworthy brain with the outline of a key to the problem.

Dear, stolid old Jan, who, given the time, could beat anyone at unravelling the hardest, hard-tied, knotted problem.

With a tale of sudden faintness he gave her into the care of Edna Talbot, who cooed and fluttered over her like the woman she was, in spite of her workmanlike appearance and her outrageous craving for a big meal. And she herded the sahibs to the far end of the court, where lay the sick man, after the big meal in which Leonie had joined right heartily; a little white about the face, truly, and shadowed about the eyes, but normal and content, with not the vaguest recollection of what had happened after the killing of the tiger.

"Oh! don't be dense," Edna Talbot said quite brusquely when Guy Dean, having brutally ignored the suffering native, suggested returning to the others. "You surely don't want to make a triangle."

"Triangle—what!"

"Well, you know the old saying about two being company, don't you?"

"Of course I do—that's where it comes in," replied the lad not over lucidly, "*I* want to make the two!"

The major laughed at the rueful countenance, as he clapped the boy on the shoulder.

"You'll get over it all right, old fellow; it's just like inoculation, a feeble taste of something which might have been ever so much worse. Trust me, you'll get over it!"

"*Never!*" stoutly maintained young Dean as he heaved a stone at something which fled across the court, his mental vision failing to register a picture of the future in which Jill Wetherbourne, daughter of Molly and Jack, occupied the principal position.

Later, Leonie, sitting with Jan Cuxson on a block of fallen masonry, smiled sweetly upon the head *shikari*, who, salaaming, prayed her to honour him by accepting a little memento of the *shikar* which had terminated so successfully upon the slaying of the tiger.

In his open palm he held two small bones about two and a half inches in length, two little superstitious tokens which ensure sons to the woman who treasures them, and which, he told her in his broken English, were only found in the tiger, one on each side of the chest, unconnected with any other bone at all.

"It is a charm, O! Mem Sahib, defender of the poor, which will assuredly bring you happiness.

"And may the sons of the sahib grow straight as the pine tree," he added slowly in his own tongue, as he felt the sahib's eyes fixed steadily upon him.

"What did he say to you, Jan?"

As the shikari turned away Cuxson caught the girl's hands and crushed them up against his heart.

"I will tell you some day!"

"Tell me *now*!"

"No! not now! It is of love that I should have to speak, and in all these past weeks you have not let me touch your hand or speak to you of love. You have put a barrier between us, a barrier of a misplaced fear, which has grown higher and stronger since I have had to confess to failure in finding any trace of your old servant. India is wide, dear, and its villages uncountable, and *I* am not distressed over the empty return of these last months; all that worries me is, that while prowling about the Himalayas out of reach of the post, I never knew what had happened to you, or that you were in India."

Leonie sighed as she opened her hand and looked at the small bones.

"Tell me now, Jan!" she insisted.

"No! Leonie, I cannot. There will be no one near us when I do tell you, and except as a souvenir of that very fine old man, you need not keep them, because my love is a still greater and surer charm to bring you the great happiness they promise."

CHAPTER XXXII

"And thou shalt become an astonishment,
a proverb, a byword."
                                                    —*The Bible.*

When Leonie returned to Calcutta she found that the tale of
her courageous act which had preceded her, and of which
home and local papers had exhausted themselves in praise, had
not served to endear her to that little white community, which
suffers from social myopia, and the self-adjusted chains of what
it most mistakenly calls caste.

Not likely that the feminine members of Jute, military,
railway, or law circles *would* open their arms any wider to this
young, and beautiful, widowed creature with the mop of naturally curling hair, now that, if so minded, she could verbally
and positively flap one of the finest tiger skins that had ever
come out of Bengal in their heat-stricken faces.

In fact some of the young ones as they wrestled with the
nightly problem of their own dank, straight particular bit of
woman's glory, would doubtless, if questioned, have upheld
the Hindu custom of completely shaving the widowed head.

Many, in fact, had been the meetings of these younger mem-
sahibs in bungalows, or flats, at Firpoes, or in clubs, where,
under the pretext of criticising the latest fashions from
overseas, they discussed the pros and cons of accepting this

person into the haven of their Anglo-Indian bosom.

The elder ones kept out of the clatter, having suffered and fought in similar crises in their own day as had their mothers, and their mothers' mothers before them since the days before the mutiny; being moreover resigned to the corrugated appearance of their faces, and the, in consequence, perambulatory instincts of their lords.

"Her *undies*," said a woman who, with the excuse of borrowing a book, had essayed to spy out the land of Leonie's cabin. "I saw her running ribbons in them—the most *ex*-quisite crepe de Chine, hand embroidered and trimmed with *real* lace!"

"How *de trop*!" had answered a matron, whose household *linge* and personal *lingerie* showed complete only in the sections of finger napkins and undervests, as is the way of a careless, untidy woman's linen stock.

"Well, that's easily understood," chimed in a third. "After all she *is* trade."

And the no's had carried it.

Wherefore, although in ignorance of the verdict, she did exactly what every other woman did, and went where they went, she most certainly did *not* have what one would call a good time. She loved the Maidan and golf at the Jodhpur Club, or Tollygunge, before breakfast; she cordially loathed shopping and duty calls; grudged the hours lost out of life in the daily afternoon siesta, and took part in dances, bridge, dinners, and all the usual monotonous effort to kill time, with the air of an indifferent, disgruntled statue.

Gossip was no joy to her, scandal she would not tolerate, and the women commenced the task of ostracism by means of half-uttered phrases and little invidious smiles; and most men voted her *odd* owing to a certain indescribable barrier which they invariably encountered when they approached her over impulsively, and which really did *not* tally with her enticing, bizarre beauty.

Yes! they voted her odd, certainly, but in the secret places of their hearts and bungalows some of them would ponder.

Had not the major sahib's bearer curled himself up on the mat beneath the bed and gone to sleep, while the major sahib, after the ball, had sat in his shirt-sleeves upon that bed until three in the morning; and over and over again mentally slid up and down the room with supple, slender Leonie in his arms, where, in the earlier hours of the night, she had rested seemingly content for one half-second before he had let her go under the palms.

And, "Damn it all, she's not a flirt," did not a certain youthful sahib who worshipped openly at her shrine exclaim, as he thought, in the unpleasantly heated watches of the night, of that moment when she had smiled down sweetly into his adoring eyes, as his cheek brushed her hand while she was arranging her habit, and he her stirrup leather.

How *were* they to know that, distracted by an ever-increasing fear, and lost in an overwhelming love, Leonie had no more remembrance than the man in the moon of the fact that she had danced with the one, and smiled upon the other.

It was the final flare of the season in the shape of a ball at Government House; one of those mixed massed gatherings to which you are invited either on account of your rank, or your unblemished reputation, or the fact that you've had the fore-thought to inscribe your name in the visiting-book.

Leonie was standing with Jan Cuxson near an open door under a revolving fan which disturbed the outer masses of the hair she had piled haphazard upon the top of her small head, catching the great coils together with huge pins, and strengthening the entire structure by means of a finely wrought, diamond-hilted steel dagger, looted in the Mutiny by a not over-punctilious forbear.

"I wonder you don't cut your hair to bits," had once remarked before a multitude, an envious dame, whose curls reposed cosily in a box o' nights, and who had grave doubts as to the sincerity of Leonie's tawny locks.

"I run it through in its sheath," Leonie had replied, pulling the sheathed dagger out as she spoke, so that her hair had fallen in a jumbled scented mantle all over her, causing the men to put their hands in their pockets, or behind their backs, and the women to mechanically pat their heads; just as you fidget unconsciously with your veil, or the curls above your ear, when someone of your own sex, and far better turned-out, happens upon your horizon.

On this night her absurdly small feet made her head look almost top heavy, just as the uncorseted small waist emphasised the width of her shoulders, and the violet shadows enlarged the opalescent weird eyes looking wearily on the scene around her.

Why didn't she go back to England if she hated it all so much?

Because she couldn't! Because India held her and she waited upon Fate as patiently as ever did Mr. Micawber.

"Lady Hickle ought to go to the hills, she's looking absolutely fagged!"

The male voice drifted in through the window upon a pause in the music.

"Well! continuous *sleep-walking's* not likely to make you look your best, is it?"

The damnable giggle at the end of the remark brought a frown to Jan Cuxson's face as he picked up somebody's wrap from a chair, put it round Leonie and led her unresistingly down the steps into the grounds.

It sounds better to say "grounds" rather than "compound" when speaking of Government House.

"I—I *hate* all this," Leonie said impulsively as she sat down on a marble seat. "I hate India—I—I—"

She flung her head back, and it came to rest upon the man's shoulder, and she shivered ever so lightly when he pressed it still further back, pinioning her arms so that she could not move.

"Leonie."

The sudden authority in the voice brought a light to the eyes on a level with his mouth; she moved unconsciously, and Cuxson suddenly letting her go caught both her hands in one of his, pulled her round sideways, and jerked them up to his chin, and she laughed softly as she fell slightly forward; and laughed even more softly when he crushed her back again against him with his hands upon her breast.

Both heedless in their love of the eyes watching, of the hidden form, and above all of that relentless will which causes some of us uncontrollably to do odd things at odd moments under the Indian stars.

If *only* he had not hesitated, if only he had turned the face to him then and there and closed the gold-flecked eyes with kisses.

But instead he held her crushed to the point of agony against him with his mouth upon the sweetness of her neck, leaving the gold-flecked eyes to open wider, and still wider as they stared straight into the shrubbery around, where the flaming poinsettia flowers looked black under the stars.

"Beloved! Leonie, listen—"

"*Don't!* please don't!"

She pulled herself free and knelt on one knee upon the bench, with both hands outstretched against him; and he, not grasping the psychological points of the moment, sat down dumbly beside her, instead of mastering her physically, or mentally on the spot as it behoved him to do.

Heavens! what fools some men can be with that jungle animal woman within their hands.

"Leonie, listen dear, I want you to marry me, dear—soon!"

The words fell upon Leonie's clamouring soul as dismally as the raindrops of your childhood fell upon the window-pane when you were waiting to start for a picnic.

"You don't know what you are saying!" she replied. "It is criminal even to think of such a thing—mad as I believe I am—mad as I shall be when I end in a padded room!"

Her voice was barely a whisper, but it cut like slate on slate, and her eyes stared straight ahead as she continued speaking rapidly, almost uncontrollably, and yet with a certain air of relief as though glad to give vent in words to the horror which pressed upon her brain.

"Although you pretend it is only sleep-walking," she went on, heedless of his efforts to interrupt her, "you know perfectly well there is something wrong with me. You know it, so did your father, so does Auntie, people here are whispering it. Yes! they are, they *are*," she reiterated, "and they are *right*. Something more than just being frightened by my ayah happened to me in India all those years ago, oh! you know it did, I'm under a spell or bewitched—sometimes I have a—a—" she struck her forehead with her open hand as she crouched back upon the bench like some animal at bay—"a—oh! my God—you see—I cannot even say what it is. Can't you tell me, Jan? Can't you help me? *You*—you say you love me—you say you have found a clue—for pity's sake follow it, follow it and save me—you—you—"

"Leonie, *look* at me!"

Something in his voice forced her to look at him, and her eyes shone like flat pieces of opalescent glass so contracted were the pupils, but they widened even as she looked into the steadfast grey eyes, and her mouth relaxed into the shadow of a smile.

Good heavens, why didn't he take her in his arms and smother her up against his heart, or put a bag over her head, or failing the bag, put his hand before her eyes?

What fools some men can be with the woman they love within their reach.

But instead he left her, hurt and humiliated and desolate, to sit half crouched by herself, whilst her eyes, against all striving, slowly veered round to the shrub.

He held her hand, it is true, whilst he talked, but what good is *that* to a frightened woman whose heart is crying for protection, and whose body is clamouring to be forced into submission?

"Dear," he said as Leonie stared at the poinsettia bush, "I am on the track at last, and in a very little time shall know exactly what happened to you all those years ago. There is only one link missing, and that I shall surely find, as I find everything when I set my mind to it. Then the whole thing will be cleared up, and this mysterious cloud lifted from you. Look at me, dear!" Leonie turned and looked at him blankly, and as he continued speaking, slowly, and as though against her will, turned her eyes back to the poinsettia bush. "I want you now in your distress. I want you in the storm as well as in the sunshine, dear; I love to see you smile, it would be heaven to *make* you smile. Marry me, beloved, *now*. Dear, won't you? Let me lift the cloud from my *wife*. Oh! Leonie, think of it—my *wife*!"

Leonie answered mechanically, as though she were repeating a lesson and had not heard one word of the man's pleading.

"What have you found out? And what is missing?"

"I have found the woman who was your ayah."

Leonie pulled her hands away, and pushing the hair off her forehead, sat quite still listening, but not hearing the music as it floated through the night air, watching without seeing the couples as they strolled about the grounds.

And then she answered, but without any real interest, although very distinctly, shivering slightly as the man put the wrap over her bare shoulders.

"Have you? And who is she, really? Of course I know her name—but—but what do you know about her? I have had no answer to my letters since I've been out here, is the poor thing still working?"

"She's—not exactly working for a living, dear, and she is—is—"

He stopped short with a world of perplexity in his eyes, then went on as slowly and mechanically as Leonie had done.

"Perhaps, dear, I—I had—better not say any more until—until I have everything quite clear."

And he drew his hand sharply across his eyes as Leonie sighed.

"Very well!" she replied gently. "Just as you think best."

"Tell me you love me, Leonie, let me be sure of that, let me just hear you say it once."

Joan Conquest

She put out both her hands, and he took them and kissed them.

"Dear, do you count me as *so* little? Don't you know, cannot you feel that a love like mine endures for ever?"

"Do you still want the little white house behind the white wall—Leonie, *do* you!"

"Oh! Jan!"

"Well, marry me—marry me, beloved, and give me the right to protect you—from trouble, and these slanderous, murderous tongues."

Leonie's face was lovely to behold, swept by a wave of colour, and with eyes like stars; but she shook her head although a little smile parted the crimson mouth.

"No! Jan! Nothing will make me change. Not until we know and until I am cured. Do you think I would risk our love, and our happiness? I shall never, never marry you as long as I have this—this longing to—this desire to—to—oh! what is it. Find out what has happened to me, find out what I do when I walk in my sleep—just how mad I am, and if the madness can be cured, and if it can, *then* I will—will—"

"Yes, dear?"

"I will—will—!"

It was no pretty sight to watch her striving to speak, her mouth opening and shutting without sound, her hands against her throat.

Then she looked at him suddenly, smiling sweetly, and put both hands in his, while he, sick with pain and unconfessed fear, changed the conversation abruptly by the grace of understanding.

"I think you ought to go away, Leonie—to the hills—for a change. It's getting frightfully hot, why don't you?"

"Yes!—I might—I think I will—I'm so tired of everything—so very—very tired!"

"Where to, dear?"

Leonie bent her head a little sideways as though listening, made a strange little movement with both her hands, then placed the open palms against her forehead and replied:

"To Benares!"

She had barely whispered the words, so quietly did she speak, as the poinsettia flowers bent slightly—to a passing breeze—may be!

CHAPTER XXXIII

"Dona praesentis cape laetus horae, ac
Lingue severa."
—Horace.

Leonie's first long-distance journey was just like other people's
first long-distance journey in India.

And being of the type which revels in the new and unknown,
she loved it.

Who wouldn't!

The seething masses of dusky humanity enchanted her; she
delighted in the glaring colouring, the clank of the holy man's
chains, the incessant call of the water carrier and sweetmeat
vendor, and the clang of iron on iron which announces the
train's departure.

She absolutely thrilled on disrobing the first night in the little
bathroom while her ayah spread her sheets and pillows and
blankets upon the lower berth; and when her bodywoman
disappeared through the door leading to the servants' compartment, she lay for a time watching the stars, and the glimmer of
passing mosque, or temple, or tomb.

Then she laughed aloud in sheer content, wedged Jan
Cuxson's box of chocolate biscuits safely into the side of the

bunk, and turned to the side table to look for light literature in the shape of a magazine.

Having acquired the pernicious habit of eating biscuits and reading before going to sleep, she frowned upon the discovery that her ayah appeared to have left the books upon Howrah Station; and had stretched her arm to rap upon the wall to summon the woman, when her eye caught sight of a paper volume lying under the opposite bunk.

India is certainly a most dusty land, but a traveller can keep his railway compartment and boots spotless by distributing a few *pice* to the dusky, cheery youngsters, who, salaaming, solicit the favour of using boot polish, or floor brush, to the mutual benefit of self and the sahib. Leonie, therefore, felt no repugnance when, clutching the table with her left hand, she made a long arm and secured the book, which proved to be a guide to India's most famous beauty spots.

She turned the leaves casually and laughed.

"Why! I'd completely forgotten it," she said aloud, turning the book sideways to look at an illustration. "The wonderful tomb Guy Dean insisted upon my visiting if I ever went to Benares. How beautiful! Must be the tomb of some ancestor of that young prince he was talking about. Oh! how beautiful, and— oh! how helpful! I suppose some Englishman must have left the book in the train by mistake."

She had picked up a bit of paper which had fallen from the book; a rough time-table with directions in English as to the best means of getting to the world-famed monument.

"That decides it," she said sleepily as she switched off the light, pulled a miniature mosquito net, deftly arranged by the ayah, over her head, and the sheet up to her neck. "We get to the station to-morrow—sometime—disembark—put luggage into cloak-room—find elephant and—and dak bungalow—and— oh! almost full moon—how—*how* delicious—ride out and see the—the—"

She slept, oblivious of the fact that she was carrying out implicitly the programme mapped out for her.

Travelling in India is real sport when the train doors are likely to swing open at no given spot, soft-footed natives to enter surreptitiously and disappear as quietly upon sight of your open eyes; and guards to clamour for your ticket, while a mob collects outside your door at the junction to look at the pretty unveiled mem-sahib awakened from her slumber by a dignified bearer with his offering of *chotar hazri*, which means the thrice blessed early tea-tray.

Her restless spirit was soothed by the rush of the train through the endless plain; strange scenes, strange sights wrenched her mind from the terrible question everlastingly throbbing in her brain; and her eye was not quick enough to distinguish one delicate oval face from another, or to notice that at each stopping place her ayah meandered down the length of the train to a compartment where, in consequence of his high caste and rank, a man sat utterly alone—unconcerned and totally oblivious of the screaming, chattering crowd upon the platform, of beggars, pilgrims, and *bona fide* native travellers.

True, for one moment at the station where she alighted for the world-famed tomb, she glanced back hurriedly at a native who placed himself between her and an unsightly epileptic; and she looked back once again as her intuition rapped out a message she did not grasp, and her ayah suddenly besought her help with the coolies.

A dilapidated tonga, drawn by a pony of the same description, took her and her servant to the dak bungalow, built on a concrete platform in a jungle clearing about two miles outside the village.

There she gave carte blanche for the arrangement of the evening trip to the guide who materialised serenely, all smiles and extreme deference. Bathed, and fed, she had her hair brushed for half an hour by her ayah; refused the offer of massage, which process she abhorred, and turned in and slept the afternoon away upon her own bedding spread on a charpoy.

Later she bathed again, attired herself in a simple low-cut, white silk dress, dined, and wrapping herself in a heavy white Bedouin cloak, wedding present from Jill Wetherbourne, who had got it from her godmother in Egypt, seated herself on the verandah to await the arrival of whatever means of locomotion the guide had chosen to take her to the tomb.

And down the jungle path loomed the shape of a great elephant, moving at a gentle shuffle but an almost incredible speed.

Without audible instructions it stopped in front of the verandah, threw back its trunk, twined it gently about the middle of the *mahout* or driver, lifted him from his seat behind its ears and placed him on the ground; then on a word, trumpeted shrilly in greeting to Leonie.

"Oh!" said she as she almost sprang from her chair in delight. "Oh!"

The *mahout* salaamed, standing in the moonlight at the animal's head.

He made a vivid eastern picture, dressed as he was from head to foot in white, with two pleated side-pieces to the turban, hanging in suchwise as to conceal half the face; and the guide, who had been squatting on the edge of the path, also salaamed, smiling in glee at the mem-sahib's delight.

"Behold, mem-sahib," he said, "is the elephant even Rama, the pearl of the prince's stables." His English was not quite as intelligible as these printed words, but Leonie made shift to understand.

"I have never seen such a beautiful elephant," she said, walking up to the great beast, followed by the guide, the ayah and the bungalow factotum.

The mem's statement was quite within the range of possibility seeing that her elephant lore had been gathered from the Zoo and other low-caste specimens with their straight backs, mean tails, and long stringy legs.

"Does the—the *mahout* speak English, because my Hindustani is not very good. I would like to have the—the beauty of the animal explained to me, and why it has its face and body painted; and why does he, the *mahout*, I mean, wear those side pieces to the turban, they are very unusual."

A moment's pause, during which the *mahout* stood like a rock, and then the guide, shuffling his feet, answered to the effect that the driver could not speak English, but that her humble servant would translate if the mem-sahib would deign to listen to his mean speech; that the man was the prince's best beloved—*mahout*, he added after a second's pause, and that the side pieces were part of the uniform worn by the prince's head-mahouts.

Not a bit of which information was true, *mais que voulez vous?*

So they all walked round Rama the beautiful, the guide translating the soft Hindustani into lamentable English.

Rama, it seemed, was a *koomeriah*, a royal or high-caste elephant, and still a youth, being but forty years of age, *vide* his ears. His height was ten feet at the shoulder, and would the mem-sahib note the perfect slope of the back down to the beautiful, long, feathery tail. Also the massive chest and head, with the prominent lump between the eyes so bright and kind, and full of knowledge. Notice also the deep barrel, and short, so very short, hind legs, the heaviness of the trunk, the plump cheeks which would indeed grace a comely elephant maiden; count the eighteen nails upon the lovely feet, and place her hand upon the soft skin which fell in folds about the tail.

Leonie did as she was bid and ran her hand also down the nearest magnificent tusk, with tip cut off and ringed about the middle with bands of gold inlaid with precious stones.

"Perfect ivory," continued the guide, "five feet in length with tip, curving upwards with the curve of the sickle moon, and sloping slightly from each other as though in anger."

Leonie smiled at the guide's verbal imagery, and put her hand upon a cream coloured mark near the base of the broad trunk.

"Why, I thought it was paint!" she said, speaking over her shoulder to the *mahout*, who, unperceived, held a fold of her white cloak in his hand. "This is paint, surely," she added, running a finger-tip down the vermilion and white lines which covered the great beast's face and sides.

It seemed that the yellowy-white blotches raised the animal's value above that of sacksful of rubies, and the painting of the face and sides served two purposes; one to render it easier for the animal to find favour in the eyes of the gods, the other to bring about the same result in the eyes of man; even as does woman when she accentuates the night blackness of her eyes with antimony; and the slenderness of her finger-tips with henna.

In state procession it seemed that Rama the perfect carried a gold and jewel encrusted howdah upon his beautiful sloping back; that what was left uncovered of his anatomy was hung with a net of silver, with tassels of pearls; that strings of seed pearls were entwined in the glorious meshes of hair in the beautiful tail; and that his nails were manicured, bracelets of golden bells hung about the ankles, and buckets of perfume poured into his bath.

"The *mahout* has placed the humble cushioned seat this night upon the back, mem-sahib, so that nothing shall be between

Joan Conquest

the mem-sahib and the light of the moon."

Leonie gave orders that a succulent cake full of currants and flavour should be brought forthwith from her hamper, and having pushed it as far back into the mouth as possible, where it was demolished to the accompaniment of the most disgusting masticatory noises, laughed aloud when the elephant stood on its short hind legs to show its appreciation, and said thank you by means of a soft purring sound in the throat.

The process of getting to the knees reminded Leonie somewhat of a sailing vessel she had seen rolling in a rough sea, but she settled herself comfortably in the cushioned seat and waited with glee for the *mahout* to get into position upon the animal's neck and order it to rise.

"What is he waiting for?" she asked, as he made no movement.

"He wishes to know where the ayah is to sit," answered the guide.

"*Ayah!*" said Leonie, and laughed gently. "But I am going alone!"

The *mahout* said something swiftly.

"The way is many miles through the jungle, mem-sahib; there is no dak bungalow, no people, the mem-Sahibs and also the sahibs go always accompanied."

"I am going alone," said Leonie quietly. "Tell the *mahout* to get up."

Upon a word of command the elephant got to its feet, and raised one knee; the *mahout* placed one foot upon it and swung himself up to his seat upon the short neck, said something to the elephant, who moved off up the jungle path, while the servants salaamed deeply to Leonie, and again even more deeply in the direction of the elephant's head.

CHAPTER XXXIV

"Some little talk awhile of me and thee
There seem'd—and then no more of thee and me."
—*Omar Khayyam.*

The elephant trumpeted before the gate.

The two halves of the door opened from within, clanged against the sides, and the *durwans* in scarlet and silver bent almost double as they salaamed before the white woman who passed under the red-stone, centuries-old gate upon the back of Rama the Great and Perfect.

The elephant knelt and Leonie stepped on to the marble pavement, placing her hand for one instant upon the *mahout's* arm to steady herself.

She looked up and down the double line of cypress trees and gave a little cry, which was almost one of pain, at the sight of the glory before her; and pressing her hands above her thudding heart, longed with all her soul for the man she loved and had denied.

For a moment she stood absolutely still, the heavy cloak swinging gently in the slight breeze, then walked down the steps, and like some ghost passed noiselessly beside the lily strewn water tanks towards the marble, wondrous Tomb. Madhu Krishnaghar, waiting until she was well out of earshot, spoke to the elephant, bringing it to its feet, and gave a sharp order to the keepers of the door, which caused them to speed from the scene as fast as their feet would carry them towards the village where they had been commanded to stay until sunrise, leaving the girl, a prey probably to that inexplicably sensuous feeling which the desolation, and beauty, and pity of this place arouses in *some*, alone with the man who loved her as men love in the East.

He followed her slowly beside the water tanks, and absorbed in his love and the joy of being alone with her, failed to catch the sharp call of apprehension when Rama, as faithful as a dog, and far more intelligent than many humans, rapped the ground smartly with the end of his trunk.

Having been told by his beloved master to stand where he was until his return, and being obedient even unto death, he did not move; but he eyed the form which had slipped in through the gates with dislike, and shuffled his feet in distrust as the man disappeared behind the cypress trees.

It was only a foolish curiosity-bitten *shudra*; a wretched member of the lowest and most servile class, who, passing on his way to his miserable hovel, had noticed the gate open at the untoward hour of midnight, and the absence of the ferocious *durwans*.

His low caste, which is the least of all, had prevented him, up to this day, from entering what he thought must surely be paradise; and now he took the risk and slipped in, not only stricken with curiosity, but obsessed with a desire to tell a wonderful tale to his patient wife and four sons, who, because they were *his* sons, were doomed to remain of the lowest servile caste; as would be their sons far, oh! far beyond the third and fourth generation.

How was he to know that a woman with unveiled face was visiting the tomb at midnight, or that she was beloved by his master whose word was life, or death, to those who served him.

Leonie passed through the silver gates into the tomb, and stood beside the marble, flower-strewn sarcophagi, which lie side by side, and over which, day and night, hangs a lighted lamp.

She did not move when a whispered golden sound fell gently through the shadows. Like a cobweb thread, so fine it was; like a thread of gold, so sweet it was; rising and falling, to rise again in one throbbing cry of love, pleading, insisting, despairing.

The echoes caught and held it in the dim corners of the marble cupola, and answered cry with cry until the place seemed full of the sobbing of lost souls. Back and forth, at the girl's feet and around her head, surging over the dead lovers, beating against the walls and roof, to die away, sobbing, sobbing like a weary child.

Leonie, transfixed with ecstasy, stretched out her hands to catch the dying notes; and for that infinitesimal fraction of a second, when the golden sound crossed the boundary of human sense, felt as though she stood upon the edge of eternity.

She turned to see the driver of elephants standing like a bronze statue outside the doorway; but speak she could not in that dim place fragrant with the loves of the past, neither could she support the divine pain alone, and picking up a rose and a sprig of bay from the marble, tucked them into the V of her bodice and walked out.

But she did speak, to remonstrate, in the sweetest, most imperfect Hindustani in the world, when the man followed her at a quite respectful distance.

"It is not safe for the mem-sahib to go alone," he answered. "A wild animal, a man, a snake, might be in hiding. The mem-sahib should have been accompanied by her guide."

Thus spoke Madhu Krishnaghar, who had not one evil

thought about, nor intent towards her, and who, having pushed the mandates of his religion into the background for this one night, was living in the intoxication of the actual moment.

Leonie walked round the outside of the marble dream bathed in moonlight, occasionally stopping to ask a question of the man who followed.

"Is it the tomb of an ancestor of the present prince?" she inquired haltingly.

"No! mem-sahib! look at the lettering in black marble inset in the white; right round the tomb run those verses from the Koran. A Mohammedan emperor built it—*I* am a Hindu," the pause was scarcely noticeable as he added quietly, "as is everyone upon the prince's estates."

She stopped in front of one of the four towers which stand at each corner of the marble terrace, and looked upwards.

"I am going up," she said.

"Nay! mem-sahib. These towers are climbed only with a guide and a lamp. They are not clean, they are not safe. A snake, a pariah dog, a man might be on the stairs which wind round and round, and are as black as a night of storm."

Leonie had climbed the few outer steps and was standing inside the door. Not once had the untowardness of the whole proceeding struck her, nor had she given a thought to the fact that the man with her was a low-caste elephant driver, not fit to touch her shoe-string.

She made no reply, and disappeared into the darkness. You can see fairly well up to one half of the tower, then pitch blackness surrounds you, and you begin to feel cautiously with hands and feet for that reason; also because just about here your head begins to whirl owing to the stifling atmosphere, and the architect's corkscrew design.

She had no idea that the man, alarmed for her safety, was following her, and she stopped and gasped near the top, wondering how much farther she had to go, and almost wishing that she had not started; and so black was it that she did not even see the white turban which was on a level with the step upon which she stood.

Then there was a glimmer of light and more. Presently it grew quite light and she staggered up the last few steps, and reeled on to the small round cupola of the tower unprotected by rails.

Well for her was it that Madhu, divining the danger, raced up the last steps in one bound, reached her as she stood swaying on the edge, and drew her quickly, roughly back into his arms, where, forgetting his role of servant, his religion, caste and colour, he held her safe and crushed against his heart.

She, with her eyes shut and her head spinning, remained there without understanding one word of what the man was saying.

"And having held thee in my arms, how am I to let thee go," he whispered, with his mouth near the scented masses of her hair. "Nay, I cannot, thou white, wonderful flower in a land of drought. Behind the purdah will I place thee, hidden from all eyes but mine. Thy body-woman shall not touch thee, for *I* will be thy servant, and *my* hands will draw the lace from about thy bosom, and *my* hands will perfume thee, and my love shall encompass thee until thou swoon upon the ground even at *my* feet. Waiting for thee I have known no woman, and I will have no wife but thee, and many sons shalt thou bear me. Yea! each year shall see thee bowed beneath the fruit of love, for I will not spare thee. And thou shalt be honoured before all men; a high estate shall be thine, and a flood of jewels and gold and grain shall flow at thy small feet which I shall kiss. And thou *shalt* veil thy face, for I would kill him, *torture* him who looked upon thee."

Leonie opened her eyes and stared at the shimmering white-ness of the tomb, and she smiled and did not move, for the witchery of the full moon had fallen upon her.

"Red!" she whispered, pointing to the dull glow of dead bodies burning somewhere near, and laughing till her teeth flashed between her scarlet lips.

The man searched with one hand and found a small flat jewelled case in the folds of his turban, and opening it, with the long, deft fingers took out two pellets.

He watched her as she lay upon his arm, and suddenly forced the pellets between her teeth, and himself laughed, as she grimaced at the bitter taste but swallowed them.

He had not the slightest intention of doing her any harm, but with the whole of his vividly mature brain and virgin body, he delighted in the effect of the drug upon the woman he loved.

There was no doubt about it that she suddenly awoke to the passion of the man looking down upon her, and responded to it.

Wave after wave swept her from head to foot, causing her body, untrammelled by whalebone, to tremble against his, and he loosened the white cloak and let it fall, holding her pressed to him in her thin silk dress, laughing down at her, delighting in her eyes, her mouth, her throat.

Handsome men are an everyday sight in India, but this man was as the gods, and Leonie, beautiful, drugged Leonie, looked at him from the corner of her eyes as looks the wanton, and laughed.

"I will not kiss thee," he whispered, watching the colour sweep her face at his words, and smiling at the thudding of the heart beneath his hand. "Nay, I will not bruise thee nor cause thee blemish until the purdah hangs between us and the world.

Look not at me thus-wise, and lift not the glory of thy lips, for I will not seize thee as a beggar seizes upon the *pice*. I am thy king and thy slave, and I will carry thee to the gate. Nay, move not thy body for fear I throw thee upon the ground and set my seal upon thee. Lie still! and yet—why not, why *not*! perchance *has* the hour struck."

The man was crazed with love, and the girl intoxicated with the drug, and they were perched up there above the world alone, in the stillness of the Indian night.

He hastily wrapped her in the cloak, and taking her into his arms, hid her face against his shoulder, and stood for a moment staring out towards the spot from whence had come the ill-omened jackal cry.

"Not yet," he whispered. "Not yet!"

Sure-footed as a goat he carried her down the winding stairs out into the moonlight, and across the terrace, and up the marble steps, and placed her upon the wide marble seat, and sat sideways upon it behind her, unwitting of the miserable wretch who watched from between the cypress trees.

Leonie sat quite still until the mystery of the place, or whatever it is, entered into the innermost recesses of her being; and she held out her arms to the light burning day and night above the dead lovers, and sobbed.

Madhu Krishnaghar laid his hand upon hers on the cold marble of the seat, and lost himself in ecstasy at the tears which welled into the strange gold-green eyes and fell, then opening the collar of the white linen coat, he lifted a necklace of priceless pearls over his turban and passed it over the girl's head, holding it lightly until one end had slid down into the scented laces of her bosom where lay a cat's-eye on a golden chain.

"Thou white doe," he said, "thou virgin snow," and added

fiercely, "give me the rose from above thy heart, that I may press it to my couch."

Obediently Leonie gave it, faded and warm, and looked at him with a strange little gleam of anger in her eyes; and he, understanding that the effect of the drug was passing, and that wrath maybe would follow love, led her by the hand down through the double row of cypress trees towards the gate.

Alas! a twig cracked under the wretched *shudra's* foot, snapping with the report of a pistol in the stillness of the night; and the man, feeling the hands of his gods upon him, fled like a hunted hare towards the gate.

Madhu Krishnaghar, with his face one blaze of fury, stood still and called.

"Rama," he called. "Rama, hold," and as the wretched creature, forgetting the animal in his fear, sped past him, Rama curled his trunk swiftly about him and jerked him to a standstill.

Useless to strive against that strength; useless to fight against the gods or raise his voice in shrieking prayer.

For had he not looked upon the unveiled face of his master's woman.

Slowly Madhu Krishnaghar led Leonie up the marble steps and stopped.

"Thou dog," he said gently, "thou low-caste dog!"

Then he drew Leonie into his arms and covered her completely with the heavy coat.

But the man, submitting to fate with the terrible resignation of the East, let fly one last poisoned arrow.

"The dog goes to his death," he cried. "But behold, the shame of the lord is great, for have not the eyes of the low-caste dog rested upon the woman's face."

"*Usko marro*! Kill quickly!" thundered the son of princes, and turned indifferently away.

But even as the elephant threw the man upon the ground, and placing his foot upon his head, tore him in twain, Leonie wrenched herself free, and flinging up her arms to the moon, laughed and laughed until the night echoed and re-echoed with the horrible sound, stopping only when the smothering folds of the cloak were thrown about her.

Joan Conquest

CHAPTER XXXV

"And thou shalt grope at noonday."
                                    —*The Bible.*

Jan Cuxson, hurt to the quick at Leonie's refusal to marry him, also at her rejection of his offer to accompany her upon her travels, shut his hurt away, and set his mind to the completion of his task.

His suspicions had been aroused by the finding of that orange and silver scrap of *sari* near the temple, when the ayah had presumably been left miles behind on the launch; and fully realising the futility of employing the methods of the West against the subtlety of the East he decided to pit native craft against native cunning.

The only result of the investigation, however, was that Leonie's present ayah had been traced back via the Ranee's house to the days when she had been in the service of the Colonel-Sahib Hetth, V.C., but beyond that was a blank wall.

She had suddenly left the Ranee's service to become body-woman to Leonie; without a single reference to the time when she had been nurse to Leonie as a baby.

Who was keeping her silent, and why? And what was she doing, and who was she with in the deserted temple in the jungle?

Whose tool was she?

Certainly not the Ranee's. She was wrapped up in her duties toward the fast ageing Rajah, and her only son, who seemed much the same as other sons of princes.

Having finally decided that the answer to the problem lay in the temple, to the temple he decided to go, more with the intention of having a look round than with any definite plan.

The decision was made with the fixed though unspoken determination that if the solving of the problem should involve a sojourn of ten years in India, for ten years he would remain.

He hired a guide and a coolie, both of whom looked exactly like any other guide and coolie, and having much to think out, and sure thinking being anything but a rapid process with him, also because he did not wish to draw too much attention to his movements, he chose as a means of conveyance the ugly flat-bottomed public paddle-boat which floats unconcernedly down the Hoogli from Calcutta, through the bigger creeks of the Sunderbunds, and up the Pusaka River to Kulna.

If you want a few days' rest, or time in which to unravel a knot, pray take that means of locomotion; you can be dropped anywhere into a *nukur* or native boat which will deposit you for a few annas on any island you choose, but don't do it if you are in a hurry, or are filled with a desire to see the lesser creeks, and the quite small ones, where tigers are supposed to sit in rows upon the water's edge, monkeys to swing across the water by means of the creepers interlacing the dark and dismal trees, and crocodiles to lie in tumbled masses waiting to be turned into portmanteau, dressing-case, or shoes.

Cuxson's method and brain were rather like his gait; as he had said in Rockham cove, he was *slow*! He could not and never had, even at Harrow, been able to run a hundred yards without becoming most uncomfortably blown; but he could walk anyone to death at a set plodding steady tramp, accomplishing twenty miles without turning a hair; while after a series of terrific spurts, and enforced periods of rest, his companions would give up dishevelled, sweating, and unpleasantly mortified miles away from the desired goal.

Problems, mathematical or medical, were treated in just the same way. The more brilliant of his fellow-students would seize upon a pen, fill reams of paper and slap the result down triumphantly at the end of an hour, to find themselves later, and again with mortification at the bottom of the list, or not on it at all; whereas Cuxson, after hours of searching here and there in the convolutions of his grey matter, would light on a thread, a grain or a speck of dust which he would proceed to turn inside out, or tear to pieces; the outcome of which process would be printed at length in the *Lancet* or some such-enlivening journal.

So he lay on the long chair in the corner reserved for sahibs, and was not too uncomfortable, nor in any way uneasy as to the result of his investigations, although all that he had to build his hopes upon was the word of a native, and a piece of orange silk picked out in silver with the dust of a sundri breather adhering, which lay in his pocketbook with a ring of seaweed, and some glistening strands of tawny hair.

The serang, meanwhile, parleyed with certain gatherers of *golaputtah* which is a special palm leaf growing in the Sunderbunds for the express purpose of thatching boats and *suapatti* huts; and having discussed the ins and outs, and pros and cons of the situation with every male upon the boat, had transferred the sahib with his guide and coolie to a native boat, after a gratifying give and take in silver rupees which are so much nicer to handle than dirty notes.

And an old priest made sacrifice of a black kid unto his god, having been apprised in the mysterious native way of the approaching arrival of the last person on earth he wished to see.

CHAPTER XXXVI

"What hath night to do with sleep?"
—*Milton.*

"What a nuisance!"

Leonie turned on her bed and frowned through the chick at the two girls who had ensconced themselves in long chairs on the verandah outside her bedroom.

Broad-minded and big-hearted, she had tried to overcome the intense irritation which the Eurasian manner of speech invariably aroused in her. Some get accustomed in time to the parrot-like monotony; some don't; and to the end of his days the young, immaculately groomed and turned-out assistant in Hamilton's will wonder why the beautiful girl with gold-flecked eyes had suddenly frowned, and placing the trifle intended for a wedding present upon the glass counter, had left the shop with an appallingly inadequate excuse.

Fortunately for him the pukka European has not been endowed with the gift of hearing himself speak as others hear him.

Like the broken flight of maimed birds over a lawn in the process of being mown is the Eurasian speech and intonation; with the inevitable dip in the middle, the rise at the end of each sentence, and the ceaseless clipping of syllables.

Joan Conquest

And Leonie frowned as she lay under the mosquito netting awaiting the warning of the dressing bell, and even felt thankful to a crow which suddenly perched itself on the top twig of a fir tree, and shrieked its condemnation of the sunset, the star just above its head, and the chatterers in the chairs.

In an effort to break through the overpowering lethargy which lately had fallen upon her at odd moments of the day, she lifted herself on to her elbow, only to sink listlessly back on the very hard bed. After all, why worry over problems to which there seemed no answer? Why fret over the silence of the man she loved when she had curtly refused his offer of companionship; for there always comes a time when mere man, subjected to the unsatisfactory daily menu of snubs and refusals, tense moods, and moody silences, will refuse it, and clear for a diet, which, although somewhat lacking in salt and spice, will have the advantage of being substantial, therefore satisfying.

Also there was no doubt about it the social ostracism of Calcutta had followed her to Benares; she had not failed to notice that the people packing the hotel looked at her furtively, smiling spasmodically when caught in the act, and seemed ill at ease when left alone with her.

Another thing which annoyed her intensely was the habit she had developed of peering into the shadows of the compound at odd moments, and listening for a sound she could not even describe to herself, and which she never heard; while through the blazing hours of the day, and the stifling hours of the night, like a black thread woven into a tissue of gold, ran the ghastly fear which had been with her since the day when a schoolgirl had taunted her, and to which she had given voice near the poinsettia bush to Jan Cuxson.

She had *done* Benares en tourist.

She had watched the worshippers thronging the Praying Steps at dawn from the deck of a boat rowed slowly up and down the holy river; had enticed the monkeys with gram from the niches in the Doorga Kond, the world-famed Monkey Temple; gazed fascinated and with reverence at the firing of the pyres about the dead bodies shrouded in white or red according to their sex upon the Burning Ghats; averted her eyes steadfastly from the bloated bodies in process of being torn to pieces by crows or vultures as they floated on the soft bosom of Mother Ganges to everlasting peace; and had passed restful hours in the wonderful ruins of the Buddhist temple some miles outside the city.

She had done all that others have done and will do, and still she waited, doing absolutely nothing and with no excuse for loitering in the hotel with its long broad verandah; learning much of the city's history from the charming manager who walks with a stick, and has the blue-green-brown shadow of the peat bog in his eyes.

"Shoo, you brute!" said one, of the girls on the verandah, and continued speaking when the crow had flown farther afield. "Well, the manager says we are not to go to the bazaar to-night on any account!"

"Why ever not?"

"Says there's a row or something brewing—something to do with the natives and their religion!"

The girl with the reddish-brown hair put a final polish to the nails, which damned her everlastingly, as she spoke condescendingly of one half of her forbears; while the other, a *bona fide* blonde as to hair, half opened the long sleepy brown eyes, which, combined with the shape of her silken-hosed leg from ankle to knee branded her even before she uttered a word.

"Don't believe it," the latter replied. "It's a do on the part of the guide to get more backsheesh; you simply can't trust these natives a yard. I'll tell you what, though," she sat up with an energy surprising in one of her kind, "let's ask Lady Hickle.

She's *such* a pet, and there's *nothing* she doesn't know about the place, she's been here a whole month."

Followed a short spell of peace in which Leonie raised her hand to summon her ayah squatting on the dressing-room matting, and put an end to the incessant chattering.

But bolts do not wait upon the clapping of hands before they crash down upon your defenceless head from out the blue, and the one destined for her from all time hurled itself at her from out a wispy cloud of Eurasian gossip.

"Oh! but we can't do that!" announced the peevish high-pitched voice.

"Why not?"

"Ma says we're not to be with her alone. There's all sorts of weird tales going round about her. Thought you knew. They say she killed her first husband, and tried to stab someone in Calcutta with that dagger she wears in her hair; that she lives on the q.t. with a native—he gave her that gorgeous necklace of pink pearls; has been seen with him in the compound after dark—Ma watched—and she's positively dotty at the full moon. Fact! Mrs. Oswald told Ma that there's no doubt that she's quite mad at times."

The blonde slid her slightly bowed, silken-hosed limbs to the ground, her face the colour of greenish putty through the superstitions of one half of her forbears.

"Let's go and find your ma!" said she. "It's full moon to-night."

And after their departure Leonie sat very still on the edge of the bed, with one foot tucked under her, and the other bare and very perfect stretched down to the matting; the netting fell in folds behind her, and her eyes stared into the corner where a one time nameless, unshaped spook, having taken form and name at last, stood mouthing at her from the shadows.

She started violently and looked down when her body-woman touched the arched instep with her wrinkled, dusky hand.

Keenly intuitive, as are all the peoples of India, she had crept noiselessly across the matting and crouched at Leonie's feet in her desire to be near the beloved child in her distress.

There was a heaven of love and a world of indecision in the monkey eyes, but not a trace of fear when the beloved child suddenly twisted the *sari* from about the sleek head and pock-marked face and shook her violently by the shoulder. Instead she rocked herself gently to and fro, crooning in the toneless cracked voice of the native woman who tends a white child and loves it.

"Missy—baba, it's ayah!" went the tuneless song, "it's ayah— it's ayah—be not afraid, baba—baba—it's ayah—ayah— ayah."

Over and over again she repeated the words with her eyes on the terror-stricken face above her.

"Why!" said Leonie, frowning till her straight brows met as she pressed the palms against her temples, "why, you used to sing that in—in—you used to call me—in the name of all the gods, woman, tell me—help me, oh! help me to understand!"

Great tears stood in the native woman's eyes, and she opened her mouth to speak, then turned her head slightly and looked towards the chick which had rustled; scowled, and bowing her head ever so little placed the palm of her hand against her forehead for an instant.

"Won't you or *can't* you speak?" said Leonie almost roughly, her voice ending on a sharp note which changed to a little bubbling uncanny laugh as she sat back on the bed holding her ayah at arm's length.

She took no notice of the dressing-bell when it clanged throughout the building, nor of the swish of the water as it was heaved into the tin bath in the bathroom, but sat on with the plaits of her hair coiled like snakes on each side of her, and the whiteness of her bare arms and shoulders shining in the light from the bathroom.

"Ayah! ayah!" she said in a dull sing-song sort of way, "do you know what they say? Do you know what they think? They think, they say I'm *mad*! And do you know I think I am. Sometimes there's the sound of drums in my brain, great big drums beaten by giants, and sometimes the sound of bells. And the sound of the bells is hot, it burns great scars on—on—and there are hours for which I can't account, and cuts and bruises on my feet and—and—"

Very quietly the native woman rose, and passing one arm behind the bare shoulder drew a hand across the low broad forehead, singing in her own tongue so softly as to be almost inaudible.

"I dream of blood, ayah," went on Leonie, "so often—so often—it is warm to the fingers and drops so—so slowly—and—"

The ayah pressed her fingers a little as she drew them behind the ears to the nape of the neck, and raised her voice ever so slightly in the Vega chant she had learnt as a lullaby.

"The women," she crooned, "that are lying on a bench, lying on a couch, lying in a litter; the women that—are—of—pure odour—all—of them we—make—sleep!"

The cracked voice sank suddenly as her child's face softened and relaxed, but the dark hand passed to and fro ceaselessly above the eyes and down behind the ears.

"It walks so softly, ayah—it's—it's in that—corner now—look! can't you see—its—its eyes—and the small—light—and she is—she is calling—calling—just as she—has—has—always—"

The tawny head fell backwards on to the white *sari* picked out in coloured silk, pulling it away from the head, and the marriage dower of thirteen silver earrings in the left ear, and the turquoise studded nose ring which shone dully in the dim light.

"And it's dark—it's—quite—"

Leonie slept, and her neighbours in the dining-room went through certain anatomical gymnastics such as lifting the eyebrows, shrugging the shoulders, and pursing the lips, all of which are supposed to denote suspicion; while the native woman kept guard behind the reed blind through which she watched a figure clothed in spotless white flitting among the shadows of the trees.

When those shadows marked the hour of midnight she sprang quickly to her feet.

With one violent uncontrollable movement, Leonie had risen to her knees with the tips of the fingers of one hand against her lips and her eyes slanting sideways towards the window near her bed.

"Hush!" she whispered. "Listen!"

Very softly, very sweetly there fell upon the night air the single stroke of a temple bell.

Once it fell, and twice, and yet again. And as it stopped the night was filled with the dull faint throbbing of many drums.

Calling! calling! calling!

Hidden in the shadows close to the reed blind, Madhu Krishnaghar watched the girl with intent half-shut eyes as, outlined against the dim light from the dressing-room, she twisted the heavy plaits of hair about her head, pinning them with the diamond hilted dagger; then stripping her flimsy garment from her, lifted the sheet from the bed, and twisted it deftly about her waist; watched her as she mechanically took a white *sari* embroidered in silver from the ayah, and without hesitation folded it in true native fashion about her body and small head.

The light of his religion flared into a flame of love and passion almost uncontrolled when Leonie, lifting the chick, stood by his side in the full light of the moon, with a smile of welcome on her lips, and the light of unholy knowledge in her eyes.

Quite close to him she stood with one hand upon his arm, as he hung garlands of scented flowers about her neck, and then with a little beckoning gesture was gone; and the ayah crouching on the floor, beat her withered breast with her withered hand, a world of doubt in her monkey eyes.

Like two white moths they flitted through the gloom and the hanging ropes of the banyan trees, down the narrow native path, and on through strangely empty streets and deserted bazaar to the Praying Ghats.

The air beat about them with the incessant throbbing of many drums, calling to prayer—calling to sacrifice.

Calling! calling! calling!

CHAPTER XXXVII

"Let us pass our lives at Benares, living by the banks of the divine river, clad only in a single garment, and with our hands uplifted over our heads."

—*The Vairagya Sataka.*

The Praying Ghats or Steps lay desolate in the light of the full moon.

Hundreds of small lights twinkled and flickered before the countless temples; hundreds of fading flower garlands, hung about the temple doors or festooned about the gods—some of which are quite indescribable—perfumed the night air; and to the right and to the left the smouldering bodies on the Burning Ghats cast a crimson glow on the slow, silvery waters of India's most holy river.

Of worshippers there was not one.

Of the countless priests who crowd the steps at dawn there was but one.

The mad priest.

Naked save for a loin cloth, he stood as he always stands from dawn to dawn with feet wide apart and hands upraised to the heavens, outlined against some one of the Rajah's palaces which crown the top and stretch the length of the terraces like a mighty rampart between the holiness of the place, and the fret and traffic of the outer world.

The holy man's arms, his legs, his emaciated body are covered with a fine ash powder, his long hair is matted with cinders and cow-dung, his mad eyes stare across the river into the infinite, at that which *we* cannot see, as he stands shouting unintelligible, maybe mad words, maybe not, to the glory of his goddess, Kali the Terrible.

Was he born mad? no one knows! What does he eat or drink? A handful of rice, a sip of water from his glittering bronze vessel! When does he sleep? No one can tell you.

Who knows! who cares!

He is a holy man! the mad priest of the Holy City!

He alone had taken no heed of the incessant resistless throbbing of the drums behind him in the city; neither did he take notice of the two white figures as they ran lightly, swiftly, hand-in-hand down the sunken, crooked, granite steps to a place between the praying rafts at the water's edge.

For a moment Leonie hesitated with the water lapping her feet on the third step, then she turned her head slowly, and looked straight into the man's eyes which had been fixed intently on the nape of her neck.

She gave a little sigh, drew out the dagger and let fall the plaited glory of her hair, and lifting the garlands from about her neck threw them out on to the waters; then with a native woman's movement pulled the *sari* backwards from her head, and unwound it from her shoulders which gleamed like ivory in the moonlight. Slowly, but without hesitation, even as the man dropped his shawl and long white garment upon the waters, she untwined the *sari* from about her body, dropped it across a *suttee* stone, and the dagger upon the step behind, and stood swaying gently with naught but the sheeting about her waist and limbs.

The man, naked save for a loin cloth, stood like some splendid bronze statue two steps lower; straight as a pine was Madhu, the descendant of princes, with a width of shoulder most unusual in the native of India, and which served to emphasise the slimness of the waist. Muscle rippled under the bronze skin of back, and chest, and limbs; and between the breasts gleamed the painted symbol of his religion, just as it shone between the brows.

The lean face with its hawk nose, and curved mouth set close in a straight line, had the look of an eagle as he stood gazing up at the girl with burning eyes, in which fanaticism, heightened by the lapping movement of the holy water about his knees, warred with an overwhelming passion roused by the slenderness of the white girl's waist, the virginity of her beautiful breast, and the satin whiteness of her skin.

And she placed her hand in his and followed him submissively down the steps.

The waters bathed her ankles, her knees, her waist, as she made a cup of her two hands and drank of the holy water; the jackals yelled from the far shore, and the unseemly body of a dead youth floated past face downwards a few yards away.

For some long minutes she stood with her face uplifted, then dipping her hands again into the water raised them and poured it upon her head until she glittered as though beset with diamonds. Strange little movements she made to right and left with both hands, circles she drew on the face of the waters, and the man within an inch of her beautiful body stood with arms folded hiding his hard clenched hands.

Raising both arms straight above her head she called aloud in answer to the spirit which moved her:

"Flowing on, devoted to it," she cried in the soft words of

India's holy writ, "by day and by night flowing on; I, of desirable activity, call upon the heavenly waters!"

From the temple above the mad priest took up her words as he scourged himself in the ecstasy of his worship, and shouted:

"Kali! Kali! Kali!"

Which eerie solitary cry brought the pigeons out of their nests in thousands, to wheel and whirl madly in their fright before resettling in the facade of the palaces, of the niches and nooks of the temples, and the slender minarets of the Mosque of Aurangzeb.

Bending backwards Leonie laughed up at the priest above, whose body was running blood, then descending the last three steps worn by the feet of thousands of pilgrims, and tilted by time and the resistless waters, flung out her arms and sank beneath the surface while the great plaits of hair floated towards the man and crept about his waist like loving, living arms.

Three times she sank, and three times she rose, singing gently to herself, while great tremors shook the man from his turbaned head to his slender feet.

Love or religion? Who knows!

Are they divided by much more than the breadth of a hair?

Leonie turned and walked up the steps, the wet heavy sheeting hobbling her about the knees and ankles, clinging to her as the skin to the peach, her dripping hair making little pools of holy water upon the holy steps; until, standing upon the one where lay the little crumpled heap of her silken *sari*, she unplaited it and shook it out in the night breeze.

She picked up the *sari* and the dagger, and ran a finger along the razor edge, looking sideways at the man who moved not an inch when she drove the point of the blade beneath the skin above his heart until the blood ran; neither did she move when he dipped his finger in his own blood and marked her between the brows with the sign of Kali.

The mad priest, frothing at the mouth, swooned upon the slanting temple roof, the drums were silent, the jackals had ceased their indecent noise, being intent doubtless upon the task of tearing some body to pieces before the arrival of the hosts of enemy pariah dogs; and Leonie, beautiful, bewitched Leonie, holding the white *sari* picked out in silver against her breast, held out her hand, and with the sweetest, maddest laugh in all the world sped like a deer up the great nights of steps.

And at the top when the man, moving swift and as surefooted as a buck, closed in upon her, her heavy drapery folded itself soddenly about her ankles so that when she essayed to save herself she twisted round and fell backwards.

Her mouth quivered in a smile, and her eyes, like stars, flashed back into the flaming ones so near her own as the man, lost to all but his consuming love for the girl, bent above her, and with slender hands crushed her back against the edge of the steps until the skin of her shoulders was torn and bruised.

"As the creeper!" he said, whispering the words of the Vega hymn with his eyes staring straight into her eyes. "As the creeper has completely embraced the tree so do thou embrace me, that thou mayest be one loving me, that thou mayest be one not going away from me!"

He smiled softly as she half raised her arms and whispered to her, the words sounding like a summer breeze blowing upon the hill-top.

"As the eagle, flying forth, beats down his wings upon the earth, so do I beat down thy mind, that thou mayest be one loving me, that thou mayest be one not going away from me!"

And his delicate finger-tips pressed about her temples as he whispered to her.

"As the sun goeth at one about the heaven—and—earth here, *so do I go about thy mind*, that thou mayest be one loving me, that thou mayest be one not going away from me!"

Slowly he bent still closer, and gently put one hand upon the gracious curve of her slender throat; and Leonie, wanton, seductive, bewitched Leonie smiled as she too whispered in the tongue of India's holy writ.

"Let yon man love me; being dear to me let him love me; ye gods send forth love, let yon man burn for me.

"That yon man may love me, not I him at any time, ye gods send forth love, let yon man burn for me!"

The silence which followed was pierced by the call of the holy conch shell, so low, so sweet, to prayer, to sacrifice.

Those who have not heard that call can never understand, those who have heard will forgive this feeble description of the intoxicating, soul-shattering, maddening sound.

Soft and sweet it will steal insidiously into your ear, your brain, and the whirlpool of your senses until you stand rooted in ecstasy in a flooded field of sweet desire. Rising swiftly and shrilly it will tear like racing waters at the ramparts we and our forefathers, have assiduously and mistakenly built around our inner selves; built until you and I and our neighbour have been metamorphosed through the ages from that mighty thing which went forth and took exactly what it wanted, to the almost shapeless slug form which, in the peace times of the present enervated century, contentedly eats lettuce in the damp seclusion of an overturned flowerpot.

Yes! that call will pull those ramparts to pieces about your feet; and at the last indescribable, insistent scream of triumph which sears your brain and soul, it would be wise to be on the look out, and to keep a strong hand upon the vows you may have vowed, and upon those of the commandments you may not already have broken; because at that strange seductive sound the solid chunks of love, honour, chastity and right thinking; everything, in fact, that is in any way decent and above board is likely to break into a thousand infinitesimal, unconsidered atoms, and be blown broadcast by the wind of indiscretion.

Leonie lay still, unconscious of the sound and the subtle change creeping over the man who bent down to her, and who, high caste, over-educated, overstrung, aflame with love and afire with the sensuality of his religion, slowly tightened his hand upon the gracious curves of the slender throat.

Years ago Kali, his dire deity, had been outraged by denial in her desire for sacrifice, and since then, in her wrath, the black goddess had scourged the land with plague, pestilence, famine, and earthquake.

Truly sacrifice of goats and buffaloes had been made until the altars and the courts of her temples ran blood; offerings had been made to her priests of grain and jewels, yet had she continued to whip the land until thousands died of hunger and disease.

Why should not his hand bring the long-desired and long-sought peace to his well-loved land, and what more fitting place and time for sacrifice than the steps of the Holy River, under the light of the full moon which is Kali's lamp?

Ah! and why should he not have his earthly reward in love, one short, full hour of the delight he had denied himself, and then, even upon the *suttee* stone, that little memorial of the burning alive of the young widow upon the funeral pyre of the beloved husband, drive the diamond hilted dagger through the soft breast in worship of his god, and through his own heart that he might follow his beloved quickly as she passed to Paradise.

Yes! sacrifice of the woman he loved that his god might be twice pleased.

He was crazed with the delirium of his religion, mad with the call of the senses lashed to frenzy by the restraint which had been unnaturally forced upon him throughout his life; his eyes had the look of the eyes of those gods who spy down upon you from the shadowy corners of India's temples, and his nostrils dilated as he touched the dagger in her hand.

Only for a moment! For even as he touched it the single beat of a drum fell heavily upon the air, causing him to sit back on his heels with a smile upon the full curved lips, and a light of sudden understanding in his eyes.

There was more toward than a mere sacrifice!

The Holy City was, and had been for days, in a positive ferment of religious excitement; the bazaars were thronged with pilgrims who, by boat and train and on foot, had hurried to the city of a thousand temples.

Something unusual was in the air although no one could clearly explain what it was; something was to happen although no one could name the hour or the day!

Rice, and flowers, and jewels cemented with blood had been thrust into and pressed down until they completely filled the great crack which had suddenly appeared before the altar of the oldest and most venerated image of Kali, the Goddess of Destruction, in the Holy City; and the foreigner had been warned not to place his profane foot within the precincts of the city upon this night of the full moon.

The native laughed as he sprang to his feet, standing bare and exceeding beautiful beside the indescribable graven images; and he laughed as he searched in the folds of his turban, and having found the pellets bent down and pressed them between Leonie's teeth, then jerked her to her feet, steadying her with his eyes.

He flung her back against the kiosk wall, and encircling her with his arms drove them fiercely down and against her as he met his splendid teeth in the whiteness of her shoulder—in love; and taking her hand sped with her to the inner places of the city, shouting as he ran in the frenzy of his religion.

CHAPTER XXXVIII

"Neither let her take thee with her eyelids."
                                            —*The Bible.*

"And making a tinkling with their feet."
                                            —*The Bible.*

The bazaars were moving in one solid mass in the direction of, but not to, the Cow Temple.

For hours the endless streams had moved inch by inch through the narrow streets lined with shops and gaily painted houses, towards the heart of India's Holy City.

Young women and old, young men and old, children, fakirs and holy men pressed patiently forward, impelled and called by some mystic summons they could not explain.

There was no pushing nor striving, neither was there laughter nor any kind of merry-making, although a flower garland hung around every neck, although the multi-coloured raiment was of the best and cleanest and brightest, and the different marks of the different religious sects shone as though fresh painted between the eyes and upon the face and body.

The holy cows walked slowly with the people, hung with garlands and painted on the face and sides; holding up the traffic as, unafraid, they snuffled their velvety muzzles in the unguarded baskets of grain, and pushed their way unconcernedly and by holy right across the human stream into the Cow Temple as they passed the ever-open door.

There was certainly no pushing nor striving to get one before the other, but underneath the calm pulsated a certain restrained excitement, to be read in the light of the thousands of eyes, and the extraordinary spasmodic, almost uncontrolled, movements of the delicate dusky hands.

Mothers would suddenly jerk their children up into their arms and press their little faces against one of the thousands of tiny shrines, where the gods sit all day and all night behind the bars through which are thrust offerings of flowers, of food, of jewels.

Men would suddenly strip themselves of all except the loincloth and, casting their clothing at the feet of some holy man, proceed calmly upon their way. One out of a number of beautiful, fragile girls, with cast-down painted eyes and half-veiled face, for no apparent reason would sidle up against some man; rest for one moment against him, and continue with him upon the road, his arm about her, crushing her body to his; and the drums throbbed, and the horns screamed in and around the temple of their goddess.

Yet one did strive, and, heedless of rebuke, did push her way ruthlessly through the throngs, slipping on the greasy pavement covered with refuse and cow-dung; sliding, ducking, squirming her way in and out, breathless and dishevelled, with a simple brown *sari* slipping from about her sleek head and pock-marked face.

Her monkey eyes flashed this way and that in search of something or someone she could not find; her withered hands beat her withered breast; the sweat streamed down her face until at last the crowd gave way, and looking upon her as one mentally afflicted, helped her stumbling passage up to and through the temple gateway.

Joan Conquest

Priests stood at the entrance to the outer court of the temple. They did not stand there, as do the ushers in the West, in order to keep the riff-raff, those humble, poverty-stricken children of God, from occupying the plush-covered seats in His House; but knowing the intimate connection between religion and the senses, and the limited space of the court of sacrifice and the temple itself, they stood there in order to keep a finger upon the pulse of that mass of humanity's passions.

The full moon flung her silver on to the stained worn flags of the roofless court; hundreds, thousands even of tiny wicks in tiny earthenware saucers flickered in the niches and on the outer edge of the walls; hundreds of torches flung a smoky veil around the restless figures passing in and out of the narrow entrance, and over dark heaps which lay at the foot of the walls and in the corners.

Black heaps which, lay upon dark carpets, heaps big and small which seemed to move, around which hung an overpowering, sickening stench of blood.

Heaps revealed when touched by the fluttering drapery of some worshipper to be the decapitated bodies of goats and bullocks lying in their blood, and from which would rise the millions of ever-moving flies which had given them a semblance of life in the torch-light.

Millions of flies, bloated offences, which settle for a second heavily on your face or arm and fly slowly back to their feasting.

It had been a day of stupendous sacrifice, and the place ran blood.

From the inner temple came the sweet never-stopping clang of a silver bell, as in one continuous stream the worshippers climbed slowly up the flight of steps, passed in, struck one note by swinging the tongue of the bell to announce their arrival to their goddess, and passed out; while babies of both sexes, naked save for a silver bead upon their rotund little bellies in the male, or a profusion of tiny bracelets and a nose-ring in the female, heaped the flower offerings in masses at Kali's feet.

Kali! Ah! formidable, terrible image graven in stone!

Pictures, highly coloured and blatant reproductions which will shock your artistic sense, can be bought for a few annas at the native shops which swarm outside the temple walls; but it is probable, nay, it is certain that not a single one of the Europeans who may read this book will ever see the original goddess in all her terror, and all that inexplicable power with which she holds the Hindu multitudes in the palms of her black hands.

Black, and crowned and heaped with jewels, she looks down at, or through, or over you with her slanting fish-shaped eyes. Her small ears, her flat nose, her arms, her pendant breasts are smothered in priceless gems; a huge red tongue protruding through the stretched mouth hangs far down upon the chest, ready to lick up the flames of sacrificial fires; a magnificent tiara binds the black hair which streams in masses behind her small distorted body; rows of pearls, flower garlands, and a string of skulls hang about her short neck; one hand holds a knife, the other a bleeding head, two are raised in blessing, while behind her shines a sun of flaming tongues of fire, and over all is spread an umbrella.

Yet it is not the horror of the repulsive physique hewn in stone which holds you breathless before her; you know it is stone you are looking at, just as you know that the Sphinx is stone; but as with the Sphinx you feel the life of centuries throbbing through the carved monster; you feel that its breath, which is about you, is the wind which has swept across the desert places and teeming cities of the East; you feel that the eyes which are upon you have seen all things; in fact you are almost mesmerised by the force of ages into falling upon your knees in worship, before you suddenly wrench yourself violently round to face the sun outside the open door; and even as you do it involuntarily put your hands to your neck, upon the nape of which, by the suggestion of unconfessed fear, you have felt the stealthy, longing, jewelled fingers.

On this night the slanting fish eyes of the goddess seemed to look through the doorway, and to linger upon the exquisite figure of a child dancing upon the extreme edge of the terrace between the two flights of steps.

Dancing!—hardly that, as she stood, her body swaying slightly in the whirl of her mixed emotions, and totally unconscious of four young men who, arms entwined, stood below, watching the beauty of her body and her movements with half-shut eyes.

Her ankle-length, full muslin skirt swung this way and that, as she moved slightly from her bare, over-slender waist, which accentuated the wonder of the young bosom out of all proportion in any but an eastern maid of ten years.

Jewels flashed in her delicate nose and ears, and on her slender fingers and parted toes, for was she not on the eve of her marriage, this little maid? Who, finding herself upon this unwonted night, alone for the first time in her life, had broken purdah, with her senses strung by days and nights of never-ceasing preparation for her marriage; during which she had been massaged by skilful, cunning hands; bathed and perfumed, forced to dance, forced to over-feed; until roused to a pitch of terrible excitement by drugs and curiosity, and the religious ecstasy of all around her, she had crept out alone, and into the temple with the teeming multitude to dance for the glory of her goddess.

Her little feet made patterns in the dust as she turned slightly, this child of ten, until her snake-like arms seemed stretched in invitation to the four pairs of burning eyes fixed upon the virgin beauty of the little body.

Who noticed in all that crowd when four pairs of hands shot up and seized her about the knees, lifting her gently down, or who, in the tumult, heard the cry smothered in the muffling cloth of a white coat in a distant shadowed corner.

And one dead body more or less in the morning, what does it signify or matter in a place which reeks of blood?

And just as this happened, and just as a dishevelled pock-marked woman stole swiftly up the temple steps, every face turned in one direction, and wave after wave of indescribable excitement swept the multitude.

And yet there was nothing, no sound, no sight to account for it; only the high priest, tall and terrible, with the face of a Roman emperor or a Jesuit, came from behind the altar and stood at the open door, looking first at the throngs and then at a mass of black cloud which, as is sometimes the way in India, had suddenly spread itself towards the east, and was slowly climbing the heavens.

CHAPTER XXXIX

"The gods approve
The depth, and not the tumult of the soul."
              —*Wordsworth.*

"What a frightful row the natives are making in the city," was the fractious comment of one heat-distracted tourist to another through the mosquito netting which divided the two beds.

"Disgraceful!" peevishly assented the other as she turned restlessly upon the thin, hot mattress, and heaved the one thin sheet to the foot of the hot bed.

A sharper note had topped the heavy murmur which, like the rumble of a distant sea, had beaten the air without ceasing throughout the night.

A film operator would have said that a crowd had woken up; a London policeman, that a crowd was turning nasty, as the sharp note went crescendo right along, until it took the definite tone of thousands of human voices upraised in unrest of some kind.

This way and that surged the multitude, bowing unconsciously before the gusts of passion which swept from every quarter.

The fret of the thousands of feet upon the paving sounded a silky accompaniment to the strange throaty murmur of fast rising religious hysteria; sharp, uncontrollable cries stood out like steel pencilling against the velvet monotony of the throbbing drums; the never ceasing tinkle of rings, and clanking of bracelets and holy chains against the blare of the horns sounded as out of place as a child singing in a thunder storm.

The high priest, with the face of Rome, with a beckoning gesture, drew towards him other priests. Some also with the face of Rome, and some with the face of the field labourer; some, gaunt and stern; some, jolly and rotund; well, just like any gathering of clergy, of any creed, you can see any day, in any country of Europe.

The chiming of the silver bell had stopped when the worshippers, upon the peremptory command of the priests, fled pell-mell out of the temple and down the steps to join the frenzied crowd; while from the direction of the Praying Ghats there arose a roar of voices as two slim figures sped swiftly up the narrow lane, which seemed to open of its own accord before them.

The woman, clad from the waist downwards in one linen piece, came running swiftly, lightly, undisturbed, almost hidden in the masses of her hair blown before her by the rising wind.

Her naked body gleamed in the mixed lights; one hand, thrust out through the hair, held a dagger with diamond hilt; the other was clasped in the hand of the man who ran evenly and steadily beside her.

There was not apparently an inch of space to spare in all those narrow streets; but by the madness of religion which drove the packed humanity back against the walls, a way was made for her who appeared to the multitude as the long-promised earthly incarnation of the Goddess of Death.

When she had passed, those who were against the wall remained there, standing crushed to death, supported by the indifferent neighbours who had helped to drive in their ribs; and those who had slipped to their knees in religious fervour, or by reason of the state of the street, also remained prone upon the ground, the mass of people treading indifferently upon their broken backs and necks, while the threatening heavens were rent with screams of physical agony and cries of sensuous delight.

Straight up the steps ran Leonie, and into the interior of the temple, just as a priest, a lad, with his face twitching spasmodically, and calling upon his god, fell dead at her feet, smitten by the force of his religion.

Leonie, throwing up her arms, laughed as she put her cut and bleeding foot upon the boy's neck—laughed until the place pealed and echoed with the unseemly clamour, causing the crowds outside, held only in check by the mental force of the handful of priests, to strain against the invisible hypnotic barrier, and cry to high heaven for a sacrifice.

Then Leonie turned about and ran out on to the terrace, standing a ghastly, beautiful figure before the multitude; and only a pair of monkey eyes, in a pock-marked face, hidden by the deep shadows of a corner inside the temple, saw the high priest with *roomal* in hand, creep stealthily up behind the girl.

No one in the tumult heard the growling of the elements; no one noticed the clouds bent on enveloping the moon; no one but the pock-marked woman understood what was towards for the appeasing of the outraged god.

"Blood!" screamed the tight packed ranks; "a sacrifice of blood! Kali is hungry! Kali is thirsty! Give unto the Black Mother that which she demands!"

Leonie flung up both arms and laughed, even as the high priest drew back one step, scowling at the averted sacrifice.

"A sacrifice!" went up the cry from thousands of throats; "a sacrifice! a sacrifice!"

Again Leonie flung out both arms, and, just as the *roomal* was slipping over the small head, with the scream of a tigress whose cub is in danger, the ayah leapt straight at her beloved child, wrenching the knotted handkerchief from the priest's hand.

A horrible cry of disappointed blood lust shook the very earth; drums beat, horns screamed, daggers flashed in the dense mass, and fingers met round many a throat.

They were mad indeed the people, but none so mad as Leonie as she stood with feet apart glaring down at the ayah's sleek head, which she held by the hair, in one hand.

So mad was she that the priests drew back as from one divine; all but the high-caste youth who stood unnoticed amongst them and who advanced one step as Leonie raised her face to the moon.

"She of the full moon," she chanted, "was the first worshipped one with depths of days, of nights. They who, O worshipful one, gratify thee with offerings, those well doers are entered into thy firmament!"

To which the waiting multitude thundered a response.

"A sacrifice! A sacrifice! A sacrifice!"

Over and over again went up the cry as men and women and children fell foaming to the ground, "and conches and kettle-drums, tabors and drums, and cow-horns blared."

Then came a silence, deep, sinister, and foreboding; only for one second before it was broken by a gasp, the catching of the breath in ecstasy of thousands of mankind.

And followed screams of pure delight as Leonie flung back her hand, in which gleamed the diamond hilted dagger, just as a terrific peal of thunder crashed upon the searing flash of lightning, which flamed from the dense clouds as they swept over and blotted out the moon.

CHAPTER XL

"Could I come near your beauty with my nails,
I'd set my ten commandments in your face!"
                                    —*Shakespeare.*

Leonie was sitting on the edge of her bed waiting for the *gharri* to take her to the station; she had lunched and breakfasted in her bedroom, in fact she had lived there since her interview with the manager, which had been indescribably unpleasant for him, in that it had been so distressing to the gentle girl as she had sat and nodded her head and looked at him out of agonised, forgiving eyes.

The hotel *en masse*, at least the feminine portion of it, had had a prior interview with the manager which had been *superlatively* unpleasant for him.

Coerced by a force which was closely allied to the brute; almost shouted down when he essayed to argue in favour of the hounded girl; threatened by the immediate transfer of the entire visiting list to the books of a rival hotel, he had ultimately owned to defeat; and Leonie sat on the edge of her bed, staring vacantly into the denuded dressing-room, while the native staff, yea! even unto him who had done her no service, buzzed round in the vicinity of her door.

Strange things had happened, things undefined, and therefore not capable of bearing the light of honest dissection or

Joan Conquest

discussion.

What *had* happened during the night of rioting—so-called—in the city? What had been the meaning of those white-robed figures which had fluttered near her door? And oh! why had her faithful ayah been found on the edge of the river the morning after, stabbed through the heart?

As if anyone in India with any sense at all *would* make inquiries about the last event.

All that and a lot more! and quite enough to slam the gates of heaven or the hotel upon any lovely woman on her own!

Yes! but—did all *that* really do the actual slamming?

Not a bit of it!

It was the most convenient excuse the womenfolk could find to hang upon the peg of jealousy which had been knocked into the wall of feminine conceit and bad intent, by the hammer of Leonie's beauty, and irritating indifference to both men and women, especially the former.

Let any woman lure to her side some other woman's own particular bit of masculine property; poach successfully upon her understocked male preserves; and figuratively, maybe verbally, most assuredly positively if she live east of Blackfriars, the claws of jealousy will be sharpened upon her; *but*—ignore the bit of masculine property, pass it by on the other side, consider it as belonging to somebody else, leave the preserves severely alone, and vials of execration, anathema, and denunciation, which are all synonyms for the same thing, will be poured upon her because of her lack of the appreciative faculty.

Fact!

Very few women can see the difference between joyfully

hoarding genuine antique pewter, and wearing a second-hand neglige.

So Leonie was fleeing home via Calcutta, and she sat without movement, hating herself and the world, even the man who, having taken her at her word, had left her alone to stumble as best she could along the crooked, lonely road which would end, as far as she could see, in a padded cell.

"How could you?" she suddenly cried aloud, and the natives made surreptitious signs, and withdrew to a certain distance out of respect to the disorder of her mind. "How *could* you leave me! Didn't you *know* that it is because I love you so that I would rather *die* than let you share my curse? But couldn't you have done *something*, tried to follow that clue, gone somewhere, oh! done *anything* just to show that—!"

The rumble of wheels cut her agitation short, and drew the native element closer to the door, in order that it should be quite near the mem-sahib when she appeared—with her purse in her left hand.

And while she sat on her bed, and later on in the train, striving to break the mental thongs which bound her to some intangible stake, Jan Cuxson was sitting in the secret places of the jungle temple, striving to break the bonds of raw hide by which he had found himself fastened to a ring in the wall.

As he struggled he speculated savagely upon that insensate sense of security, common to most Britishers, which had caused him to try and find the Hindu temple under the guidance of an unknown native.

He mentally reviewed his journey from the boat to the temple, fighting through the tiger-grass, breaking through the delicate impeding branches of the sundri trees, crushing the sundri breathers under his heavy boots as he tramped behind the guide, having failed to notice, owing to the resemblance that exists between one ordinary native and the next, that the guide and coolie of the jungle were not the guide and coolie of the paddle boat.

He remembered that once he had stopped dead and laid a detaining hand on the guide's shoulder, as through the darkening forest had come a cry, eerie as it wailed through the shadows, to be taken up ahead of them, and echoed and re-echoed until it became faint in the distance and died away altogether.

"What's that?"

The native had not hesitated.

"The cry, O Sahib, Protector of the poor, of the jungle owl as it seeks its food!"

Cuxson, unobservant for once, and anxious to get to the end of the trail again failed to notice that it was still far too light for any member of the owl family to be abroad.

Also, when he sat down on a fallen tree trunk to readjust his boot strap, he had mistaken for the booming of a huge jungle insect something which whizzed through the space where his head had been a second before.

It is true he had questioned the guide as to the route they were taking, pointing out that it was not the one traversed in the *shikar.*

To which the guide had replied that doubtless the *shikari* had taken the sahibs many miles out of their way to ensure a big toll to the sahibs' guns, and those of the mem-sahibs.

Jan Cuxson had accepted every explanation.

Extraordinary is this complacent sense of security of the British male when he butts into the paths and customs of countries of which he knows literally *nothing;* and he had arrived at the temple all in good time.

Silence, intense and rather overwhelming, had hung about the forbidding place which allied to the abomination of desolation had disconcerted him, and made him turn to the guide for further reference.

He had frowned, and involuntarily recoiled towards the wall when he found that his guide had disappeared, and that he stood alone in the heart of the jungle.

But strangely enough, even as he stood staring at a white wall in front of him, a sudden apathy had fallen upon him, also a strong disinclination to move hand or foot; in fact, he remembered laughing stupidly, and pulling out his cigarette case with the intention of soothing a distinct sense of irritation aroused by something which hammered incessantly upon his inner consciousness, warning him to be on the look out.

He remembered also looking once or twice in the direction of the temple door with the feeling that someone was on the point of coming out towards him, and then he had slipped contentedly to the ground, yawned, and gone to sleep.

All the sounds of a jungle dawn had greeted him on his awaking: a monkey had swung itself up to the top of the ruined wall where it had sat grimacing at him; an adjutant bird had clapped at his boot with its huge bill as it stalked past him towards the door; and he had found himself bound by waist and wrists to a stout ring in a wall which still held traces of brilliant colouring.

CHAPTER XLI

"And unto wizards that peep and that mutter."

—The Bible.

Like some infuriated bull he had fought and tugged at his chains and shouted for deliverance, until clouds of birds flew skywards in fright, and blood had spurted from his finger-tips and stained the shirt about his middle.

Thongs of hide sound inadequate against the strength of a man, but steel chains are weak compared with them for resistance, and to strive against them simply results in pure agony if they have been thoroughly soaked by the Indian dew which almost amounts to rain, and dried by the Indian sun which almost amounts to a furnace.

Of course, in a properly constructed novel he would have been left in a position which would have enabled him to gnaw the hide with his strong white teeth, or rub it until it wore through against some sharp stone.

But this he could not do because his wrists were bound behind, leaving the space of a foot or two between his waist and the wall; and when he leant back he had the tragic outline of a modern Prometheus bound; when he strained forward, that of one of Muller's pupils undergoing treatment for the development of the chest.

Neither could he, contort himself as he might, have brought his teeth within gnawing distance of deliverance; moreover, ruins exposed for centuries to the soft manipulation of a jungle climate, show no sharp stones; they are rounded and polished by the passage of time, soft feet, and that which crawls upon its belly.

At length, however, peace quite strangely fell upon him, and though he could not move, the agony of his hands and lacerated waist vanished entirely; such perfect peace that he leant back against the wall and idly tried to count the myriad tiny dainty hoof marks in the dust between the doorway facing him, and the ruined archway on his left.

He did not think it strange when turning his head he discovered an ancient priest seated against the wall with his mahogany coloured old body outlined against the dull blues and reds of the painted stones; and his eyes, bright with religious fervour, fixed through the crumbling arch, beyond the delicate sun-dried leaves, the blazing sun, and the steel blue heavens, upon Eternity.

The fine old man had no intention of torturing the white man, he had merely bound him to the ring until his goddess should inspire him, her servant, with her wishes concerning this stranger who was intimately connected with the white woman in the care of his beloved disciple, even Madhu Krishnaghar.

Neither did he intend to starve the white man nor bring him to the point of madness from thirst; but accustomed to hours and days of self-subjection in which he neither ate, drank nor felt the need of material sustenance, he failed to take into account the inner cravings of a man when he had been tied for two nights to a ring in the wall.

And he sprang to his feet and crossed the floor when Cuxson, after an interval of forty-eight hours during which he had neither eaten nor drunk, tortured by cramp from his waist to his feet caused by the strangling hold of the hide thong, with his heart pounding the blood against his brain until it shook, and his arms feeling like burning staves ending in blocks of ice, suddenly scrambled somehow to his knees, shouted, and fell forward with the soles of his feet against the wall, and the whole weight of his heavy body hanging upon the wrists.

It was but the work of an instant and a flashing knife and he lay face down upon the floor at the feet of the priest who passed swiftly through the doorway out into the jungle, and returning as swiftly, bound great green shining leaves about the wounds, and squatting on his heels gently massaged the black and swollen arms.

A holy man! a Hindu priest touching the contaminating flesh of an infidel! Impossible!

There are many methods of purification from contamination, but the main point in the priest's mental process of self-extenuation *was* that an infidel awaiting the verdict of the Great Mother should not be allowed to *die*.

Therefore more green and glistening leaves were placed upon the floor, and food, and water in coarse earthenware, set upon them, until Cuxson had revived sufficiently to eat, and enter into conversation with the priest, who, seeing no reason to withhold the information sought, and secure in the knowledge that the spreading jungle tied the sahib to the temple even more securely than the thongs of hide, gradually unfolded to him the dark history of the girl he loved.

"Eighteen years," began the tranquil voice of the old man, "as the sahibs count the passing of the moons, have gone since a high caste woman knelt at full moon in this temple at the foot of the altar of Kali, the Goddess of Destruction.

"Kali the Black One; daughter of the Himalayas, wife of Siva! Durga the inaccessible, Uma so sweet!

"Chandika the fierce, Parvati who steppeth lightly upon

the mountains.

"Bhairavi the terrible, Kali of death, Kali! Kali!"

The old priest, who had leapt to his feet under the exaltation of his worship, sank down again upon the floor, and continued his tale in the Indian tongue.

"The high caste woman, chief wife of a great prince of Northern India, held in her arms her first, her only son, a weakling, a sickly babe nigh unto death. Thrice had she been shamed by the birth of a woman child, and now her crown, her glory, her great gift unto her lord was like to die.

"Followed only by her body servant she had sped from her palace in the shadows of the Everlasting Hills, even unto the southernmost limits of Bengal, a pilgrim to this holy, secret temple where I pass my last days in sacrifice and worship; I, even I, foremost *guru*, once teacher of the Thugs, those beloved servants of Kali—before the law of the white man forbade their sacrifices unto the goddess."

Jan Cuxson, knowing of the sacrifices both human and animal offered in bygone days to the terrible goddess, shivered as the horror of the place seemed to close in upon him.

"The high caste woman demanding from the Goddess of Death the boon of life for her son, cast her jewels upon the altar and made promise of cattle and grain and her three daughters as handmaidens in the secret places of the temple. And I, aforetime great among the Thugs, lamented that I had but a coal black kid to offer as a sacrifice, for behold, Kali demands *life for life*, and *will not be denied*.

"Flowers flung by the woman, O white man, strewed the stone floor upon which I have worn a path during the passing of the years; hundreds of small lights flickered in every corner, causing the shadows to dance about these weary feet and the eyes of the great gods to shine from the corners of the roof;

and without I heard against the wall the rubbing of the great tiger as it waited for the blood sacrifice which it nightly devoured before the dawn, the striped cat upon which Kali rides forth at night on her journeyings through the jungle.

"Even as I plunged the sacrificial knife into the neck of the unworthy sacrifice, I heard footsteps as of one running swiftly; and behold, there came a low caste, pock-marked woman up the middle of the temple, who flung herself at the feet of Kali, laying a sleeping babe upon the altar steps."

"Ah!" barely whispered Jan Cuxson with his eyes fixed upon the fanatical old face.

"And behold, the low caste woman was ayah in the services of one, even a great colonel-sahib, who, being raised above his fellows, was hastening back across the Black Water to his own land, taking with him his one wife, and the one child of their union.

"Loving the white girl child with the great strange love of the servant of India for the offspring of the *feringhee*, the ayah had secretly brought the babe in the absence of the mem-sahib upon visits of farewell, that I might dedicate her to the goddess, binding her in spirit for ever to the land of her birth."

The white man sat in silence when the old man sprang to his feet, standing relentless and formidable in the light of the one lamp.

"See'st thou? See'st thou, sahib, my sin? The sacrifice was within my hands, and yet I spared the child because of the woman's beseechings. I hesitated, yea! I even asked a sign. Aye! and the sign was good, twice pleasing to the Goddess of Death, for behold the owl hooted not, neither was the voice of the jackal uplifted as the doe, coming from the *right*, looked through the open door.

"With the high caste woman I made covenant, that her male

child in return for his life should be a servant of the Black One, obeying in all things the mandates of her priests.

"And I held those sleeping babes upon my arm, and within the lips of the girl child I placed the *goor*, the sacred sugar, and around her neck the *roomal*, the noose of sacrifice. And I cut the sign of Kali between the breasts of the man child and between the breasts of the woman child, and marked him between the brows with her blood, and marked her upon the forehead with his blood, so that his mind should be her mind. And her will I bent to *my* will, that her eyes should open in sleep at the light of the full moon, and that she should go forth upon the mission of the Black One, making sacrifice to the spouse of Siva.

"And yet, though she be bound to the secret temple and to Kali, and to the son of princes until death shall release her, the Great Mother is not pleased, nay, her wrath is terrible at the averted sacrifice, and India, my land, has suffered through my fault."

The priest stood motionless, staring down unseeingly upon the man at his feet who spoke softly.

"And what became of the white child?"

"The white child, the infant *feringhee*? She lay asleep in my arms with eyes wide open, and the high caste woman, picking up a jewel, even one of the colour and shape of cat's eye, smeared it with the blood of the kid, placed it above the heart of Kali, and then hung it by a slender golden chain about the neck of the woman child. And the women, content, departed, bearing with them the united babes, but since that ill-begotten night my land has travailed in agony, stricken with plague and pestilence and famine!"

"And?" Cuxson scarcely breathed the word.

The light of the moon slipped over the ruined wall, drawing a nimbus round the old white head as the tall thin figure in the snow-white garments swayed slightly.

"I waited for the command of Kali, and after many years I sent my beloved disciple, the son of princes, across the Black Water to bring the white woman by the force of his will back to the land of her birth and up to the altar steps. And now I wait—I wait—for a little, little while."

The old voice rose to a thin shout of triumph which lapsed into silence as, totally oblivious of his prisoner, he sank to the ground, lost, quite suddenly, in that wonderful abstraction of the East in which the native can find escape from the trials of life at odd moments, and in unaccountably odd places.

During the long silence that followed, Jan Cuxson sat patiently puffing at his pipe and trying to piece the strange tale together, until at an advanced hour of the night he once more felt the hawk-like eyes fixed upon his face.

Eagerly he picked up the thread of the story as though there had been no lapse.

"You mesmerised her, you say, eighteen years ago, and you pretend you can still bend her to your will?"

"Nay, Sahib! Through me Kali the Terrible imprinted her will upon the babe's tender mind those many moons ago!"

Cuxson shook his head.

"You can't make me believe *that*—it's rubbish—like the mango tree and rope trick—it's impossible, simply *impossible* to make strong-minded, level-headed people do things against their will."

In such wise does the westerner account to his own satisfaction for the mysterious workings of the East.

The old man said no word, but looked steadily between the young man's eyes.

"If the sahib will look to his right hand!"

Cuxson turned his head and started.

Eyes glaring, tail thrashing the ground, and ears flattened to the great head, a tiger half crouched.

"The devil!" he ejaculated, as the mouth of the great animal twisted spasmodically. "Here's a fix."

"The sahib will place his hand upon the tiger's head."

"Not much!"

"The sahib is afraid!"

The quiet scorn of the words struck Cuxson like a whip, and he stretched out his hand impulsively towards the smooth head with flattened ears and glaring eyes.

There was not a sound, though the tail swished the ground, and the huge mouth opened slowly, showing the splendid ivories.

"The sahib, if he is not afraid, will close his hand firmly upon the throat!"

Cuxson's hand closed gently upon the striped skin; then he exclaimed sharply on perceiving that the only thing his hand grasped was air.

"Why—what—how the—!"

The old man nodded his head gently, and answered without a smile. "It was the will of the Black One that the sahib should see the steed upon which she roams the jungle at night!"

But Cuxson was British, and would not be convinced.

"I don't believe it," he said shortly. "That was a tame animal, which strays in and out of the temple like a tame cat."

"Will the sahib look at the dust upon the ground. Is there sign of feet, marks of the body, or the lashing of the tail upon the dust?"

Truly the dust, save for the deer marks, was undisturbed, but Cuxson shook his head stoutly, and refused to believe the evidence of his own eyes.

"The sahib will not believe! Then will I make her, the white woman, see thee, the man she desires as husband, a prisoner in the House of Kali, covered in blood, and she will hasten forthwith to thee—and to me!"

Cuxson sprang to his feet with murder in his eyes, but stopped and flung out his hands as though to thrust aside some obstacle.

The priest laughed softly.

"O babe in wisdom! Behold, thou shalt not be bound, yet shalt thou not stir beyond yon temple wall until she come, and with her the son of princes who yearns for her; then shall I lift my will from thee and tie thee to the wall that thou mayst behold the double sacrifice of *love* and *life* made to Kali the Terrible."

The priest was gone, and Jan Cuxson sat down upon a fallen block of masonry, covering his face with his wounded hands; and faintly from the temple echoed the voice of the priest as he prayed to his god before projecting his will across the space that divided him from the white woman.

Only for a little moment of despondency, and then he sat back and shook his great shoulders with the light of battle in his eyes, and grim determination in every line of the powerful jaw.

How he was going to circumvent the priest and save his beloved he did not know—he had no plan, but—he was going to pull it off.

"The son of princes," he said, addressing a monkey which had flung a stick at him from the top of the wall, "why I'd trust my dear, bewitched or not, with a thousand sons of princes. I love her and she loves me, you gibbering bit of fur, and d'you think *anything* could stand against *that*. Let her come! Just let her be within reach of my arms, *then* you'll see what you will see. Let the priest play into my hands, and bring her here, the sooner the better, for *that* is exactly what *I* want."

And he laughed as he refilled his pipe, blessing the old priest for his consideration in annexing naught but his rifle and revolver.

Which is just about the simplest way of starting to get out of a tight corner.

Ignoring all obstacles, owning to no defeat. The splendid heritage of the English speaking race.

CHAPTER XLII

"A good name is better than precious ointment."
                                    —*The Bible.*

"And in its light the Star of Love aglow,
Shone with her beacon fire, a guide
and guardian still."
                                    —*Dante's Inferno.*

In the middle of the night Leonie lay face downwards upon
her bed in the great Eastern Hotel.

All the luggage she had brought with her from England was
stacked around the small room, and even in the dressing-room;
in fact, there was that unfinished, unpacked air about the
whole place which is inseparable from anyone in India who is
in the throes of going home.

She had returned on the wings of panic from Benares, only to
find that the gossip which had been circulated about her had
arrived well in advance; and that, like crows after a dust cart,
what remained of the city's female population was busy pulling
her to a thousand pieces with claws and beaks sharpened by
the million irritations of the hot weather.

A dignified bearer had salaamed gravely, and handed her a chit
upon her arrival at the bungalow, where her friend was braving
the pestilence of the hot weather in comradeship with her

husband, who, in the secret places of his heart, wished to goodness she had gone to the hills with the rest of 'em.

Her luggage, the letter stated, had been shifted to the hotel, where a room had been taken for her, and there would, it seemed, be plenty of accommodation on the *City of Sparta* which would be sailing in three weeks' time for home.

And that was all!

It is wise in the hot weather to pull the purdah, which is the Indian way of saying to shut the door, in the face of a young and unattached girl with a tawny head and opalescent eyes; especially if the dust has long been undisturbed upon the threshold of the secret places of the male heart supposed to be entirely in your keeping.

For days she had remained in her room, not daring to face the curious glances, and subdued whispers, of the few visitors to be met with in the marble desolation of the front hall; and not for worlds would she have used the telephone for fear of the direct snub the wire would surely have transmitted.

Food she hardly touched; sleep she did, heavily, waking dull and unrefreshed; and for hours she would sit and stare into the corners, or peer over her shoulder into the stifling shadows, or study her face in the mirror, wondering if her strange eyes were the eyes of a mad woman.

The bearer had caused her long moments of worry.

The morning after her arrival at the hotel, instead of the little, dusky, nimble, monkey-eyed man of the night before, there had entered one, tall and dignified, who had cleared a space on the table beside her bed, deposited a bunch of flowers and the *chotar hazri*, or early tea, and raising his hand to his turban had departed.

Quite a usual procedure! But wakeful Leonie, who had

indifferently watched him through the mosquito curtain and from under the pillow frill into which she had burrowed her head, frowned when something familiar in the man or his movements had particularly attracted her attention.

Most natives look alike to the newcomer in India, but she frowned again as she chewed the crust of buttered toast and racked her brain fruitlessly for a clue.

One by one she went over each city and place she had visited, each railway journey she had made, each hotel she had stayed in. Then had poured out a cup of tea and given it up.

Having fruitlessly worried over this seemingly insignificant detail of an Indian day's routine, she had impatiently counter-manded the early tea for the following mornings, and had indifferently left the really lovely flowers which came up regularly on every tray, to the fantastic arranging of the little dusky man who looked at her like a wistful monkey, and slipped nimbly about the room in her service; and who, likewise, rejoiced greatly over certain backsheesch which he, with the joy the native has in all intrigue, imagined to be the outcome of love.

I wonder if Europeans in India know with what interest their bearers or ayahs watch, and what detailed accounts they could and do give of their masters' or mistresses' love affairs, great and small, legitimate and illegitimate.

It is to be surmised that they do *not!*

They were not the eyes of the nimble little bearer that were watching from the bathroom on this particular night, when Leonie very quietly raised herself in her sleep and, flinging back the netting, sat staring silently into the corner nearest the door.

She half knelt, half sat, with a faint look of surprise on her face, which changed slowly to absolute amazement, then to the faintest suspicion of love and happiness, during which transition her smile reflected the glorious lights of the seventh heaven.

"Oh, beloved!" she exclaimed, and laughed softly, the sound falling eerily in the absolute stillness of the night, the shadows dancing eerily upon the plaster walls as she threw out her arms.

She flung them out in a beautiful abandonment of love, and the hidden eyes glistened as they watched the fingers slowly curl and clench as a look of horror crept gradually over the whole face, blotting out its sweetness and light, changing it into a veritable mask of terror.

A horrible dream! A nightmare!

If you like! The label of casual explanation, tied by the string of ignorance, never did much harm to any psychological package.

Leonie was apparently asleep and evidently seeing things, so perforce she must have been dreaming, for what else *could* she have been doing!

Anyway her heavy, unrefreshing sleep, induced by fatigue, mental weariness, or a super-will, was very gradually being turned into a thing of moving shapes.

The shadows in the corner had lightened and darkened and lightened again, lifting at last to show a half-ruined, roofless room and a banyan tree outside an almost perfect archway.

A wick in a coarse earthenware saucer flickered feebly in one corner, two deer pattered swiftly across the flags and out of the door, and very slowly a man jerked himself on to his knees and twisted his death-white face towards the coming dawn.

Jan Cuxson suffering the tortures of the damned, chained by his rashness and his love to a ring in the wall with thongs of raw hide, which were drawing blood from his wrists and staining his shirt about his waist.

This way and that he wrenched and tore, then stopped quite still glaring into the shadows.

This way and that again, hurling himself back, against the wall, flinging himself forward until the agony of the thongs seemed to be beyond all human endurance.

Just for one ghastly instant, one second, he stopped, staring straight into the eyes of his beloved, seeming to call insistently for help, his face distorted until it lost all human semblance; then pitched forward, hanging unconscious upon the thongs just as a priest, thin and gaunt, with knife gleaming in his hand, rushed towards him; and Leonie, with a piercing shriek, sprang straight out of bed, flung herself violently against the wall, and woke up with her hands feebly groping over the coloured plaster.

And next evening the news that Lady Hickle had left the hotel without her luggage, destination unknown, streaked like lightning through the almost deserted Chowringhee, the Strand Road, the Maidan, and clubs and bungalows.

What a godsend is a bit of gossip in the hot weather, when your neighbour's looks, wardrobe, and morals have been threshed bare; when the mail has not arrived; and the hill news has only served to upset your temperamental digestion; in fact there were little whirlpools of excitement in the Saturday Club's stifling atmosphere, serving to add a passing zest to the heat-stricken evening hours and pegs which no amount of ice seemed to cool.

Every man, high or low caste, white or not, who met Leonie, figuratively cast himself at her slender feet.

Men ran to do her service, they smiled in doing it, they mopped their heated brows and cheered up, even at one hundred and two in the shade, when she happened along to ask some good office with a smile on her red mouth.

She had paid her outrageous bill, left orders concerning her outrageous luggage, and walked out of the hotel almost unnoticed, because of the witchery of her most gracious manner which served to make her path easy—where men were concerned of course; and without let or hindrance she had cashed an outrageous cheque at her bank which left a few rupees to her credit, and had walked through the building to give orders as to her mail, and ask advice of the fair-haired, courteous young Englishman who rose from his table as she turned away with the sweetest words of thanks for the trouble he had taken in finding out for her how to get quickly to the Sunderbunds.

"I wonder why she's going there, of all places, in this infernal heat, and in such a desperate hurry, and I wonder if she's going alone!" he said half aloud as he drew beetles on his blotting-paper, and frowned as somebody, breathless from heat, sank heavily into the chair on the other side and slapped some documents on to the table.

Leonie was acting quite subconsciously in all she did on that blazing morning.

Which does not mean that she was still walking in her sleep with her eyes wide open, or that she was not aware of her own movements.

Not at all. She was wide awake with a fixed determination to get to the temple in the Sunderbunds as quickly as she could.

Why?—well, who knows?

As far as the dream was concerned her mind had been a perfect blank when she had awakened the previous night groping over the plastered walls; but branded across it, in letters of blood, had been the one word Sunderbunds, standing out clearly against the fog which surrounded something terrible she could not understand. No, she did not understand, but she knew that everywhere she looked she saw the lettering; and that every sound she heard, the soft slur of the lift, the throb of the motor engine, the call of the indefatigable kite, cried the one word aloud; and that in some inexplicable way the resistless summons was connected with the man she loved.

What was she to know of the working of an eastern mind in the secret places of a Hindu temple?

Neither did it strike her as strange that a taxi, with its flag up for hire, should be standing opposite the bank door, blocking the way for arriving vehicles; or that, having persistently refused many irate would-be hirers, and patiently listened to the asperity of their remarks, the driver should have opened the door and held it back as she walked straight across the pavement, got in, and, without hesitating gave the address of the Whiteway Laidlaw Company.

It might have seemed odd to a stranger; still more odd would it have appeared to any chance passer-by if they had overheard the following short conversation as Leonie got out at the shop.

"Can you drive me afterwards to Kulna?" she asked in her best but inefficient Hindustani.

"Even so, mem-sahib," promptly replied the lithe, good-looking son of the East as he salaamed. "If the mem-sahib will pardon her servant he would advise driving to Jessore and resting the night there at the dak bungalow, that is if the mem-sahib is not in too great haste!"

Leonie frowned, only understanding half of what was said.

"Don't you speak English?"

"No, mem-sahib; but my brother, who lives near the New Market but a minute's drive from here, speaks the mem-sahib's language. Also, he is a good bearer, having travelled widely. If the mem-sahib permits, I will call him to accompany her on her journey to Jessore."

"Very well!" said Leonie, beckoning to a boy, who sprang towards her with a huge basket which, for a few annas, he would carry round the entire building after her, and into which she would throw her purchases of all sizes and shapes.

He emerged some time later jubilantly staggering with basket and hands full.

What a priceless mem-sahib who had not once complained about the price!

The brother had materialised! Oh, those brothers and fathers, and mothers and sisters, and all those relations who are always so strangely near at hand in India!

"If I may offer a suggestion," said the soft voice in the delightfully choice English of the educated native of India who has sojourned in England, "it would be that we drive only to Jessore, stopping at Bongong dak bungalow for tiffin. If the mem-sahib is sight-seeing, I will arrange everything in the most convenient and pleasant manner for her. From here to Kulna in one day would be a long and wearisome journey in this great heat."

Leonie half turned with the slightest frown as she passed her hand over her eyes.

Once again had come that suggestion of something familiar—a suggestion too fleeting to be caught.

"You can do exactly as you think best as long as I start for the Sunderbunds to-morrow morning."

"The public boat does not start for three days, mem-sahib."

"I can hire a private launch, can I not? Money is no object, only speed."

"Easily, mem-sahib. Consider it arranged!"

Leonie lifted her head for half a second, showing her face deathly white, the crimson line of her beautiful mouth and the shadow-encircled eyes emphasised by the dark green silk lining of her topee.

She glanced quickly at the dignified figure beside her on the pavement and looked away.

You do not, as a rule, recognise people you have met in your sleep; neither had her memory been impressed with the passing glimpses she had caught of the handsome face in the British Museum and during the *chotar shikar.*

No, in spite of the tugging of her memory, there was nothing to link this person in the spotless white turban and full-skirted coat of the bearer to her fastidious self.

Neither did that strange anonymous gift of glorious pearls which was round her neck even then, or an unaccounted for mark upon her shoulder, help her in any way.

She leaned back listlessly as her newly acquired bearer arranged the newly bought suit-case and the various packages.

It was an absurd way of starting out on a jungle trip, picking up a car any old how out of the streets, and a bearer from the labyrinths of the bazaar without even glancing at his chits, which, even it she had, would probably have been forgeries.

She had certainly had the sense to put on her knee-high boots and knee-length skirt, a low collared shirt waist and sports coat, also a topee; but, wishing to leave no clue as to her future movements at the hotel, she had slung everything else pell-mell into her trunks, locked and left them to be fetched and stored at her bank.

It had obviated the calling of a car and the giving of an address to the hall porter, but it had forced her to buy everything she might be likely to require for a day or two's sojourn in the waste places of an Indian jungle.

She had thought of everything with one exception, and that, of course, the one item which should have been the most important on the list.

Of weapons of defence she had none.

But then, what was she to know of the workings of the mind of the man sitting with his back to her as the car turned and sped swiftly down the streets, which seem to stretch endlessly, until you strike the heavenly tree-lined road which leads you through Dum Dum and other well-known places to the river edge.

CHAPTER XLIII

"Thence shall I pass, approved
A man, for ay removed
From the developed brute; a god,
Though in the germ."
                                        —Browning.

Blazing hot simply did not describe the degree of heat which pressed down upon and around Leonie as she sat totally unconscious of it on the verandah of the Bongong dak bungalow.

For the benefit of those who have not experienced the assorted joys of travelling in India, a dak—pronounced dork—bungalow is a travellers' rest, humble or spacious, presided over or not, as the case may be, by a simple and courteous native. They are to be found dotted about everywhere—in jungles, on roads, and outside ruined cities; and there you can stay for an hour or a night, sleeping in comfort, provided you have brought your own bedding and mosquito netting; eating according to the contents of your hamper.

In the cooler hours vivid flashes of orange and black, or black and red, or turquoise blue and green, or white flit across from tree to tree; parrots chatter, crows scream, and the brain-fever bird soothes or irritates you according to your mood, and you tap your fingers on the table in time to the metallic anvil cry of the coppersmith bird, until a tiger-ant or some such voracious insect claims your undivided attention.

In the heat of noon the only sounds to break the intense stillness are the metallic anvil cry of the aforesaid coppersmith bird, and the never-ceasing call of his brain-fever brother.

Except for your own there is no movement whatever—the voracious insect is always with you.

Quite alone in the bungalow, with her back to the open bedroom, Leonie sat undisturbed, with her eyes fixed unseeingly upon the tree-lined road, and a torrent of disconnected thought swirling through her mind.

Exactly what she was doing, and why she was doing it, she had no idea; she only knew that do it she must, and was content to let it rest.

Programme or plan she had none, only an intolerable desire to get to the ruined temple in the jungle.

For what?

She had no notion! She had to get there quickly, that was all she knew.

She sat on, with her elbows on the table and her chin in her hands, without stirring; in fact you would have sworn she was asleep so still was she in the silence broken only by the two birds.

She could see the car a little way down the road awaiting her, with the driver curled up sound asleep beside it at the foot of a tree; the bearer asleep too somewhere, she surmised hazily, as the sound of the packing of the hamper had altogether ceased.

And then something, instinct maybe, or whatever you like to label the incorporeal look-out in our psychological crow's nest, whispered to her that it might be wise if she awoke to her surroundings.

There had not been a sound, nevertheless she felt that somebody stood quite near to her.

She did not move her head, but her eyes flashed quickly to right and left, and she frowned ever so slightly when she remembered that her revolver had been left behind in Calcutta, safely tucked away at the bottom of her dressing-case.

As is the usual way when a revolver is owned by woman.

Nothing stirred except the little curls on the nape of her neck, which quivered when she shivered involuntarily.

It happens every day in India! The land where curtains take the place of wooden doors, and a deferential servant on noiseless, unshod feet glides into your chamber unannounced, and stands patiently behind you until it pleases your august self to turn and acknowledge his humble presence.

That's what you think, anyway.

And it takes quite a time to become accustomed to the noiselessness of this proceeding, and to control the start which gives you away completely.

Leonie could stand the uncertainty no longer, she suddenly swept round in her chair, and remained quite still with her mouth slightly open, and her eyes fixed upon the face of her bearer.

He was just behind her chair, his white full-skirted coat touching the back of it, his arms folded; but as Leonie turned he took one step back and salaamed with both hands before his face, completely hiding the blazing eyes for the one second sufficient for them to regain their normal placid, indifferent look, as he gently made it known that all was ready if the mem-sahib desired to depart or to sleep.

Yes, his eyes *had* blazed as they rested upon the gracious lines of this woman he loved, but whom, before he had known her, he had vowed, in the transports of his religion, to bring unto his god.

Yes! and the whole body of this magnificent being, vowed to holiness by his parents, *had* trembled as he stood close to her sweet-scented person; so close that it had seemed as though he stood knee deep in a bed of clover at dawn.

Yes! and he was alone with her, with the knowledge of his power upon her mind; yet he would not have touched one hair of her head, nor laid a finger upon her against her will, even though she was absolutely at his mercy, and the inner room was misty with shadows.

They are gentlemen of the finest type, these pure bred sons of India; not the ravening beasts of prey towards women described so minutely, and with such nauseating detail, in various religious and altruistic pamphlets; little literary atrocities written mostly by men and women who have gathered their experiences of the East from an exhibition or two at the White City or Earl's Court, and their data from their own scurrilous minds.

Bad types there are in every country! But for pity's sake let these social reformers stick to the West, and start on those who make it unpleasant, if not unsafe, for an honest, well-groomed woman, with pretty feet and veiled face, to walk slowly by day, or by night, through the so-called decent streets of London town.

Let them leave the fine, cultured men of India to their own gods and their own customs, remembering that their ways are not our ways; for which those of them who have tarried in our country, return thanks as, laying an offering of thanksgiving before their god, they lift the purdah, behind which awaits the modest, gentle little maid; perfumed with the scents of the East instead of the aroma of whisky or brandy pegs allied to the tobacco of Turkey or Virginia; and unbesmirched by the close embrace of the fox-trot which caused a certain Maharajah, on a visit to England, to remark to an Englishwoman:

"Why! I thought—"

Well, perhaps 'twere better that the damning commentary should be left unwritten.

It was late in the evening when Leonie questioned her servant.

"Does the serang know exactly where I want to go? And how quickly can he get there?"

She was having dinner, and quite a good one, in the front part of the living-room in Jessore's dak bungalow. This room can be divided into two by means of a curtain drawn across, and you can listen, in fact you are obliged to listen, if there is another party ensconced behind, either to the furtive love-whispers of those who should not be there, or the frank abuse of each other of the *bona fide* couple suffering from intense heat and long years of matrimony.

Leonie spoke over her shoulder in the direction of the bedroom, where the bearer was arranging the mosquito net, her toilet things, and her new-bought dainty night attire.

It you are the right type or caste everything always goes smoothly for you in India; if you are not it most emphatically does *not*; so she had not given a thought to the extraordinary ease with which her wishes seemed to be carried out, in fact forestalled.

"It is the same serang who took the mem-sahib when she went on the *shikar* and killed the man-eating tiger. The two coolies to carry the mem-sahib's luggage have been hired, and the boat will be moored to-morrow night!"

"To-morrow *night*," said Leonie, the light from the adjoining room throwing up her white face against the shadows of the quickly falling night. "But it took us *two* nights to get there last time."

"We are going a shorter way, mem-sahib. The launch will be moored in a big creek on the front of the island at which the mem-sahib landed last time. A small boat will take us through the very narrow creek, which encircles the island, to the other side near which the temple stands. There will not be much walking for the mem-sahib, she can proceed immediately to the temple in time to see the sunrise, or pass the night in a *suapattah*—"

"Oh! never *that*!" said Leonie most decidedly, thinking of her last experience.

"But this hut is clean, mem-sahib!"

Leonie turned right round in her chair.

"How do you know that the last hut was not?"

"All huts are dirty, mem-sahib."

There was not a sign of confusion on the calm well-bred face, and he stood like a statue as Leonie, unconsciously striving for light in the darkness, continued her questioning.

"How did you know I wanted to go to the same place—to the temple, I mean?"

"I did not know, the mem-sahib told the chauffeur!"

At the last word Leonie lifted her head, and her eyes rested intently upon the handsome face in the doorway between the two rooms.

"No! I did not!"

"The great heat of the day doubtless caused the mem-sahib to forget the order she gave to her servant."

Never argue with a native of India, because educated or not he will invariably, and with the utmost courtesy, make you feel at the end of the argument that, if not a born, you are at least an excellent temporary liar.

"Did your parents have you taught your remarkable English?"

"The mem-sahib is too kind to inquire."

In India you do not show curiosity about your servants' private affairs or their families, it is not expected, it is not understood; and at the silence which followed the answer Leonie, feeling herself rebuked, rose from the table, and walked out on to the verandah to hide the colour which swept her face from chin to brow.

In the middle of the night, when suddenly and unaccountably aroused from a restless doze, she spoke sharply as her eyes rested on a white figure prone upon the floor in the reflected light of the moon.

"*Bearer!*"

Her voice was indignant, and the man with one movement rose to his feet and salaamed.

"What *do* you mean by sleeping in my room?"

Dear heaven, how he loved her as she sat like an image of wrath behind the mosquito net with the sheet pulled up to her neck.

"There are three doors to the mem-sahib's bedroom, and as the blinds fit badly, except for the presence of her servant, there is nothing to prevent a pariah dog, a jackal, or a thief from entering."

"Please leave my room and sleep somewhere else. I do not like it, and I am quite safe."

Leonie, feeling acutely the want of dignity in her bunched-up attitude, did not know what to say when the man refused suavely, but point-blank, to leave her.

"I regret that I cannot obey, as the mem-sahib is in my care, and I am responsible for her safety; but until the day breaks I will keep watch at the foot of the bed where the mem-sahib's eyes cannot rest upon her servant!"

Oh! Leonie! Leonie! With that strange, angry, and unaccounted-for mark still upon your shoulder, if only you knew what a fuss you were making over nothing.

But she said thank you quite nicely when *chotar hazri* was placed beside her bed in the early morning, to the refreshing sound of water being heaved into the tin bath in the dressing-room.

CHAPTER XLIV

"If thou faintest in the day of adversity,
thy strength is small."
                              —*The Bible.*

Jan Cuxson was walking round and round the ruined chamber,
pausing at the doors as he passed them to look out at the
seemingly never-ending jungle; he would have reminded any
onlooker of some caged beast as he went monotonously round
and round.

He was rather a desperate sight, too, with harassed eyes in a
gaunt face, and his open shirt exposing a somewhat emaciated
chest; not that he had been starved, far from it; but eat you
ever so heartily, fill your interior with all the fatty substances,
real or artificial, in the world, worry will push in your cheek
and temple, draw canals of woe from your nose to your mouth,
and force your cheek-bone, nose, and ribs into high relief.

Of course he ought to have had a many days' growth of beard
all over the face; but, owing to one particular fad, he had not;
and thank goodness! for it would have been simply appalling
to have had to end the book with the hero looking like a
woolly hearthrug.

His fad which saves the situation was that when travelling
either for hours or for days his safety razor invariably travelled
in his pocket; and the old priest had smiled when he caught

him in the act of lathering his face, less successfully, it is true, than more, with a finger tip smeared in ghee, which is clarified fat; and had come back later with a handful of stuff which looked for all the world and felt almost as sticky as French almond rock, a certain vegetable root, slightly acid of smell, which lathers beautifully in hot or cold water, and which, in some districts, the natives use as soap.

He was simply in an agony of mind.

He had stormed, and threatened, and pleaded in turn, and offered the whole of his kingdom in exchange for her safety—all of which had made about as much impression upon the priest as a few snowflakes would upon the Himalayas.

His one and only attempt at escape, which had taken place twenty-four hours before, had been a dire failure.

Roaming around the courtyard outside his chamber, which seemed curiously near, and yet cut off from the rest of the temple, he had heard the tinkle of silver anklets, the sound of a native woman's high-pitched laugh, and the bleating of a goat.

And the thought struck him that if a woman had come to seek counsel of the priest she must have come through the jungle by some safe road known to the native, and she would have to go back by the same road; and if he could only find the way into the temple itself, and watch her from the shadows, what would be easier than to follow her and reach Leonie in time to save her from the disaster and death threatening her.

Although the thought of the death straight to which Leonie was coming, blindfolded by the curse upon her, made his blood run cold and turned his heart to stone at the knowledge of his own impotence, the picture of what might happen to her at the hands of the native crazed with religion and love well-nigh drove him frantic.

He was absolutely at the priest's mercy.

A stronger will than his own allowed him to wander so far and no farther; indeed, he had been powerless even to reach the block of stones from behind which the priest appeared when upon visiting bent, and around which he disappeared when he went to worship before his god.

"I am like a damned hen with a chalk circle drawn round it!" Cuxson had exclaimed when he tried over and over again to pass the invisible line; and he cursed aloud as he felt the deep sleep creeping upon him at various hours of the day and night, and from which there was no escape, try as he would to keep awake.

But upon the day when he heard the tinkle of silver anklets and the bleating of the goat, something, just as curiously incomprehensible, had urged him to walk to the ruined mass of stones which hid the priest's entrance and exit; and he had walked across the sun-stricken court without let or hindrance, or covering to his head, and had found on the other side a low doorway almost choked with jungle growth.

He had not paused to think nor plan; he had merely bent his tall figure and crept through and down the narrow, decaying passage, along which, dotted irregularly here and there, shone little lights in tiny earthenware saucers. He had paused once or twice, sickened by the sight of offerings of which a description is not necessary, and shivered, strong man though he was, when he had met the eyes of gods leering, or glaring at him from little hewn-out shrines in the crumbling masonry.

His feet made no sound, for the narrow way was choked with the dust of ages, and he gave no thought to what might lurk in the shadows in the shape of beast or reptile, so intent was he on reaching the place which held the woman, and which had seemed near when she had laughed, and unaccountably far away as he stole stealthily forward.

The passage twisted at every few yards, and once he had found himself at a dead end in what he thought must be the priest's living room, as far as he could make out by the dim light coming through a tiny aperture high up in the wall. He had dimly seen a bed of leaves, a single covering, and an earthenware platter and jug, before he turned quickly and retreated when something hissed softly and rustled among the leaves.

Having got back into the passage and made some considerable headway, he was almost choked, when on turning a corner he had been enveloped in a sickly sweet smell of many flowers, allied to some sickening odour to which he could give no name; and then he had stopped dead, and flattened himself against the wall as he realised that he had come out by the side of the altar into the temple itself.

Arranged neatly on each side of the doorway were glittering brass vessels, brass trays, and little piles of tiny earthenware saucers; to his left was tethered a black kid, which lay contentedly upon a heap of dying flowers; near it was what appeared to be a miniature guillotine stained almost black; and above his head, in front of him and hanging from a hook in a huge, upstanding block of granite, glittered, a short, needle-pointed knife.

One knife?

Nay! two, three, a dozen, scores, thousands, thousands of glittering knives whirled around his head; and hundreds of goats grinned from corners and capered about his feet, and millions of evil eyes winked at him from the dusky shadows; and voices rose in choirs, male and female voices, whispering, laughing, singing. Louder, still louder, rising like some all-conquering flood, while silver anklets clashed until the brain was nigh to splitting with the din.

He must see, he *must* see, and watch the women who laughed shrilly and often; he must see the front of that great block of stone which barred his way to Leonie. Yes! Of course that was it, just that one great block of stone which kept him from his love.

Jan Cuxson made a mighty effort to move his heathen foot over the inch of threshold which separated him from the holy place. His breath came in gasps, and the veins stood out in knots upon his forehead as he pushed with both hands at the empty air; he fought like a mad dog to overcome that mighty force arrayed against him which neither advanced nor retreated, but was just *there*.

Then as something out of the void struck him cruelly between the eyes he gave a mighty shout which made no sound at all, and fell with a crash, scattering the brass vessels and tiny earthenware saucers to the four corners of the space around the altar.

Sunstroke?—well, *hardly*.

Because the next morning, when he awoke with the hide thongs fastening him by the wrist and the waist to the ring in the wall, he felt fit, and fresh, and extremely wide awake.

Perhaps it was that the blow, or whatever had struck Jan Cuxson down on the threshold of the temple, had served to sharpen his wits; anyway, for some unknown reason, words uttered by the priest on the first day of his imprisonment began to repeat themselves over and over again in his brain, as he sat uncomfortably with his back to the wall and his eyes fixed with a certain crafty understanding upon a piece of rusty metal half hidden under a fallen brick.

Wherefore he wheedled and cajoled when the priest came to visit him until the thongs were unfastened and his somewhat prescribed liberty restored.

"Only until the shadows fall, sahib," the old man said as he gathered the hide thongs in his hands. "Tonight is the night of the full moon and the white woman is even now approaching."

"Leonie—I mean the mem-sahib—is in the *jungle*—with whom?"

"Verily, sahib, with the man who loves her!"

"Oh, my *God*!" said Cuxson slowly. "How do you know?"

"*We* need no wires or poles to carry us news, sahib! We have a surer way, aye, and a quicker one. Struggle not to-night, sahib, when I tie you to the ring in the wall. Bound you must be, for the Black One has spoken; and it is her pleasure that I shall lift my will from you, even as I did by mischance yesterday. India has suffered through this white woman; my people have been tormented by her, and Kali, the Black One, has commanded that the sufferings of the land shall be wiped out in the white woman's blood, and the torments of the people in your torments."

It has been said that Jan Cuxson was plodding to a degree akin to slowness.

He was! But you may be sure that if an idea came to him even at the eleventh hour it would be a good idea and would be developed until it reached an advanced stage of perfection.

Some time after the priest had departed he drew the piece of metal, which proved to be the broken blade of a knife, from under the fallen stone, slipped it into his pocket, and was as well content as his harassed mind and overwrought imagination would allow him to be.

CHAPTER XLV

"Behold, thou art fair, my beloved,
thou art fair!"
                    —*S. of Solomon.*

"Yea! he is altogether lovely."
                    —*S. of Solomon.*

With her bearer's hand to balance her, Leonie stepped off the
gangway into the rocking, canoe-shaped boat, made in the dim
past by digging out the interior of some tree trunk, and in the
bows of which were huddled the coolies with her luggage.

Two bronze-hued rowers, nude save for the loin cloth, paddled
the boat round the bends of the narrow creek with a dexterity
due to habit; and then by chance or misfortune wedged her
firmly into a glutinous mud-bank from out of which it took
the five men two hours and every ounce of their united
strength to push her.

It is not wise to wade waist or knee deep in a Sunderbunds
creek, and clear a boat with a yo-heave-ho, for fear of some
festive mugger, which means alligator, lurking in the mud.

She had therefore no option but to pass the night well above
the jungle perils in the *suapattah* hut, like a cockatoo
screeching defiance at a cat from the safety of its perch; and to
which safety you climb almost flat on your face by means of a

rocking, slender bamboo ladder, and with about as much grace as a monkey manipulating a stick.

There was a sharp tussle of wills after the dinner of which Leonie partook on the small platform which comes between the top of the ladder and the low door of the hut.

Having arranged her bedding and mosquito curtains as best he could, and seen to it that one of the low caste coolies negotiated the ladder with a gourd of water upon his head and placed it upon the floor in the mem-sahib's bed-chamber, her bearer, when Leonie retired for the night, drew up the ladder and curled himself up in a corner.

Almost stifled by the heat of the interior she came out again in search of fresh air, and stared in amazement at the white figure as he sprang to his feet perilously near the edge of the platform.

No! nothing would move him from his post during the night, nothing.

"But I am perfectly safe up here," remonstrated Leonie, "when you have gone to the other hut I can quite easily pull the ladder up!"

"Even so, mem-sahib," quietly replied the man, "but the mem-sahib is not accustomed to these heights; there are no railings to the platform, and one false step would send her crashing to the ground."

"But I am going to *bed*," Leonie persisted. "Besides, if I did move I can see quite plainly, it's almost full moon!"

There was a barely perceptible pause and then;

"Yes, mem-sahib, it is the full moon!"

Leonie, stricken dumb in the belief that the story of her mental plight had reached even to the bazaar, turned back and re-entered her so-called bedroom, drawing a purdah made of *golaputtah* leaves across the door, and leaving her bearer to his own devices and thoughts.

Which were utterly of her as he divested himself of his outer raiment, and nude save for the loin cloth, sat like a bronze statue in the overpowering heat of the night; and even as "the eagle flying forth beats down his wings upon the earth," his thoughts beat down so forcibly upon her mind that at mid-night she arose in her sleep and lifting the purdah walked out on to the platform.

She walked straight forward, too far from the man for him to pull her back; and in too deep a trance for him to have stopped her with safety to her brain. His face was that of one tortured as he rose to his feet and threw out his hands; and the sweat came out in great beads upon his forehead under the supreme effort of will, which pulled her up within an inch of certain death.

For one long moment she stood with arms upstretched to the moon shining in all its glory, then swung round and crossed to where he stood against the hut.

"Yes?" she said gently. "You called me!"

The man drew his breath quickly as he looked at her, and forgot his gods in his love, and his passions in the innate nobility of his soul.

She looked for all the world like a mere schoolgirl in her over-long, kimono-shaped, diaphanous night garment, with her hair hanging in two great plaits, and her eyes and mouth lit by the suspicion of a smile.

"Sit down!" he said gently, and she sank to the ground as easily and with all the graceful suppleness of a native woman.

"Yes!" she repeated. "You called me! What is it you desire?"

She made a little gesture inviting him to sit beside her, and he sank to the ground, lying prone at her knees with his chin in his hands, staring straight into the green eyes which shone strangely, and looked at him unblinkingly.

"Tell me what you think of me," he said, speaking in the merest whisper out of the depth of his love. "Tell me, and I will tell you what I think of you—thou lotus bud," he finished desperately in his own tongue.

Leonie answered in the sweetest, purest Hindustani, using the beautiful strange metaphors of India to describe the human body.

"Thou art," she said. "Thou art—how can I tell thee I—"

She stopped, laughing down at him as she put both hands out on a level with her chin, palm upwards, towards him, in a little supplicating gesture.

"*Tell* me!"

"Behold," she said softly as she passed the tips of her fingers from his forehead to his chin. "Behold is thy face softly rounded like the egg of a bird, and thy brow is even as a tautened bow—"

A great tremor shook the man at the touch of her hand, but he made no movement as he broke across her words.

"And thy face so fair, so dear, is even like the *pan* leaf, and thy dark brows like the *neem* leaf disturbed by the wind, when thou art displeased with him who so loveth thee. Yet when thou art not angry, are thy drooping lids like the water-lily in their sweet repose. Thy ears, those can I not see—ah!"

Leonie laughed softly as the very tips of her fingers passed down the side of his face.

"And thine are like vultures with drooping head, and thy nose—"

"Thine," he interrupted, twisting his head to evade the exquisite agony of her touch, "is like a *sesame* flower, and thy nostrils even unto the seed of the barbarti, and thy lips—oh! thy lips are the *bandihuli* flower."

He raised his face with agony in his eyes, closing them as she lightly touched his mouth.

"*Thy* mouth is even as the *bimba* fruit, which is warm and soft, and thy chin is like a mango stone, and thy neck like unto a conch shell which I encircle with both hands."

She spanned his neck with the outspread thumbs and little fingers of both hands, and laughed as he pulled them apart and buried his face in his arms.

"Dost fear?" she said. "Dost fear that I shall strangle thee? *Dost fear?*" she repeated with a certain sharp note in the voice which caused the man to look up quickly and straight into her eyes, upon which she laughed quietly.

"Tell me," he insisted gently, "tell me what thou thinkest of me!"

"Ah!" she whispered, "thy shoulders are like the head of an elephant and thy long arms are as the trunk, and the strength of thy breast is even as that of a fastened door—which love perchance may open," the heavy lids half-closed over her eyes as she slowly drew the finger-tips of both hands down towards the slim waist, and the man's teeth drew blood from his under lip.

"Thy middle is like a lion's, so slender is it, and—"

He stopped her fiercely as he twisted on to his right elbow and seized both her hands in his left.

"And the suppleness of thy arms, and the softness of thy limbs are like the young *plaintain* tree, and thy fingers are the buds of the *champaka* flower." He spoke rapidly, crushing her hands cruelly. "The bone of thy knee showing whitely through thy garment is shaped even as the shell of a crab, and the whiteness of the bone from thy knee to thy slender ankle is like a full-roed fish—"

"And thy feet and thy hands, O Lord, are as the young leaves of plants!"

To which he replied through the teeth that were closed.

"And thine so small, so dear, are as lotus buds—lotus buds swaying at dawn in the wind of love."

She smiled divinely as she stretched one perfect bare foot from under her garment, and bent her head to catch the words as he passionately whispered the Vega hymn.

"Want thou the body of me, the feet; want thou the eyes; want the thighs; let the eyes, the hair of thee, desiring me, dry up in love.

"I make thee cling to my arm, cling to my heart; that thou mayest be in my power, come unto my intent.

"They—"

He stopped, convulsed with passion, and bending kissed her feet.

"Ah! thy hands, thy feet, are like lotus buds—lotus buds which I love, even if they be drenched in blood."

He leapt to his feet and caught Leonie's wrist in the vice of his hand as she sprang upright in one movement, laughing as she pointed at his mouth.

"Blood," she whispered, "blood—it is warm—it drops slowly—slowly—"

She ran her fingers across his mouth, and shook with hideous silent laughter as she showed him the tips stained red.

"Come," she said, "come—she is calling—calling—" and she struck at the hand which gripped her shoulder, and tried to shake herself free.

"Come!" said the man, looking straight into her eyes, "come with me."

She slid her hand into his, and followed him docilely as he lifted the reed purdah and entered her bedroom.

"Lie down!"

He lifted the netting and pointed to the bed.

As he towered above her the scarlet mouth in the uplifted face was on a level with his shoulder, as she smiled distractingly and raised her hands palm upwards in a little supplicating gesture.

"My Lord!" she whispered. "My Lord!"

The temptations of all the ages, and the overpowering passion of his own glowing East rose about him like a flood; he shook from head to foot as she laid herself down and drawing the sheet about her whispered again, "My Lord!"

They were alone in the jungle, and his will was hers; she was as a bit of wax upon which he might imprint his seal; there was no one to say him nay if he should draw her unto his intent.

And he loved her.

Yes! he loved her, and because of the overpowering strength of this love he knelt beside her and placed his fingers upon her temples.

"Sleep, beloved," he whispered, "sleep—the women that are of pure odour—all of them—we—make—sleep."

And Leonie slept peacefully and undisturbed until the dawn, because Madhu Krishnaghar, with his face buried in his arms, who lay across the threshold of her bedroom, was one of the splendid type that India breeds—an Indian nobleman.

CHAPTER XLVI

"Out of the abundance of the heart,
the mouth speaketh."
                        —*The Bible.*

One thing after another happened to prevent Leonie from continuing what remained of the journey during the cooler hours of sunrise.

One coolie strayed and was not retrieved until the other two men were hoarse from shouting, then another ran something into his foot, which was only extracted after a mighty fuss, and something akin to a major operation, skilfully performed with the bearer's knife and a few thorns plucked from the bush.

Last but not least, as they were on the point of starting, a snake about two yards long had blithely wriggled its shining length across their very path; and nothing short of hours of prayer and offerings to their gods would move the coolies along that path after such a sign of ill omen; no! rather than budge an inch they would have laid down in their tracks and died of snake-bite, or a marauding tiger; and Leonie was far too wise a traveller to lose sight of her luggage for one second—in India.

Although she had no idea why she was in such haste, she inwardly fretted at the hours lost, but passed them with outward patience in the shade of the jungle trees; eating what was brought her, and sleeping away the afternoon stretched on a rug; unconscious of the fact that her bearer sat behind her head, fanning her face gently, and with the lightest and deftest of fingers removing the various insects, long and short, fat and thin, smooth or horny, which seemed to have taken unlimited return tickets for the journey over her body.

They had been for some time on the way, the coolies trapesing behind to the tune of some monotonous chant; and the moon was beginning to fling handsful of silver out of her heavenly mint when Leonie, overcome by a most unromantic craving for tea, gave the order to halt.

"How much farther is it?" she asked, as she busied herself with a spirit lamp and a tin of evaporated milk.

Her bearer looked up at the moon.

"Another half-hour, mem-sahib, and we reach the outer walls of the temple—ah! allow me—"

Leonie had dropped a teaspoon and was bending to pick it up, but instead, straightening herself with the kind of snap an over-strung violin string gives when it breaks, took one step forward and fixed her eyes on her servant's face.

"Of course," she said, speaking half to herself, "of course—no wonder I thought I knew you—I saw you in London once— and it was you I saw on the station—and your voice—" she clasped her hands together and took a step quickly back- wards—"you were the guide in the tiger hunt, you—you have been following me—you are dogging me—hunting me down—why—tell me why? What harm have I done you?—tell me?"

Her eyes, which were shining strangely in the quickly falling night, swept the man before her from head to foot, and she instinctively threw out her hands and took another step back- wards as she realised at last his extraordinary beauty.

"Why is the mem-sahib *afraid*? What has her servant done to cause trouble to her soul? He meant but to lighten her load, and make smooth her path."

Leonie, with the desire common among women to hide the tell-tale expression of their faces by the movement of their hands, knelt and began fiddling among the tea things.

"Sit down," she said abruptly, pointing to-the ground on the other side of the earthy tea-table, "and tell me everything."

"Nay, mem-sahib! A humble native may not sit in the presence of a white woman."

Leonie lifted her head.

"Sit down," she said simply.

And there in the heart of the jungle, by the side of the fire that had been lighted to scare off any animal, they sat, those two splendid specimens of two splendid races divided by custom and colour, while he told her the strange story of the night on which they had both been dedicated to the Goddess of Destruction, and the happenings thereafter.

"Do you mean to tell me that you willed me to come to you in the museum that day in London?"

He looked straight into her perplexed eyes as he answered slowly:

"I felt that if I could draw you through the ebb and flow and the floods of London traffic, I could do as I would with you on the plains of India. I did not know you—*then*!"

"And the priest has made me come to the temple—against my will?"

"Even so."

"And what is to happen to me there to-night?"

"A danger threatens you, beautiful white woman, a great danger threatens you from which I alone can save you, yea! and will in spite of all the gods!"

"*You* will save *me*—*you*—and why?"

"Because I love you!"

The words were out, and Leonie, springing to her feet, drew back as the man rose and stood motionless in the dancing shadows thrown by the fire.

"What do you mean? Oh, how dare you—"

"How dare I—*dare* I—tell you that I love you and want you for wife? Why should I not love you from your beautiful head to your perfect feet? Why should you not be my wife? Because I am what you call *black*? because of this colouring of my skin which, outside my own land, damns me to eternity, and bars me from all that I desire? Nay, you *shall* listen, and you *shall* answer! You *will*, will you not?"

The voice had dropped from the pitch of fierce denunciation to the sound as of a deep river flowing in pleasant places, and Leonie nodded mutely, succumbing, as is the way of woman, to the entrancing pastime of playing with fire.

She closed her eyes and clasped her hands tightly together when the man, stepping across the barriers of interracial convention, came and stood just behind her shoulder without touching her withal, and spoke in his own tongue.

"Ah, woman, I would call thee wife. Behold, I have much to offer: a great name, vast wealth, palaces, broad lands, jewels, elephants, villages; the esteem of my people, the love of my father and of my mother, of whom I am the only son. All of which is nothing, nothing compared with my love for thee. A love as virgin as the snow upon the Everlasting Hills, swifter than Mother Ganges, deeper than the Indian Ocean, and higher than the vault of heaven. What matter custom, or law, or regulation, or colour, when such a love as mine is offered? Thou as my wife, *thou*, and thy children my only children. Am I not beautiful? even as beautiful a male as thou art a female? Would not the days and the nights, the months and the years be as heaven—together? *Love me*—nay! say but that I may call thee wife. Give me thy promise and I will save thee!"

"Save me?—from what?"

Leonie turned and faced this splendid lover, shivering slightly as a low moaning wind rustled the leaves of the trees and stirred the undergrowth.

"Even from death!"

"Death?" she said quietly, looking straight into the man's eyes. "*Death*—for *me*? Why I thought I was being willed to the temple to make sacrifice to your god?"

"To-night thou must surely die unless I save thee."

"Oh! you are mistaken," came the quick, decisive reply. "Why, if I was murdered, the whole Empire would be up in arms."

"The British Raj would not know," was the quiet answer.

"Oh! but—"

"You have not seen the Fort of Agra, the sad, dead palace. There, in the dungeons, is a beam stretched across the hidden wells and marked with the fret of a rope. Many a beautiful woman has swung from that beam by neck, or feet, or wrists, and her body dropped through the well into the Holy Jumna without the knowledge of any save her master and her executioner."

"Oh!—oh! don't—"

"Twice," continued the quiet voice relentlessly, "the sacrifice has been averted, but *now* the hour has come. Thou art here alone, none knowing, and I—I *alone* can save thee. And will not Kali, our mother, raise her hands in blessing upon us united, even as we were united when babes, and being appeased, lift the curse from off the land. She is soft and gentle, treading lightly upon life's stony paths, Uma so sweet, Parvati, daughter of the eternal snows. Oh! woman, say that thou wilt be my wife, for behold, are we not marked with the same mark which—"

"Mark? *What* mark?" Leonie questioned abruptly, looking back over her shoulder, her mouth perilously near to his as he bent his head slightly towards her; and there fell a little silence in which the thudding of his heart could be felt against the silk thread of her jersey.

"Between thy breasts, thou white dove, hast thou no mark?"

Leonie tried to speak, and failing, nodded her russet head.

"Even so, it is the mark of Kali which the priest cut upon thee and me, uniting us all those moons ago in the Mother."

She turned completely round and faced the man with a little look of wonder in her eyes.

"I have so often wondered about the—the little mark," she said. "But you see—how could I marry you—I could not, do not—love you!"

"Love," he said quietly. "*Love!* Thou wilt love me, aye! thou wilt love me in thy waking hours, even as thou wouldst have loved me in thy sleep if—if the gods had not intervened."

"You—have—been   with   me—in—my—sleep?"   she whispered.

"When thou didst walk in thy sleep!"

CHAPTER XLVII

"For jealousy is the rage of a man;
therefore he will not spare in the day
of vengeance."
                    —*The Bible.*

Suddenly she was struck with the full horror of those lost
nights in which the man beside her had been her companion.
She stretched out her hands and turned them over this way
and that, scrutinising them with horrified eyes. She touched
her mouth with her finger-tips and drew them with a shudder
down her neck, and her breast, and her waist, as she looked
upon the beauty of the man before her with his passionate
mouth and gleaming eyes.

"You—you have been with me when I have walked, unconscious in my sleep; you have—"

He interrupted her hastily, divining her thoughts.

"Yea!" he said, "I have been with thee when, under the
influence of *my* god, thou hast walked in thy sleep. I have
watched over thee and helped thy cut and bleeding feet over
the roughness of the roads, as I would help them over the
perilous road of life. I have not touched thy hand save in
support; I have not touched the glory of thy mouth with my
mouth, because thou couldst not give me thy *consent* so to do!

Joan Conquest

"Dost think it has been a child's task to keep my hands and my kisses from thee? Behold, I had but to make a sign, and thou, in thy unconsciousness, would have come unto my intent! Oh, thou bud of innocent fragrance; thou fruit ready to the plucking of loving hands! Aye, thou wert, thou art in my power; and even have I seen thee in—"

"Ah!" said Leonie sharply as her hand slid to her shoulder and the words came through her closed teeth—"You *lie*!"

"Lie!"

"Yes, *lie*! You have not touched me you say; neither have you kissed me, but *you*, and *only* you, can tell me what the mark is on my shoulder—a mark I shall carry to my grave."

The man threw back his turbaned head and was about to make reply, when, with those shrill cries which betray great fear, a troop of monkeys passed them, chattering as they ran swiftly on all fours, or swung even more swiftly from tree to tree; and the native looked after them, and up to the sky, and over his shoulder along the narrow path by which they had come, showing black and white in the alternate lights and shadowings of the moon.

"Answer me!" said Leonie more sharply than she knew, and with a woman's superb indifference to any event or signs of approaching event outside her own love orbit.

"Nay, answer thou me!" replied the man who, expert in the knowledge of jungle signs, yet put aside all thought save of his love for the woman. "Tell me that thou wilt be my wife and the mother of my sons, thou beautiful woman! Tell me that thou wilt come unto me this night, wedded to *me*, by yon old priest; and that, within the arms of Uma so sweet, of Parvati who steppeth so lightly, I may set my seal upon thee.

"Lifting from thee, as I and the priest *only* may lift, that which thou callest the curse from about thee, bringing thee to happiness in the shadow of the temple."

But something had happened to Leonie, bringing her to a pitch of excitement foreign to her in her waking hours. She looked swiftly to right and left, and over her shoulder, and up the narrow path they must go to the temple; and up to the sky she could see faintly through the trees, and into the eyes of the man watching her intently. Then she clasped her hands tightly and moved close to him, her face as white as death.

"And the sahib, the white man, where is he?"

The native of India weaves and fashions the cloth of his cloak of love out of many colours. Gorgeous colours, blinding, dazzling, in which predominate the scarlet of passion and the emerald of the supreme male's jealousy. And all, from the sweeper to the highest of birth and caste, wear this wondrous garment in India, though not one out of the teeming millions fashions his cloak upon the pattern of his neighbour's.

Madhu Krishnaghar, the son of princes, with eyes dimmed by the brilliance of his own particular garment, failed to perceive that Leonie, too, was wrapped in a love mantle.

The occidental mantle, made of honest homespun, uniform in colour, and with a wide hem to allow for shrinkage; but guaranteed to stand all weathers and to last a lifetime.

He might have been flicking a fly from his sleeve, so indifferent was his answer in his blindness.

"The white man? He is bound to the temple walls, awaiting the woman he allows to walk unveiled and alone throughout India."

"Ah!" said Leonie, with that little hush in her voice which is heard in the mother's when she first sees her new-born babe. "I am sorry," she continued quietly, "so sorry I have not been honest with you. I cannot marry you because—"

She stopped and turned as with a sound like the tearing of silk a flock of birds suddenly flew from the tree tops and whirled away into the night.

"Because? *Because*, woman?"

For a moment Leonie unconsciously watched the flight of the birds, then swung round, arms stretched wide, eyes shining, and her face aglow.

"Because I love the white man in the temple who is tied to the wall, *that* is why!"

Her voice rang clear and true under the sky, and she stepped back quickly and threw out her hands as the man spoke. For the banked-down fires of his passion and his love, and the hurt to his race, and his own sudden-born agony flared in one half-second into a mighty, awful conflagration. The flame of his words licked at her feet and the hem of her garments, blazed across her hands with which she hid her face, and swept right over her from head to heels, and yet he did not touch her nor raise his voice one half tone.

"Thou *woman*! Then shall no man have thee, for I will drive my dagger through the white man's heart before thine eyes, and watch thee, thou beautiful thing, wed him in the shadow of death."

And Leonie, catching the look in his eyes and the set of the mouth, knew that he meant what he said; and she laid her hand on his arm, so that his agony was increased a thousand-fold as he looked down upon her whom he had lost.

"You would not, could not do *that*?" she whispered.

"Could not kill the *feringhee*?" and the hate in the old mutiny word was terrible to hear. "What else should I do to him who has stolen the sun from my sky, the fragrance from my rose?"

The man seized her by the wrist, and, pulling her to him, bent down, whispering soft, passionate words.

"Shall I tell thee, love flower, what love is? It is the gold of noon, and the silver of night, the might of the lion, and the soft cooing of the gentle dove. As the slender vine around the straight palm, so will my love twine around thy heart. Yea, and even as the banyan tree sends out branches to draw dew from the rounded breast of earth, my love shall yearn towards thee. Day and her lover, Night, with the Dawn and the Sunset their children; the stag and the gentle doe, with their fierce horned offspring, and their offspring as round and smooth even as thy throat. So will our union be, for behold, my love for thee is so surpassing that our sons could but be of the most perfect manhood, and our daughter, why, she will be after thine own fashioning."

The man's eyes shone as he felt the trembling of the girl, and he pressed her, tempting her, revelling after the strange way of the East in the agony of the defeat his victory would bring him.

"And to save the life of the white man, thou opening bud of the passion flower, wilt thou not come unto such a love as mine; to the shadowed corners of my palaces, to the fragrance of my courts, wilt thou not?"

Then a strange thing happened, unheeded by the two sorely tormented souls.

A great form crashed across the path behind them, followed by the bounding passage of a herd of deer; and from all around came the sounds of animals fleeing in panic, as Leonie lifted her face to the man's with a desperate resolve in her stricken eyes.

And the man, reading the answer, bowed his head to her stone cold hands and crushed them to his heart.

"Thou wilt marry *me—to-night?*"

"For the sake of the man I love," came the steady answer; "to save his life I will be—your—your wife. No, wait! On these conditions. That he is set free and shown a way to safety—that I follow him in secret—and see that he is safe—and that you tell him that I am dead. Swear that to me before your gods and I will keep my promise; swear that you will tell him that I am dead."

And Madhu, the son of princes, put both hands to his forehead and bowed before the woman; then stood erect, with hands upraised to heaven, silent, wrestling with temptation; and having won, he spoke, his face transfigured, his eyes half closed in agony.

"Thou star of heaven! Thou highest point of the Everlasting Hills, behold hast thy great love triumphed. I love thee, but my heart could hold no wife who loved another as thou hast shown thou lovest this man. I—"

But, alas! Leonie, swept off her balance in her great relief, broke across his words.

"Let us hasten quickly, quickly. You will tell the priest; you will help me to set him—the man I love—free. Oh, come quickly, quickly!"

In her callous but uncalculated desire to use this man as a lever wherewith to heave aside the mountain of trouble which threatened to overwhelm Jan Cuxson; and, with the inexplicable cruelty of the woman who loves, and will blissfully put a whole community to torture as long as her beloved is saved a single hurt, she asked the one impossible thing.

He moved so quickly, fiercely, closely to her that she backed until she stood in a patch of moonlight which shone upon her face.

Higher she raised her face, and still higher, as she looked back straight into the eyes intent on hers.

And Madhu Krishnaghar laughed savagely as he looked down upon her.

"Go!" he commanded; "go up the path to the temple gate to meet thy fate. The Mother claims thee, and may thy blood and the blood of the white man who has stolen thee from me flow upon her altar before she shakes the earth in the fury of her displeasure."

Tortured, his soul sought relief in the fanaticism of his religion which flared in his eyes; consumed with love, he called her back as she turned to do the bidding of a stronger will than her own.

"Come!"

She stopped and turned, gave a vacant little laugh, and crept into his arms when he held them out, and closed them about her without touching her.

"Ah!" he whispered, "now that thou comest to me unkno-wingly I will have none of thee. I love thee, love thee, love thee! Go to thy death that my task may be well finished, and that everlasting torment may be fastened upon the soul of him who stole thee from me! Go, beloved of my soul, rose of the morning, delight of my heart! Ah, my love, my love, go to thy death—!"

And he opened wide his arms and pointed up the path, and Leonie went where he pointed; and never once looked back at the man standing with his arms stretched out towards her, whilst monkeys chattered, and parrots screamed, and the jungle teemed with flying, frightened shapes.

CHAPTER XLVIII

"A whirlpool of uncertainty,
a prison of punishment,
a basket of illusion,
the open throat of hell."

—The Spring Sataka.

A brick and some plaster clattered about Jan Cuxson's feet as he crossed the temple chamber and stood looking out at the jungle, and the animals of all sizes and shapes which were hurtling through the undergrowth. For a minute he stood twirling the rusty knife blade between his fingers, then hid it carefully behind a block of broken masonry.

"Better so," he muttered, "not much good as a weapon of defence, but better than nothing; might put the old man on the track if he happened to find it on me when he comes to tie me up. My God! to think of it; I, strong and healthy and sane, at the mercy of that old priest, actually under his will—hypnotised, forced to do exactly what he tells me. Please heavens the ghee will hold the plaster together round the ring, and oh! I can't stand *much* more of this suspense."

He had come to the end of his endurance.

Day had followed night, and night had followed day monotonously, without a change in the heartbreaking dreariness of their round.

During the day he had watched the jungle over the outer wall for hours, rewarded by an occasional glimpse of deer; once by a striped yellow shade which had slunk between the trees, causing him to yearn for his rifle; at night he had lain gazing at the stars, comfortable enough upon a thick bed of leaves, untroubled by the mosquito which, as he had learned, does not thrive in the Sunderbunds Jungle; and day and night over the wall, or up at the stars, he strove to look into the future and found a dreary blank.

But upon *this* night he turned with a smile and a question on his lips when the priest suddenly emerged from behind the heap of stones and hurried across the flags towards him.

"Haste, sahib! The Mother is infuriated at the long waiting, and I go to make sacrifice to appease her. *Haste*, for it is not good for man if she stamps with both her holy feet. Come, and struggle not! Nay, look not at me in such fashion lest I lay the stress of my will upon you."

He looked so frail, that for an instant the white man had been tempted to fling himself upon him, and find deliverance for himself and his beloved by choking the wizened neck, or cracking the old pate against the stones.

But one is rather at a disadvantage when thoughts are liable to be read, and plans disclosed before they are even matured; and he walked submissively towards the ring in the wall, and seated himself abjectly upon the floor, just as a handful of plaster inserted itself between his neck and the open collar of his shirt, and the back of his head bumped the wall.

"Something like a slight—"

"Haste, sahib! I must away to placate Kali, the Goddess of Destruction. There is not long now to wait for the great sacrifice for which she has waited all these weary years; and then, and only then, shall the plague, and the pestilence, and the famine be ended, and the people of India return to their

Joan Conquest

old-time happiness."

He never once removed his eyes from those of the man beneath him, and Cuxson sighed with relief, well content that the glaring eyes should not move beyond his face.

Having knotted the thongs tightly, the old man straightened himself, and smiled up at the silvery heavens in the ecstasy of his worship.

"Such sacrifice, O Mother, as thou hast longed for, and which has long been forbidden thee through the might of the white man who rules us. The temple is strewn with flowers, and the flames of hundreds of lights shine in thy fish-shaped eyes, thou daughter of the eternal snows." He looked down suddenly to Cuxson, and bending, whispered in his ear. "The white woman approaches, O *feringhee*, even she who has caused this land to travail in agony all these years. And you shall see her, she shall come to you and know you not, and you shall hear her voice upraised in worship as she lies upon the altar at her Mother's feet while you are bound to the ring in the wall. She has done well in worship, even in sacrifice, but it is in her rich warm blood that Kali the Terrible would lave her hands. Struggle not, for behold, although I have lifted my will from you that you should be tormented even as my race has been tormented by a woman of your land, yet will the ring and the hide hold you fast."

Like some huge bird of prey he ran swiftly back across the flags and disappeared behind the mass of stones, and Cuxson, not daring to move for fear of tightening the thongs, sat almost numb with anxiety as he wondered if his luck would hold at the crucial moment.

Except for the crash of the frightened animals as they fought their way through the undergrowth, there was no sound whatever in the place, but as the moon took her seat above the exact centre of where once had been the temple roof, he moved, and leant forward as far as the two feet of raw hide would allow him, and from between his clenched teeth there came one word:

"*Hell!*"

For the silence had been suddenly broken by a girl's sharp, hysterical laugh, and though the sound was but a travesty, yet it was surely Leonie's laugh.

Twisting his arms in the space the two feet of raw hide allowed him, the slow, sure, desperate man with a mute appeal to *his* God, sought and caught the iron ring in his hands.

And in the jungle clearing where the fire smouldered dimly, and the coolies, flat on their faces from abject terror, refused to move, Madhu Krishnaghar sat, garbed as a servant, his brain in a whirl of religion and hate, and his heart filled with love of the white girl he had sent to certain death.

Suddenly he sprang to his feet, and tearing his raiment from him flung it wide, and stood nude save for the loin cloth about the slender middle, and the turban which outlined his tortured face, looking like some lost bronze statue in the deserted places of the jungle. He raised his hands to heaven and prayed.

"O Mother, spare her! O great god, have pity upon her," and the suddenly risen wind took up his words and lifted them above the tree tops, wafting them perhaps—and why not—to the God of Infinite Love.

Yet even as he prayed Leonie crept up to the doorway of the temple, staring unblinkingly at the far end of the interior illuminated by the flickering wicks of the hundreds of little lights. She inhaled deeply, and half closed her glaring eyes as the overpowering sickly perfume of flowers, and some other indescribably sickening odour went to her head like cheap wine.

"Yes?" she said questioningly, although no sound had broken

Joan Conquest

the intense stillness, and stood quite still with her head a little on one side, then dropped to one knee and commenced to unlace her high boots, the slap of the laces pulled through the holes cutting the silence like a knife.

With her hands clasped to her breast, and walking on the tips of her bare toes, she moved through the shadows towards the light, alone and obedient to a will that had no pity. Flowers were strewn thick in every direction, and over them she passed to her death, while the eyes of the priest never once left her face as he crouched in the opening which led to the secret places of the temple; he even smiled when she came to a standstill in front of the altar and swayed, slightly overcome by the heavy atmosphere even in her trance; and he nodded his head gently when she bent down and gathering handsful of the flowers, flung them up above her head and laughed the hysterical, crazy laugh which had reached the ears of the man she loved.

At her feet were *thalees*, brass plates laden with offerings of grain, of woven stuffs, of gold and silver; at her right hand a crimson silk *sari* lay upon a heap of fallen stones, and upon it was a garland of white flowers; and the slanting mother-o'-pearl eyes of the Goddess Kali looked down from out the black face at this girl who was to be sacrificed in atonement for the misery she had unwittingly brought upon the land of India and her people.

Leonie's hands moved mechanically to her hair, which she unfastened and shook out in all its glory; then they moved to the fastening of her jersey, and one by one her garments slipped to the floor, leaving her nude save for the covering of her hair.

Leaning down she lifted the *sari*, and with one quick movement twisted it about her waist and across her breast; slipped the garland of white flowers about her neck, and flinging back her hair raised her hands above her head and shouted.

She did not sing or cry aloud, she shouted with her mouth wide open, and her head thrust forward between her uplifted arms, a degrading picture of religious sensuality; and gathering up armsful of flowers from the floor, ran lightly over to the priest upon the tip of her bare toes which were stained a hideous red, and putting the palm of one hand against her forehead salaamed and said "Yes?" questioningly.

He laid no hand upon her, he made no sign and spoke no word, but she, as drugged by another's will as if she were under the bane of opium, followed him unhesitatingly into the secret places of the temple. Her bare feet made no sound on the dust of centuries; her eyes looked back unwaveringly into the eyes of the gods who leered down upon her; her hair caught around those others of which it is not seemly to write; and before them all she cast her flowers, and upon them all she laid her open palm.

And Jan Cuxson held his breath when she quietly sidled round the block of fallen masonry, and standing in a moonray glanced at him from the corner of her eyes. Hung with flowers, she looked like a bacchante, with one beautiful arm and shoulder showing bare through her mantle of tumbled hair.

And his eyes caught the shadow of the priest cast by the passage lights on to the floor as he stood hidden by the fallen stones, and he kept still, but he called to his beloved, striving by his will to break her chains, and truly at the sound of the loved voice the frozen horrors of her face seemed to break like ice-floes before the sun in spring.

"Leonie," he called gently, "Leonie, come to me, come here to *me*!"

Her eyelids suddenly closed upon the staring gold-flecked eyes; her mouth quivered in a little smile as she let fall the flowers about her bloodstained feet and ran swiftly across to Jan; kneeling she touched his face gently with her finger-tips, and stretched her hands across his shoulders towards the thongs which bound him to the ring in the wall.

Her hair fell upon him as she leaned towards him, and a memory of the day he had found her in Rockham Cove flashed across his mind; her mouth, her beautiful scarlet virgin mouth had almost touched his when the priest's power, closing down, jerked her back into the horrible travesty of her sweet, gentle self.

She sat back upon her heels and laughed, and said one word in Hindustani which is best translated as dog, although it means infinitely more and worse; and having uttered it she smote him across the mouth with the flat of her hand and rose to her feet.

She stood for a moment laughing silently, looking down upon him, and turning, ran swiftly across the flags to the block of fallen stones. There she paused and glanced at the white man bound to the wall with the light of battle in his eyes, before she disappeared, beckoning to the priest who followed as she ran down the passage of the gods, making obeisance before them as she passed.

CHAPTER XLIX

"The soil out of which such men as he are made is good to be born on, good to live on, good to die for, and to be buried in."
—*Lowell.*

Leonie lay motionless on the stained stone before the altar; her hair, pulled back clear from her neck, swept behind her head like a cascade of rust-coloured water to the floor; her hands were clasped between her breasts, and her great unfathomable eyes stared up into those of the stone woman who looked down at her and seemed to laugh with joy at her long coveted prize.

In every corner black shapes danced; advancing, retreating, springing towards the roof and vanishing utterly. The place seemed infested with goblins, or devils, things of untold evilness and vice, although, in reality, they were but the shadows thrown by the little lights which were like tongues licking the lips of darkness in sensuous anticipation of the coming feast of blood.

The old priest stood looking up at his god with perplexity in his sunken eyes.

Arrayed in snow-white garment, with long hair hanging down, he held the knife of sacrifice in one hand, and in the other the sacred *roomal*.

Joan Conquest

The terrible picture shone softly in the light of the full moon which struck straight down upon the altar through a hole in the ruined roof.

"Tell thy servant thy pleasure, O Black One!" prayed the priest, swaying slightly to and fro. "Make him understand it the *roomal* shall be knotted about the neck of this white sacrifice, or if the knife shall draw a necklace of red about the white neck and upon the white breast. Give me an answer, O Mother, that I may right the wrong of many moons ago. A sign, a sign, O Mother!"

As he spoke; and for no apparent reason, Leonie's hands unclasped, her arms opened and fell towards her sides, leaving the beautiful breast bare with the jewel in shape and colour of a cat's eye winking craftily with the cunning and knowledge of the sins of all ages, just above the heart.

The priest shouted in worship, and his words, caught, echoed and re-echoed from the dome, drowned the sound of footsteps running at high speed across the flower-strewn floor.

Madhu Krishnaghar, naked save for the turban which bound his handsome head and the loin cloth which girt the slender middle, sped like the wind to the rescue of his beloved.

In the black shades of the jungle, understanding at last that for him there could be no life outside the life of the white woman he loved, and no happiness outside her happiness, he had raced Time down the jungle path, through the outer gates and temple door, pausing not for the fraction of a second; realising, as he ran, that upon his speed alone depended the life of his beloved. And even as the priest flung back his arm with a scream of ecstasy, the knife was wrenched out of his hand from behind.

O Madhu, you splendid heathen, who defied the anger of your strange gods for the love in your noble heart.

"Ha!" said the old man as he swung round in fury; then he smiled and opened wide his arms. "Thou! O my son! *thou!* Thou wouldst offer the great sacrifice thyself to our most gentle mother. And art thou not in the right? Thine has been the task and the toil, therefore is it meet that thou shouldst have the reward."

He laid his hands upon the shoulders of the youth, who straightway gripped the veined old wrists and raised the withered arms high up above their heads, while their eyes met in a sudden-born, subconscious enmity, and the knife lay glittering along the wrinkled brown skin.

Only for an instant, and Madhu let go his hold, and turning, stood looking down upon the jewel above the woman's heart. As he looked, the thing, catching the reflections of the lights, shone strangely bright upon the snow-white skin, and the lust of blood swept him from head to foot.

He longed to drive the dagger through the breast above the shining jewel; he craved to see the whiteness of the skin stained with red, to throw himself upon the still form and shut the dead mouth with kisses.

He was mad with passion, intoxicated with the heavy perfumed air, drunk with the atmosphere of his surroundings, and his slim body shook as he ran the needle-point of the dagger into his own breast.

He closed his eyes in the ecstasy of that pain which is twin to the ecstasy of desire fulfilled, and in their closing woke suddenly to the purity of his strange love. He turned with a snarl and hit up the old man's hand as it almost touched the nape of his neck, and stretching wide his arms made a shield of his body between Leonie and the intent he read in the priest's eyes, just as a brick fell and split to pieces at their feet.

"Linger not, my son," said the old priest fiercely. "Behold! the rites have been performed, the chants sung, and the offerings made. Drive the knife home, and give drink to thy mother of that which she loves. Hasten! for she is angry at thy slowness, and the very earth trembles at her wrath."

But Madhu Krishnaghar looked straight back into the fierce, suspicious old eyes, and moved quickly towards the priest who, taken by surprise, retreated hurriedly.

"Father!" came the words in the musical, steady voice. "O servant of the Black One, I cannot, nay, I will not, for I love yon white woman with a love passing all understanding. Nay, hearken! A sacrifice there must be this night, and there shall be one. Even me, O my Father. Let it suffice, for behold is my love so great, that she, the slender white flower, seems but one with me. Let her go, let her go, and lay me on the stone, warm with the life of her dear body, and drive the knife through my heart, that through my love peace may be made with thy god and my god!"

The whole world seemed bound in a great terrible silence as the two men stood staring at each other in the soft silver light of the moon; then the old man smiled gently, with the cunning of all time in his eyes, and creeping close to his pupil spoke in the merest whisper; tempting, as have always tempted, those who desire to gain their own ends, and who justify all means as long as that end is gained.

"Thou lovest her, my son. The infidel white woman, the sacrifice long dedicated to thy god. And why not, for thou are marked even with the mark which shows between the breasts like lotus buds. But thinkest thou, O son of princes, O descendant of the great, that thou art fit to mate with her. She is white, a daughter of the all-conquering race; thou—thou art black—a pariah—a dog—thou wouldst be whipped from her presence, thou high-born son of India."

The old man never moved his eyes from the young face, and neither the one nor the other saw the great striped terrified beast which slunk past them and disappeared into the shadows, seeking protection in its terror.

"But why shouldst thou let this woman, whom thou lovest, go? Why not make sacrifice of love as well as life to the great one? Behold is she soft and white and all-pleasing! Why, therefore, should she not come unto thy intent neath the eyes of the Sweet One, while I make offerings in the shadows towards thy well doing; so that the Black One will be twice pleased."

Of all the horrible temptations in that place of horror! And where in the name of all the gods did the native, unshackled by convention or code, find the strength to resist?

For while the priest whispered the young face was swept by a flood of conflicting emotions—which passed—leaving it as pure, as soul-stirring as the Taj Mahal at dawn.

"No! O Holy One! I will not—I love her—I love her—I will not!"

The words were firm and the young mouth like steel, and the eyes looked steadily back into those of the priest as the latter rushed upon him in mighty, inhuman wrath.

"And I say that thou shalt, thou begotten son of evil. I say that thou shalt encompass this woman with thy might, and then offer her in sacrifice to Kali, the Goddess of Death. I say that thou *shalt*."

It was a case of will pitted against will, for the old man knew that the younger would not dare raise hand against him for fear of everlasting damnation.

And Madhu Krishnaghar girded himself for the battle by putting his love for the white woman in the forefront of his mind.

And as they fought, desperately, with one last terrific pull which caused the hide to cut down to the wrist bone, Jan

Cuxson wrenched the ring he had loosened from the wall, and stood swaying, sick with pain. Sweat poured down his face and bare chest, and blood flowed from his wrists while his burst finger-tips fumbled clumsily with the deep embedded thongs.

"I did it—I did it," he kept on repeating savagely, as his knees trembled and his body turned cold in agony. "I did it—I did it—God grant I am in time—in time."

Free at last, smothered in blood, dragging his heavily booted feet with difficulty, he sought and found the broken blade, staggered across the floor, stooped, and entered the passage of the gods where the imprint of his beloved's bare feet marked the dust of ages.

And Leonie lay quite still; to all appearance dead, with her open eyes turned back beneath the lids and her mouth half open showing her even teeth.

Not a word passed between the two men as they fought for her, one for her life, the other for her death. This way and that they moved; the one trying to escape from the direct range of the relentless will-power, and yet keep himself between the girl and the religious fanatic; the other striving to press his opponent back even to the altar stone.

Like iron to a magnet Madhu's hand was closed about the dagger hilt, and try as he would he could not relax the grasp nor fling the knife far back into the shadows; neither could he keep his footing, for strive as he would the priest's magnetic power, developed and trained through years and years of study and practice, drove him back inch by inch towards the god who looked down upon them with her fish-shaped eyes.

A glint of triumph shone in the eyes of the priest, and twisted the corner of his mouth as the heel of his enemy thudded against the stone upon which lay the white girl; and he concentrated every ounce of his strength for the last moment when, by sheer force of his will, the knife should be lifted and driven down, deep, even to the hilt. And the white man hastened as best he could, reeling at every step, with blood streaming from his wrists and spattering upon the stones beneath the leering eyes of the gods. Not one of the three heeded the low moaning of the wind as it swept past the temple and through the trees, to die away into a great, uncanny, unnatural silence, unbroken by sound of beast or bird.

Fate feeling for her shears, and peevish through want of sleep maybe, or mayhap irritated by their obstreperous behaviour, jerked the strings which bound those marionettes called humans to her palsied old fingers.

The old priest, misjudging the pull given to his string, in what he mistook to be his triumph, *laughed*.

It is better to laugh last indeed, but oft-times it is best not to laugh at all, for who can foresee the particle of dust which may enter your indecently and injudiciously wide open mouth to choke you in your ill-timed mirth.

Only for an instant did he triumph above his enemy, but for just that instant he loosened his will power; and Madhu Krishnaghar, sensing the relief, and whipped by the laugh to one final desperate effort of his failing powers, raised his hand and flung the knife far back to fall with a clatter in some distant corner.

It was done.

Youth had mocked at experience, life at death, love at opposition, as it has done since the beginning of time, and will do, let us hope, until the end.

For as the knife hurtled into the shadows, Madhu bent swiftly and lifted Leonie into his arms, holding her in this his last moment of heaven upon earth, tenderly and firmly, as he glared defiance over her head at the priest.

And he, understanding at last that he had failed, cast himself at the feet of his god who, in her fury, stamped with both her blood-stained feet.

CHAPTER L

"Greater love hath no man."
—The Bible.

There was a shout from the doorway leading to the secret places of the temple as Cuxson, covered with blood and dust, half-crazed with horror, paused for a moment as he took in the awful picture before him.

Leonie, with her hair almost sweeping the ground, lay half clothed and seemingly dead in the arms of a native, whose face was a picture of triumphant love for all to see; and a wild-eyed priest beat his breast before the horrible image of the terrible, all powerful Goddess of Destruction.

He sprang forward with another shout, which was lost in the shriek and crash of the raging elements.

For even as he moved there was a terrific roar as of tons of exploding dynamite, and a shriek of wind as it tore through the building, blowing out the little flickering lights, leaving the place pitch black save for the steady light of the full moon.

Then he swayed like a drunken man as the floor rose in a great wave and yet another, heaving the flags this way and that, cracking and splitting in every direction as it subsided.

"Leonie!" he shouted, though no sound could be heard above

the appalling din. "Leonie! Leonie!"

He saw her lying in a pool of moonlight as though asleep, and near her knelt the native, with arms outstretched above her, sheltering her.

There was a moment of complete dead silence, and then with a tearing, rending sound the dome and the temple walls split from top to base; and with a thundering crash the great block of stone upon which was carved the image of Kali the Terrible split in two, toppled over and fell upon the kneeling priest.

Herds of screaming beasts hurled themselves through the riven walls and fled across the temple floor, fighting blindly to escape. Monkeys in hundreds scrambled over the mounds of fallen bricks, chattering and calling like lost, frightened children; a tiger with one bound landed noiselessly a few feet from those two in the moonlight, half reared with a short coughing roar and bounded as noiselessly away. And God alone knows what saved the three from instant death among the tottering ruins.

The power of Love perchance.

The son of princes sheltering the girl slowly, oh! slowly straightened himself, when a prolonged silence seemed to indicate the end of the greatest earthquake that ever swept the Sunderbunds Jungle.

Blood streamed from the side of his head, battered in by a broken fragment of the high altar that had been hurled through the air; his left shoulder was in splinters, crushed by the collapse of the roof which must have killed Leonie if he had not covered her with his body; blood spouted from some great severed artery in the arm which seemed to hang by a thread from the splintered shoulder; yet was his face aglow with light and love, and his eyes afire with happiness as he raised a tawny tress of hair and pressed it to his lips.

He was dying, quickly, yet he turned his head and smiled at the sound of Jan Cuxson's boots scrambling over the impeding heaps of stone. For one second only the torture of the sacrifice required of him flared in the soft brown eyes; and then in the pride of his great race, and with an effort of will beyond all telling, he put his unbroken arm round the woman he loved so well, lifted her, got somehow to his feet, and walked, aye! walked steadily across the few yards which separated him from the white man.

Cuxson, not realising his terrible plight, with eyes only for the woman *he* loved, wrenched Leonie from his hold and swept her from head to foot with frantic eyes.

"What have you done to her?" he demanded fiercely. "Before the earthquake what did you do to her? Tell me—or by God I'll—"

He stopped the bitter words in time to save himself from everlasting remorse.

For Madhu Krishnaghar suddenly straightened his battered body, and looked the white man in the eyes.

"She is safe, O white man, safe and unharmed. Take her, keep her—carry her by the—the short road without the—the temple gates—to—happiness, *I* give *her*—to—you—because *I*—I love—her—for ever!"

There was a moment's terrible silence in which the two men stood divided, yet united, in their great love for the one woman.

The native of India put his hand to his forehead and salaamed before the woman for whom he had sacrificed all, then turned slowly around towards the place where the image of his god had so lately stood.

"Kali!" he called, and his young voice was as the clashing of golden bells at sunset. "Kali! Mother of all—I come!"

And unwitting of the great reward awaiting those who attain everlasting peace through the victory of the greater love, he crashed face downwards, dead, upon the flower-strewn floor, and passed for ever into the safe keeping of the one and only God.

CHAPTER LI

"When the day breaks and the shadows flee away!"
—The Bible.

Jan Cuxson lifted Leonie's face to the light of the moon, and caught his breath at the sight of the turned back eyes and drooping mouth.

This was the outcome of it all! *This* was how she was left to him; saved from physical hurt but with her mind for ever bound by the will of yon dead priest. Hypnotised, mesmerised, to be under the influence of the Goddess of Destruction until her death; maybe to pass her life in the security of a padded cell; she, his Leonie, his love, his wife-to-be.

He crushed her in fierce despair against his heart as the ground moved gently under his feet, and prayed aloud to his God to bring the riven walls down upon them there in the moonlight, that in merciful death the awful fate of his beloved might be lifted from her.

The only answer to the desperate prayer was silence and shadows enveloping them like a mantle, and he lifted his stern face to the radiance of the moon, with the light of battle in the grey eyes.

"I will find a way out, dear heart," he cried, as he turned her face gently against his shoulder. "There is a way and I will find it." And he strode as hastily as the masses of fallen stone would allow him towards the door and the short path which would lead him to the water's edge and safety.

As he skirted the half of the fallen altar which lay across the body of the priest, he paused for a moment and looked down upon the man who had won even in death.

As he looked the fingers of the out-flung hands twitched, and a violent shiver shook the old frame. Slowly, very slowly the gnarled old arms were gathered in under the breast as inch by inch the Hindu priest raised himself from the floor. The lower limbs were hidden, crushed under the fallen stone, and the old head hung down between the shoulders, the grey hair tangled in a wreath of jasmin flower.

He lifted his face, and the dim old eyes looked wistfully up into the grey ones staring down at him out of the shadows.

"Thou hast conquered, sahib, thou hast conquered in love," he whispered. "And she is safe, for behold my—my power—has gone—from her. I—even I—have not obeyed, and my god— has destroyed me!"

Lifting his voice he cried aloud and died.

And as he died Leonie turned her face from the shelter of her lover's shoulder and closed her eyes, and opening them again laughed sweetly as she looked up into his face.

"You, Jan, *you*! Why—whatever has happened, and—why— wherever are we?" And he looked down into the sweet face and laughed aloud, an exultant, ringing laugh which was caught and echoed and re-echoed from the dome until the place seemed filled with the sound of happiness.

"There has been a bit of an earthquake, dear, and you got hit on the head by a piece of falling brick. See, sweetheart," and he swept the masses of hair together and twisted it between her head and his coat, "turn your face this way until I have you safely out of here, it's nice and soft, and shut your eyes, darling—"

"Yes! but," said Leonie, as she turned her face as bidden and closed her eyes with a sigh of great content, "but—but how did we escape?"

"You were saved, dear!"

"Saved!—from what? By whom?"

She tried to turn her head, but he held it pressed close against his heart.

"From death—dear heart!"

"And by whom—tell me—Jan—by whom?"

Jan Cuxson paused a moment as he looked across towards the still figure of Madhu Krishnaghar stretched peacefully upon the ground.

"By the whitest man that has ever lived, dear!—by him!"

And he turned without another word and strode through the temple and out of the gates to the narrow way which led to safety. And where the trees met in an arch above his head he stopped and looked back, and Leonie, turning her face, passed her hand wonderingly over the tousled masses of her hair and the silken drapery about her body.

"Where are we going to? Where are you taking me?"

He shifted her completely into his left arm, pulled at a golden slender chain round her neck with his right hand, caught it in his strong white teeth and wrenched it in two.

And he answered her as he flung the jewelled cat's-eye far out into the jungle.

"To Devon, beloved, to Devon and happiness!"

And as he closed her red mouth with kisses the earth shook gently under his feet, and the temple, with a terrific crash, caved in; burying for ever the dead priest, the broken image of Kali, the Goddess of Destruction, and Madhu Krishnaghar, son of princes, her splendid Indian lover.

Choose from Thousands of 1stWorldLibrary Classics By

A. M. Barnard
Ada Leverson
Adolphus William Ward
Aesop
Agatha Christie
Alexander Aaronsohn
Alexander Kielland
Alexandre Dumas
Alfred Gatty
Alfred Ollivant
Alice Duer Miller
Alice Turner Curtis
Alice Dunbar
Allen Chapman
Alleyne Ireland
Ambrose Bierce
Amelia E. Barr
Amory H. Bradford
Andrew Lang
Andrew McFarland Davis
Andy Adams
Angela Brazil
Anna Alice Chapin
Anna Sewell
Annie Besant
Annie Hamilton Donnell
Annie Payson Call
Annie Roe Carr
Annonaymous
Anton Chekhov
Archibald Lee Fletcher
Arnold Bennett
Arthur C. Benson
Arthur Conan Doyle
Arthur M. Winfield
Arthur Ransome
Arthur Schnitzler
Arthur Train
Atticus
B.H. Baden-Powell
B. M. Bower
B. C. Chatterjee
Baroness Emmuska Orczy
Baroness Orczy
Basil King
Bayard Taylor
Ben Macomber
Bertha Muzzy Bower
Bjornstjerne Bjornson

Booth Tarkington
Boyd Cable
Bram Stoker
C. Collodi
C. E. Orr
C. M. Ingleby
Carolyn Wells
Catherine Parr Traill
Charles A. Eastman
Charles Amory Beach
Charles Dickens
Charles Dudley Warner
Charles Farrar Browne
Charles Ives
Charles Kingsley
Charles Klein
Charles Hanson Towne
Charles Lathrop Pack
Charles Romyn Dake
Charles Whibley
Charles Willing Beale
Charlotte M. Braeme
Charlotte M. Yonge
Charlotte Perkins Stetson
Clair W. Hayes
Clarence Day Jr.
Clarence E. Mulford
Clemence Housman
Confucius
Coningsby Dawson
Cornelis DeWitt Wilcox
Cyril Burleigh
D. H. Lawrence
Daniel Defoe
David Garnett
Dinah Craik
Don Carlos Janes
Donald Keyhoe
Dorothy Kilner
Dougan Clark
Douglas Fairbanks
E. Nesbit
E. P. Roe
E. Phillips Oppenheim
E. S. Brooks
Earl Barnes
Edgar Rice Burroughs
Edith Van Dyne
Edith Wharton

Edward Everett Hale
Edward J. O'Biren
Edward S. Ellis
Edwin L. Arnold
Eleanor Atkins
Eleanor Hallowell Abbott
Eliot Gregory
Elizabeth Gaskell
Elizabeth McCracken
Elizabeth Von Arnim
Ellem Key
Emerson Hough
Emilie F. Carlen
Emily Bronte
Emily Dickinson
Enid Bagnold
Enilor Macartney Lane
Erasmus W. Jones
Ernie Howard Pie
Ethel May Dell
Ethel Turner
Ethel Watts Mumford
Eugene Sue
Eugenie Foa
Eugene Wood
Eustace Hale Ball
Evelyn Everett-green
Everard Cotes
F. H. Cheley
F. J. Cross
F. Marion Crawford
Fannie E. Newberry
Federick Austin Ogg
Ferdinand Ossendowski
Fergus Hume
Florence A. Kilpatrick
Fremont B. Deering
Francis Bacon
Francis Darwin
Frances Hodgson Burnett
Frances Parkinson Keyes
Frank Gee Patchin
Frank Harris
Frank Jewett Mather
Frank L. Packard
Frank V. Webster
Frederic Stewart Isham
Frederick Trevor Hill
Frederick Winslow Taylor

Friedrich Kerst
Friedrich Nietzsche
Fyodor Dostoyevsky
G.A. Henty
G.K. Chesterton
Gabrielle E. Jackson
Garrett P. Serviss
Gaston Leroux
George A. Warren
George Ade
Geroge Bernard Shaw
George Cary Eggleston
George Durston
George Ebers
George Eliot
George Gissing
George MacDonald
George Meredith
George Orwell
George Sylvester Viereck
George Tucker
George W. Cable
George Wharton James
Gertrude Atherton
Gordon Casserly
Grace E. King
Grace Gallatin
Grace Greenwood
Grant Allen
Guillermo A. Sherwell
Gulielma Zollinger
Gustav Flaubert
H. A. Cody
H. B. Irving
H.C. Bailey
H. G. Wells
H. H. Munro
H. Irving Hancock
H. R. Naylor
H. Rider Haggard
H. W. C. Davis
Haldeman Julius
Hall Caine
Hamilton Wright Mabie
Hans Christian Andersen
Harold Avery
Harold McGrath
Harriet Beecher Stowe
Harry Castlemon
Harry Coghill
Harry Houidini

Hayden Carruth
Helent Hunt Jackson
Helen Nicolay
Hendrik Conscience
Hendy David Thoreau
Henri Barbusse
Henrik Ibsen
Henry Adams
Henry Ford
Henry Frost
Henry James
Henry Jones Ford
Henry Seton Merriman
Henry W Longfellow
Herbert A. Giles
Herbert Carter
Herbert N. Casson
Herman Hesse
Hildegard G. Frey
Homer
Honore De Balzac
Horace B. Day
Horace Walpole
Horatio Alger Jr.
Howard Pyle
Howard R. Garis
Hugh Lofting
Hugh Walpole
Humphry Ward
Ian Maclaren
Inez Haynes Gillmore
Irving Bacheller
Isabel Cecilia Williams
Isabel Hornibrook
Israel Abrahams
Ivan Turgenev
J.G.Austin
J. Henri Fabre
J. M. Barrie
J. M. Walsh
J. Macdonald Oxley
J. R. Miller
J. S. Fletcher
J. S. Knowles
J. Storer Clouston
J. W. Duffield
Jack London
Jacob Abbott
James Allen
James Andrews
James Baldwin

James Branch Cabell
James DeMille
James Joyce
James Lane Allen
James Lane Allen
James Oliver Curwood
James Oppenheim
James Otis
James R. Driscoll
Jane Abbott
Jane Austen
Jane L. Stewart
Janet Aldridge
Jens Peter Jacobsen
Jerome K. Jerome
Jessie Graham Flower
John Buchan
John Burroughs
John Cournos
John F. Kennedy
John Gay
John Glasworthy
John Habberton
John Joy Bell
John Kendrick Bangs
John Milton
John Philip Sousa
John Taintor Foote
Jonas Lauritz Idemil Lie
Jonathan Swift
Joseph A. Altsheler
Joseph Carey
Joseph Conrad
Joseph E. Badger Jr
Joseph Hergesheimer
Joseph Jacobs
Jules Vernes
Julian Hawthrone
Julie A Lippmann
Justin Huntly McCarthy
Kakuzo Okakura
Karle Wilson Baker
Kate Chopin
Kenneth Grahame
Kenneth McGaffey
Kate Langley Bosher
Kate Langley Bosher
Katherine Cecil Thurston
Katherine Stokes
L. A. Abbot
L. T. Meade

L. Frank Baum
Latta Griswold
Laura Dent Crane
Laura Lee Hope
Laurence Housman
Lawrence Beasley
Leo Tolstoy
Leonid Andreyev
Lewis Carroll
Lewis Sperry Chafer
Lilian Bell
Lloyd Osbourne
Louis Hughes
Louis Joseph Vance
Louis Tracy
Louisa May Alcott
Lucy Fitch Perkins
Lucy Maud Montgomery
Luther Benson
Lydia Miller Middleton
Lyndon Orr
M. Corvus
M. H. Adams
Margaret E. Sangster
Margret Howth
Margaret Vandercook
Margaret W. Hungerford
Margret Penrose
Maria Edgeworth
Maria Thompson Daviess
Mariano Azuela
Marion Polk Angellotti
Mark Overton
Mark Twain
Mary Austin
Mary Catherine Crowley
Mary Cole
Mary Hastings Bradley
Mary Roberts Rinehart
Mary Rowlandson
M. Wollstonecraft Shelley
Maud Lindsay
Max Beerbohm
Myra Kelly
Nathaniel Hawthrone
Nicolo Machiavelli
O. F. Walton
Oscar Wilde

Owen Johnson
P.G. Wodehouse
Paul and Mabel Thorne
Paul G. Tomlinson
Paul Severing
Percy Brebner
Percy Keese Fitzhugh
Peter B. Kyne
Plato
Quincy Allen
R. Derby Holmes
R. L. Stevenson
R. S. Ball
Rabindranath Tagore
Rahul Alvares
Ralph Bonehill
Ralph Henry Barbour
Ralph Victor
Ralph Waldo Emmerson
Rene Descartes
Ray Cummings
Rex Beach
Rex E. Beach
Richard Harding Davis
Richard Jefferies
Richard Le Gallienne
Robert Barr
Robert Frost
Robert Gordon Anderson
Robert L. Drake
Robert Lansing
Robert Lynd
Robert Michael Ballantyne
Robert W. Chambers
Rosa Nouchette Carey
Rudyard Kipling
Saint Augustine
Samuel B. Allison
Samuel Hopkins Adams
Sarah Bernhardt
Sarah C. Hallowell
Selma Lagerlof
Sherwood Anderson
Sigmund Freud
Standish O'Grady
Stanley Weyman
Stella Benson
Stella M. Francis

Stephen Crane
Stewart Edward White
Stijn Streuvels
Swami Abhedananda
Swami Parmananda
T. S. Ackland
T. S. Arthur
The Princess Der Ling
Thomas A. Janvier
Thomas A Kempis
Thomas Anderton
Thomas Bailey Aldrich
Thomas Bulfinch
Thomas De Quincey
Thomas Dixon
Thomas H. Huxley
Thomas Hardy
Thomas More
Thornton W. Burgess
U. S. Grant
Upton Sinclair
Valentine Williams
Various Authors
Vaughan Kester
Victor Appleton
Victor G. Durham
Victoria Cross
Virginia Woolf
Wadsworth Camp
Walter Camp
Walter Scott
Washington Irving
Wilbur Lawton
Wilkie Collins
Willa Cather
Willard F. Baker
William Dean Howells
William le Queux
W. Makepeace Thackeray
William W. Walter
William Shakespeare
Winston Churchill
Yei Theodora Ozaki
Yogi Ramacharaka
Young E. Allison
Zane Grey